PRAISE FOR VENGEANCE ROAD

"Relentlessly readable, *Vengeance Road* is a perfect Western. You won't be able to turn in until you get to the very last page!"

—Saundra Mitchell, author of *The Springsweet*

"Teens sick of books that coddle them will enjoy sinking their teeth into Bowman's latest . . . the book demands the same stoicism from its readers as the heroine herself possesses."

—*SLJ*

"Thrilling. . . . Kate is a heroine to be reckoned with."

—Jessica Spotswood, author of The Cahill Witch Chronicles

"[Kate] is a hard-riding, tough-talking young woman who can shoot to kill. The story is hers to tell."

—*VOYA*

"Flinty and fierce, Kate is a formidable addition to the pantheon of tough young adult heroines. Her story and voice crackles to life."

—A. C. Gaughen, author of the Scarlet trilogy

"Gold madness, a good-for-nothing posse, and frontier justice: *Vengeance Road* is everything you could want in a Western."

—Jodi Meadows, author of the Incarnate trilogy

"This is the kind of book I'll re-read again and again."

—Susan Dennard, *New York Times* bestselling author of *Truthwitch*

Vengeance Road

Erin Bowman

HOUGHTON MIFFLIN HARCOURT
BOSTON   NEW YORK

For my father—
Thanks for all those spaghetti Westerns, Dad!

www.hmhco.com

The text was set in Cheltenham.

The Library of Congress Cataloged the hardcover edition as follows:
Bowman, Erin.
Vengeance road / Erin Bowman.
p. cm.
Summary: "When her father is killed by the notorious Rose Riders for a
mysterious journal that reveals the secret location of a gold mine, eighteen-
year-old Kate Thompson disguises herself as a boy and takes to the gritty
plains looking for answers–and justice." —Provided by publisher
[1. Frontier and pioneer life—Fiction.
2. Adventure and adventurers—Fiction. 3. Robbers and outlaws—Fiction.
4. Revenge—Fiction. 5. Secrets—Fiction. 6. Sex role—Fiction.
7. Gold mines and mining—Fiction. 8. West (U.S.)—History—19th
century—Fiction.] I. Title.
PZ7.B68347Ven 2015
[Fic] — dc23
2014046835

ISBN: 978-0-544-46638-8 hardcover
ISBN: 978-0-544-93840-3 paperback

Printed in the United States of America
DOC 10 9 8 7 6 5 4 3 2
4500735501

Not all that tempts your wand'ring eyes
And heedless hearts, is lawful prize;
Nor all that glisters, gold.

— THOMAS GRAY

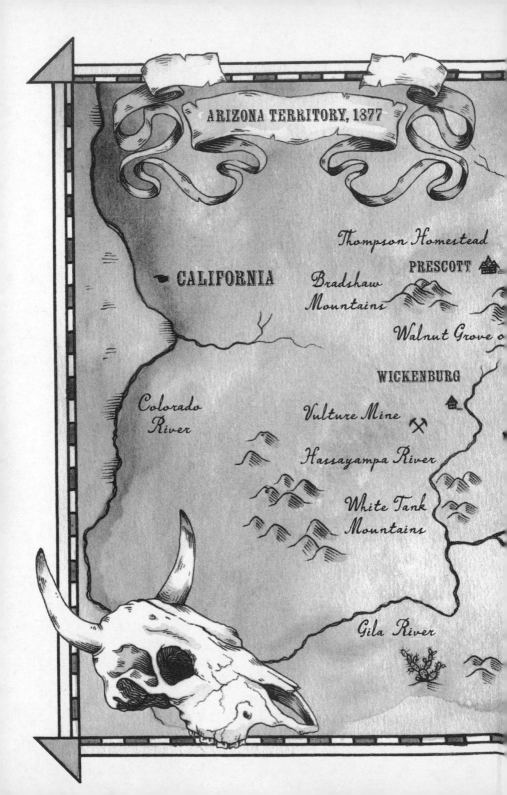

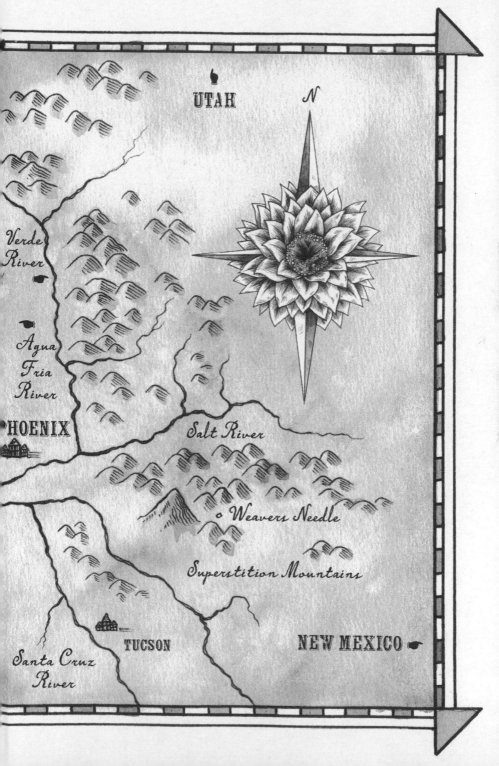

CHAPTER ONE

It werent no secret Pa owned the best plot of land 'long Granite Creek, and I reckon that's why they killed him.

I was down at the water, yanking a haul 'cus the pump had gone and stuck dry again, when I saw the smoke. It were billowing up over the sick-looking trees like a signal to God himself. I heard the yelping next—men squawking like hawks attacking prey. The crows were flying frenzied too.

I whistled for Silver and she came running from where she'd stooped for a drink. We rode outta there like two bats fleeing hell, but it were too late when we got back to the house. They'd only been hollering 'cus the job were already done. The house sat burning to its timber frame, and Pa were hanging from the mesquite tree out front, eyes wider than the moon. Dust puffed up to the south.

I jumped from Silver and pulled my rifle from the saddle scabbard, then dropped to one knee. Eyes on the trail, sight, deep breath, exhale and squeeze. Just like Pa taught me. Just like we practiced for years and years and years. One dark shadow fell from his horse. The rest kept right on riding.

"Who'd you say you were looking for again?"

I glance up at the bartender. "I didn't. More whiskey."

I push the shot glass at him, and he don't seem too pleased 'bout that. But I got some coin and a vengeance strong enough to cut any throat that tries to cross me right now.

The bartender tips a bit more my way and I take a slug. Tastes like fire.

"It's too early on a Sunday to be drinking like this, boy."

I ain't a boy, but I sure am dressed like one. Trousers and boots. One of my flannels. A flat-brimmed Stetson. Helps I got my hair stuffed up under the hat too. When I ran into the house to try to save a few precious items, my hair caught fire. Now, with its singed ends hidden from view, I reckon I look like any other greasy, tired, drink-seeking gent on Whiskey Row. And a scrawny one at that, without so much as a whisker on my chin. But if I's learned anything, it's that drunk men don't notice much in the way of details. Shame the bartender's sober.

"How old are ya?" the bartender nudges.

"Old enough."

And I am. I turned eighteen two days ago. What I can't figure is why they killed Pa only to run off without taking nothing.

I itch at my ribs through the flannel and watch the son of a bitch in the cloudy mirror mounted behind the bar. He's sitting in a corner, one grimy hand clutching a shot glass, the other wrapped round his stomach. It's well past noon and the heat's infernal, but he's got a jacket on over his wool shirt. I can't see his eyes 'cus his hat's pulled down low, but his breathing's uneasy. And he's shivering. I give him another hour or two. Three tops. He fell from his horse hard when I shot him. That weren't on account of an arm graze or shoulder nick.

I thought for sure I'd shot him dead, but when Silver and I came up the trail after I buried Pa, it were nothing but dust and weeds and a few blood splatters leading to Prescott. The bastard was so hurt, tracking him those five miles were easy. Once in town, he rode up Whiskey Row. I found his horse outside the Quartz Rock Saloon —blood smeared on the saddle horn, another speckle or two showing his move inside.

The bartender's right 'bout one thing—the place *is* busy considering it's the Lord's day. What the stout fella don't seem to realize is that a strong drink can numb the soul as good as any prayer. Hell, I muttered "Oh, God" 'bout a dozen times after I found Pa swinging, and it ain't like it brought him back to life.

He crumpled like a sack of grains when I cut him down. I had to press his eyelids shut and roll him onto his stomach 'cus I couldn't bear looking at his face— bruised and beaten, blood trailing from his nose, what looked like a coiling spiral carved right into his forehead from when they tortured him for heavens knows what.

They'd cleaned out his pockets and stolen his Colt right outta his belt. It were a beauty of a pistol—polished white grip, engraved barrel, a finish so pretty, it shined. The weapon in my holster matches. They were a set, and Pa split the pair to give one to me, and now I can't even rejoin 'em.

It weren't easy work, digging the grave. Ma's buried right beneath the mesquite tree Pa died swinging from. He put her there 'cus he said a soul should rest where it's sheltered in the winter and shaded in the summer. He said it were a peaceful place, and I knew he'd've wanted the same. I was sweating like a hog by the time it were done, knowing right well that those men were slipping free as I shoveled earth. But Pa deserved a proper burial. More than any man, he deserved things to be done right in his memory.

He landed slumped on his side when I rolled him into the grave, limbs bent at all the wrong angles, but at least he was facing Ma. He'll sleep for all eternity with his eyes on her. After throwing earth back over him, I fashioned a wooden cross for the grave. I marked it with my pock-etknife—HENRY ROSS THOMPSON, DIED JUNE 6, 1877—hammered it into place with the backside of the shovel, and then rode into Prescott without a backwards glance.

"More?" the bartender says, eyeing my empty glass.

"More," I says. But I don't drink none of it this time. The first two distracted from the pain, but I need my mind sharp.

Behind me, prospectors carry on 'bout elusive gold

and lode claims businessmen won't no longer bite at. A pair of uniforms from Fort Whipple sit to my right, hammering 'bout the Apache. And the girls—they're weaving between the men, kicking up the folds of their dresses and bending down to show off the goods.

I'm half jealous. The wrap I got over my chest to keep my shirt from looking suspiciously full is itching like hellfire. I paw at it again, knowing right well I shouldn't carp. Pa and I rode into Prescott every week for supplies. I's never set foot in the Quartz Rock before, but now ain't the day to risk being recognized. Not with the deed my fingers are itching to do.

I check the mirror.

A whore's approaching my mark. She bends and says something I ain't in range to hear. He grumbles a response. She frowns but then slings an arm behind his neck anyways and tries to squeeze onto his lap.

"I said I ain't interested!" he growls, shoving her off.

"Aw, come now. Ain't no reason to be all ornery." She pushes his hat back and I catch a glimpse of his eyes —narrowed and beady, gleaming like a demon done the devil's work. "Just 'cus it's Sunday don't mean you can't have no fun."

The whore reaches for his jacket. She's meaning to haul him to his feet and lead him to the back rooms, but her hand hits where he's injured.

"Yer bleeding," she says, looking at the smear of red on her fingers. She reaches for him again. "Jesus, yer—"

He backhands her so hard, she goes flying into the

prospectors' table. Drinks clatter and crash. Cards fly up like snowflakes. The men take one look at the whore's welted cheek and then they're jumping to their feet.

My mark draws his gun first. The prospectors freeze solid. The uniforms next to me tense. A stillness spreads through the saloon like a wave of heat rolling over plains, and alls this while I'm stoic at the bar, pretending to be interested in nothing but the glass clutched in my palm.

Keeping the men in his sights, the murderous son of a bitch hobbles toward the door. He don't take his eyes off the men, and they don't dare draw their guns. It ain't too early for drinking, but a shootout's a different matter.

My mark slips onto the street. Soon as the doors swing closed behind him, time unsticks. The whore stands. The prospectors right their table.

I toss some coins onto the bar and follow the bastard.

"Take care, kid," says the bartender.

I shove out the saloon without a word back.

The heat's pressing down like it's fixing to suffocate, and the pale dirt street gleams up almost moonlike. Stirrups and rigging rings wink at me from the saddled horses lining Whiskey Row. Like they know. Like they're urging me on.

I trail the son of a bitch round the corner, where he stumbles for an outhouse and ducks inside.

It's quiet back here. Not even a breeze.

I walk cautious, step nearer. Till I'm so close, I can see every last grain in the flimsy outhouse door. Till I swear I can smell the sweat and blood coming off the wretch on the other side.

My revolver hums on my hip.

I'll kill him for you, Pa. I'll kill him, I'll kill him, I'll kill him.

I draw the pistol with my right hand, grip the door with my left.

One deep breath and I yank it open, sighting the man before the door bangs to a stop 'gainst my shoulder. He's sitting there on the pot, but his pants ain't lowered. He's checking the wound, shirt hanging open, fingers prodding flesh. Alls I can make out is a bloody mess 'long his left side that's starting to soak the top of his trousers.

He goes for his gun but sees mine's already on him and that he ain't got a chance. He freezes, showing me his palms. There's blood covering 'em, and I wonder how much of it's Pa's.

"Reach down real slow-like," I says, "and unhook that pistol belt."

His lip twitches, but he does right in the end. The belt clatters onto the wooden seat the pot's set into. I grab it and toss it onto the dirt behind me.

"Who were you riding with?"

He grunts.

"I said, who the devil were you riding with?"

Still nothing.

I stare into his dark eyes and don't see an ounce of remorse. My father died alone. Alone and cornered and in an unfair fight—a gang 'gainst one. This man could be the very same who slipped the rope over his head, heaved him high, and left him swinging. Blood's pounding in my ears.

"Why'd you do it?" I says. "You didn't take nothing but his pistol. You just killed him and rode on, and for what?"

"You don't know?" The son of a bitch actually laughs. "A man lives with a secret like that his whole life and never tells his own son? Oh, that shines!"

"Yer friends," I says through a snarl, praying I look like I know whatever secret he's on 'bout. "Where are they headed?"

"You'll never catch 'em, and if you do"—he grins up at me, flashing dark teeth—"they'll string you up just like yer Pa."

I kick him right in his bleeding side and he howls.

It weren't a random raid. It were a hunt, with Pa being the target.

"How did you find us?" I says.

The bastard grunts.

"I ain't asking it twice."

"A clerk at Goldwaters," he says. "Real cordial fellow. He pointed us to yer pa with a smile."

Morris.

"Seems you ain't the only boy ignorant of what's walking round yer town," the bastard says. He's still grinning at me with those tarred teeth, and I wanna knock every last one loose.

"Now you listen, and you listen good," I says. "I'm going to Goldwaters, and I'm gonna get what you ain't giving up. Then I'm gonna ride after yer friends and do to them exactly what's in store for you—what's in store for *every* yellow-bellied coward who goes round stringing up innocent men."

"That sounds real nice, boy," he says. "Now for the love of God, lower that damn pistol."

"All right," I says.

And I do.

Right after I shoot him through the skull.

CHAPTER TWO

I let the door bang shut, but it don't block out the image of his face—leathered skin and dark beard, vicious eyes that went wide the moment he realized my intentions.

I kick his pistol belt aside and spit at the base of the outhouse.

"See you in hell, mister."

And that's where I'm going, sure as the sun will rise, 'cus I feel *nothing*. No remorse. No guilt. Not even a sliver of doubt. He deserved it, and I'd do it again. I'd do it over and over, and I wonder if something's wrong with me.

I ain't killed before, and it shouldn't've been so easy.

I quickly head for Silver, and we ride north 'long Whiskey Row, then cut a block east. At the next corner, I tie her up and stalk into Goldwaters. It's a hell of a general store. Anything you could ever need is crammed on these

shelves—flour, spices, jerky, tobacco, ammunition, hard-
ware. There's a grand-looking rocker in the front window
too, handmade of wood and sanded smooth as marble. I
sit in it every time I come in, and today the desire to own
something so meaningless stings through to my ribs.

Morris is at the register, a starched shirt tucked into
his trousers.

"He's a fine young man, Morris," Pa said last week. A
spark were dancing in his eyes with the suggestion, just
like the last twenty times he'd brought it up as we purchased supplies in town.

"You can quit pushing me on him" was my answer. "I
ain't marrying and leaving you alone."

Only now *I'm* alone, honest and true, and Pa never got
to see me off into something stable. I know he wanted
better for me, but I ain't never had a problem with our
homestead. The thought of being confined to town—
standing behind a grocer's counter or waiting at home
for a husband to return—is stifling. Every day the same.
Marrying for security and nothing more. I can fire a rifle
as good as any man. 'Parently I can kill another just as
dead too. I don't see why I should act like I can't just 'cus
it ruffles everyone else's feathers.

I shove my hands in my pockets. The whiskey's caught
up with me now, and my feet don't feel so steady as I
cut up the aisle of flour and canned goods. Morris spots
me easy and inclines his chin. When coming into town,
I'm usually wearing one of my fitted blouses and nicer
skirts, and my hair would be hanging below my hat, dark

and silky and reaching almost to my waist. If Morris don't even do a double take at my current state, it's only a matter of time till another recognizes me—or, worse, places me as the "boy" trailing that bastard at the Quartz Rock.

I check over my shoulder and there ain't no one left in the store but a little old lady examining a bag of flour with such care, I doubt she's got good vision.

"Kate," Morris says. "Yer looking . . ."—he eyes my flannel—"*serious* today."

"Well, I'm here on serious business" is all I says back.

"That so?"

"Did anybody come in asking after my pa recently?"

"Just yesterday," he says. "Someone were inquiring about an old friend by the name of Ross Henry Tompkins. I said, 'Henry *Thompson?*' and he goes, 'Yeah, that's the one. Been a while.' So I told him you two had a place 'long the creek, up past Fort Whipple."

"Did he give his name?"

"No."

"What'd he look like?"

Morris frowns. "Is something wrong?"

"What'd he look like, Morris?"

"Pretty rough. Trousers and chaps. A long black coat. Skin like he'd been working land or running cattle most of his life. Might've been in his late thirties or early forties. He had one heck of a scar below his right eye."

"And he was alone?"

"No, there were a few others riding with him, all packing." Morris pauses. "They weren't friends of yer father's, were they?"

The pistol's humming at my hip again. *Goddamn you, Morris. You as good as killed him.*

"Kate?" Morris reaches 'cross the counter and touches my hand. "Did something happen?"

I pull away. I need to get outta here. I need to leave before I put a bullet between poor Morris's eyes.

"Yer sure everything's all right?" he prods.

I think of what he'll say if I tell him the truth. *Talk to Bowers. Report the raid to Fort Whipple.* But Bowers, like the honest sheriff he is, left a few days back to track a horse thief who rode through town, and Whipple's soldiers protect settlers 'gainst Apache raids, not attacks from their own kind. Not that I got the time for neither. The longer I stand here yapping, the farther south those bastards slip, riding to the devil knows where. I gotta go home and load up my horse. I gotta ride after 'em before the trail goes cold.

"Kate?" Morris says again. "Did something happen?"

"Nah, everything's dandy."

I even buy ammo and supplies just to make him shut pan.

In the last bit of remaining sunlight, I dig through what's left of the house. Pockets of ash are still warm, and certain pieces of furniture fared better than others. Half my bed frame's still standing. Our kitchen table ain't nothing but coals, but the kettle's sitting there atop the rubble, like a hen on eggs.

In what used to be Pa's bedroom, I find what I'd run into the flames for originally: an old metal lunch box he kept stocked with valuables and tucked beneath his mattress. He'd also had a worn leather journal always stowed beside it, but there ain't a sign of that left. Bet it made some mighty fine kindling.

I pluck out the lunch box and bang on it with the fire poker till the warped latch gives. Inside is a drawstring pouch holding a dusting of gold. Pa never liked to talk much 'bout the early days, but I know he spent some time prospecting down in Wickenburg before he and Ma came north and settled near Prescott. The meager funds he earned then helped raise our house 'long the creek, and I reckon nearly everything he had left got spent trying to save Ma from consumption. I were nearly four when she bit.

I shake the pouch, making the gold dance. Looks like there ain't more than a few dozen dollars here, but that's more than I's ever called my own. I pocket it and find a picture of Pa, Ma, and me—still a bundle of a baby—beneath the pouch.

I touch Pa's black-and-white face with my thumb. He's standing all protective-like, one arm wrapped round Ma's shoulder and the other touching the grip of his pistol. I'm a perfect blend of the both of 'em: dark hair from Ma, but extra inches in height gained from Pa. Skin that's caught somewhere between his fair complexion and her golden bronze. She were Mexican, living in Tucson when Pa passed through running cattle years back. The way he told it, there weren't a more beautiful woman in all the Territory. Truth be told, there still ain't many women in Arizona, but Ma *was* pretty. I glance back at the photo. Piercing eyes and high cheeks and a sternness 'bout her that makes me proud.

In a way, it's a blessing she died young. Prescott ain't taking kindly to Mexicans lately. They're run outta town or spat at on the streets. I been seeing less and less of 'em since I were a kid, and the cowardly part of me's happy half my features are Pa's. That I talk like him too.

The only thing left in the box is documents—a deed for our acreage, secured through the Homestead Act a few years ago; notes and ledgers tracking money Pa spent over the years; a small slip of paper folded in half.

I open it. Pa's handwriting shines up at me.

Kate, if you're reading this, stop. You know where you should be. Get on Silver and ride.

"Aw, Goddamn it!" I says.

Silver starts beyond the wrecked frame of the house, ears perking. I look back at the note, now crumpled in my fist.

If anything ever happens to me, you go see Abe in Wickenburg.

That's what Pa always said when I were growing up. Abe in Wickenburg. Wickenburg for Abe. Over and over till my ears were practically bleeding. So many times I had the name and place memorized before I could even pronounce 'em proper.

"But what's gonna happen to you?" I was always asking.

"That ain't the point," he'd say.

Now I'm sitting here wondering if maybe this was exactly what Pa feared—if someone were after him. For what and why I ain't got the slightest. Heaven forbid he'd've explained anything to me.

I slam the box shut. The sun's setting and I can't do nothing 'bout the note till tomorrow. Only a fool would ride south through the mountains at night. You'd need a light, and fire's nothing but a beacon for the Apache.

I grab Silver's reins and lead her down to the barn, which the murderous bastards thankfully didn't burn. Pa's horse, Libby, is still standing there in front of the plow, half saddled and looking confused, and that's when I break.

'Cus this is where they found him, right here. This was where Pa's life began to end.

The saddle stand is on its side. There's boot marks and gouges in the dirt, marking a struggle. A few drops of blood are now so dark, they mostly look like drying mud.

The fog of whiskey's long gone, and yet I unravel like a drunken fool.

Screaming, I throw my hat 'cross the barn and rake my hands through my hair. My fingers snag on the singed and melted ends, and no matter how hard I yank, I can't fight 'em through. I pull out my knife and hack it off. Shorter and shorter, till my hair hangs at my jaw line and I can't feel no evidence of the fire. The bandage round my chest comes off next, and then I'm breathing easy, the tears and gasps free and fast.

I pull blankets off the shelves for the horses, and one for myself. I unhook Libby and lead her to her stall, then curl up at the foot of Silver's and sob. When she lies down beside me rather than sleeping upright, I know I need to pull it together. I can't be so far gone even my horse knows I'm lost.

I count to ten and stop crying. Just like that, I'm done.

When I were first learning to shoot a rifle, Pa told me that nearly every battle people face is in their heads. If you think you can't do something, you won't. If you believe you can, it's only a matter of time before you will.

We'd set bottles on the fence and Pa'd tell me to shoot 'em off. Every time I did, I had to move back three paces. Lately it's been weeks and months between a successful shot—the distance ain't something to shrug at—but I always strike true eventually. *Always.*

But that's physical, and physical is easy. It's just focus and confidence. The emotional stuff, Pa warned, gets under yer skin and poisons yer mind. And I can't stand for that. I made a promise to that sick bastard in the outhouse. If my word dies with him, it'll be as if I never said it, and I have no intention of letting that murderous gang ride free.

But I'll do right by Pa, too. I'll go see Abe. Maybe he'll even know what Pa was spooked by and who I'm up 'gainst. Maybe I can head off informed rather than blind.

I hunker into my blanket. First thing tomorrow, I'll go see Abe. But I ain't staying. Pa never made me promise to stay.

The horses sleep, but I don't. All night I keep a hand on my pistol and my senses sharp. Only thing I hear is Pa chiding in my ear. *Wickenburg, Wickenburg, Wickenburg. If anything ever happens to me, you go see Abe in Wickenburg.*

I think I hate Abe, and I ain't even met him yet.

CHAPTER THREE

I ride south with the dawn and don't look back. Not at the burnt house or Granite Creek or even the streets of Prescott as I tear through 'em.

Soon I'm entering the Bradshaw Mountains, the world going green round me. The shrubs get denser and the trees more vibrant. Pines sprout up as we climb, thicker and taller and making it difficult to see if there's trouble waiting ahead.

The trail I'm following has been used by prospectors and settlers traveling to Prescott for well over a decade, plus the stagecoach. Freighters come by this pass too, taking goods over the mountains by wagon once they unload from steamboats 'long the Colorado. I seen 'em winding into town like sluggish snakes—Murphy wagons loaded up with barrels of whiskey, and bags of flour and salt. It's been a while since Apache raids were a guaranteed occurrence, and I can't remember the last time a freighter lost a haul to a burnt wagon on account of Indians, but I still got a hand ready to draw my pistol or rifle. This is the kind of route where unsuspecting folk can get cleaned dry.

"You'll let me know if you hear something I don't, won't you, girl?" I says, patting Silver 'long the neck. I got my chest wrapped tight again, and I'm hoping I look like a boy to anyone I cross. Not that one boy can't be gutted as easily as one girl, but a girl trekking through the Bradshaws by her lonesome sure's gonna stick out more. Hell, I'll be safest pretending I'm a boy the rest of my life. The frontier ain't for the faint of heart, and it certainly ain't kind to women. Sometimes I think the whole world's 'gainst us.

I look back at Libby, who's trailing me and Silver with her head somewhat droopish. She's older now—Pa had her longer than he had me—but I weren't 'bout to leave her behind to starve. Besides, her and Silver get on like a pair of old maids. If Libby makes it over these mountains, I think she'll fare all right on the plains.

The trail winds higher, and by midday I ain't seen nothing but a shining view of the downward slope of the Bradshaws and the valley that waits to the south. The Hassayampa leads the way, cutting through shrubs and brambles, looking dry from my perch even when I know right well the water don't go underground till closer to Wickenburg.

Hassayampa. *The river that flows upside down.*

I ain't fond of having to follow it. Indians like the water.

Crooks like the water. *Trouble* likes the water. The sooner I get to Wickenburg, the better, and it ain't a short ride. I'll be lucky if I make it to Walnut Grove by dusk. Still, I ain't pushing the horses hard through this pass. Not where the trail is rough and roots crop up and a busted ankle will strand me like prey for vultures.

The descent is even slower than the climb. The heat's rising and the landscape's drying up. Shrubs start to outnumber the pines, and soon the land's looking more parched than fertile. When the trail levels out 'longside the Hassayampa, the dry creek bed's twice as wide as the narrow trickle of water running south. I let the horses drink while I eat a bit of jerky from my pack.

When I look back at the mountains, I swear I see someone crouched on the trail, so far off that they're nothing but a speck of tanned skin. I pull my rifle from the saddle scabbard and the figure lurches upright, disappearing into the vegetation, graceful like a deer.

I click my tongue for Libby and turn Silver south with hair raised on the back of my neck. How long were that Indian tracking me? I didn't hear a sound in them mountains—not beyond my own horses' shoes and the wind rustling Ponderosa needles.

We gotta move. We gotta fly.

I put my heels into Silver and hope Libby can keep up.

Walnut Grove is the saddest little town I's ever seen.

The center's made up of only a few buildings, two

of which are saloons. A half-dozen settlers have set up homesteads where the land is level enough to allow it, and they're the only things that look promising in the community. Most of the vegetation here ain't higher than my hips, and tilling this earth don't look like much fun. It's all sand and bone-dry dirt.

I reckon the place were buzzing once. All these abandoned mining towns were. When prospectors first descended on Arizona Territory, they dug and drilled any which place till they struck gold. Then, no matter how small the lode or weak the vein, they'd file a claim, sell the rights to the supposed "mine" to some wealthy pioneer businessman, and move on in search of a new one. I reckon them rich folk eventually started realizing not all claims are equal, or even worth their time, 'cus sorry excuses for mining towns like Walnut Grove crumpled. The prospectors rolled out. Communities dried up like creek beds, till all that remained were the folks too lost to go elsewhere. The mining towns to survive were the ones with substantial gold, like in Wickenburg, or places like Prescott, held strong by decent farming land and the fact it were our capital once and is again now.

I tie Silver and Libby outside the dingier of Walnut Grove's two saloons and push through the doors. Inside, there's a bartender and three patrons: Two wide men and a lady wider than the both of 'em put together. She's sitting on a piano with her skirt hiked up so high I can see the garter above her knee. One of the men plucks out a song on the ivories while she sings boldly outta tune. I tip my hat at her like the gent I'm pretending to be and walk up to the bar.

"What can I do you for?" the bartender says, pouring himself some whiskey.

"Just a touch of information, I hope."

He sips his drink and it leaves his handlebar mustache dripping like a cattle dog come outta a river.

"I's wondering if you could help me find someone in Wickenburg," I says. "Goes by Abe." Just in case someone *were* after Pa, I figure it's best to be asking things in Walnut Grove, where there ain't no one of consequence, 'stead of a bustling mining town like Wickenburg.

"Abe?" the bartender parrots. "Josie, you knew an Abe, didn't ya?"

She stops singing and the man quits plucking keys.

"Abe ain't worth yer time, boy," she says. "Have a drink and join us. You know 'Rose of Alabama'? Play it, Claude. You know that's my favorite."

Claude goes back to stroking the keys, and the three of 'em howl like coyotes.

"I ain't in town for a singsong," I says. Or more like shouts. "I'm looking for Abe."

Josie hops from the piano and hits the floorboards with a thunder. By the time she saunters up to me, I's decided that she could kill me by sitting on me.

"You just might be the prettiest boy to come through town all decade," she says, eyeing me up and down.

I knew I shoulda roughed myself up more, patted my face with dirt or even given myself a cut or two. I make a note to drop my voice more in the future, speak deeper and lower.

"I reckon I might remember where Abe's place is for a kiss." Josie offers me her cheek.

"I reckon you might be overestimating how badly I wanna find him."

I turn away and the men hoot in the corner. Josie laughs too, deep and rich.

"Aw, heavens, boy. I ain't been turned down in a coon's age."

"I'll take that drink," I says to the bartender. He pours it. This is turning into a damned disaster.

"Last I knew, Abe was on the outskirts of Wickenburg," Josie says. "His place'll be the first you pass when you ride into town. Claude—Claude! Back to it," she says. "Oh, brown Rosey"—Claude joins in on the keys—"Rose of Alabama . . ."

The trio squawk on together.

"Quite a concert you got yerself," I says to the bartender.

He grunts and downs more whiskey.

"Say, I'm trying to catch up with a friend."

"Abe. We know."

"Nah, someone else. He likely rode through yesterday. Has a crew with him and a scar beneath his right eye."

Claude hits a wrong key and the song crashes to a halt behind me. The bartender's expression goes so sour, you'd think I pulled my Colt on him. He reaches below the counter and brings out a shotgun as though I have.

"You go on and get," he says, jabbing the barrel at me.

I hold my hands up. "I ain't even paid for my drink."

"It's no matter. Just get. Yer kind ain't welcome here."

"My kind?"

"The Rose Riders," he says. "Now, you's got till the count of ten to get outta my place before I fill you with this lead plum."

He starts counting, and I back out calm as ever. I tip my hat at Josie in the corner, who's still staring.

"Thanks for the concert, miss," I says. Then I push out the saloon doors and hop on Silver.

The bartender and the trio step outside to watch me ride out, and even with a shotgun aimed at my back I can't keep a grin from creeping onto my face.

'Cus my so-called friend came through this way, and now his gang's got a name.

I'm one step closer to tracking his yellow ass down and sending him to rot in hell.

'Bout five miles outside Walnut Grove, I realize I'm in a bad place.

The sky's losing its color and there's another twenty miles or so between me and Wickenburg. I'm gonna have to make camp for the night.

I ride till I find a small gully bordered with shrubs and prickly pear. I lead the horses off the trail and throw both sets of reins round the branches of a short mesquite tree. Then I run back to the trail and look down at the potential camp. Silver's ears are still visible, but in the dead of night nobody's gonna be looking this way. And I certainly won't be visible once I'm lying on my bedroll.

I get a small fire crackling, and as I scarf down some jerky my thoughts drift back to what the bartender said. *The Rose Riders.*

I think that's Waylan Rose's band, notorious for robbing stagecoaches all 'cross New Mexico. As gold strikes started cropping up in Arizona, the posse came west, preying on the lines between mining towns and looking to clean out treasure boxes full of fresh ore. I know it 'cus I overheard Bowers complaining 'bout Rose once, even though Prescott ain't been booming with prospectors for at least a decade now. I thumb my lip, trying to wager what mighta brought Rose north of his normal routes and to Pa.

I make sure my coals are scattered long before the sky goes dark. As the evening cools, I hunker into my bedroll and watch the bats swooping in the last bit of twilight. The sky's so big, I swear I could swim right into it.

It's quiet, but not in the way I'm used to. When Pa were still alive, his voice were the last thing I'd hear every night. "Sleep well, Kate," he'd say, and tug my bedroom door shut with a creak. Dreaming always seemed easy after that. But without Pa's words, there's too much nothing—too much sky and space and endless parched land.

Sleep well, Kate, I tell myself. *Sleep well, sleep well, sleep well.*

I tip my Stetson down to cover my eyes and wait for sleep to find me.

I wake to a tumbling in the brush.

Eyes bolting open, I reach for my rifle, but it's big, and tucked away beneath my blankets. Worried about making too much noise, I draw my pistol real quiet-like and strain my hearing. And there it is again, someone grunting or struggling, not more than a few dozen paces away. I push my hat up slow and let my eyes adjust.

Silver and Libby are awake, both sets of ears sharper than spindles in the moonlight. I see the movement next —shaking brush at the far end of the ditch, right where the earth starts to steepen. Standing careful, I keep the pistol ready and my steps silent. Whoever it is hears me coming, though, 'cus the rustling quits.

"I know yer in there," I whisper. I reach out to pull back the branches. "Come out with—"

A dark shape darts outta the brush and charges my legs, squealing. I get knocked down hard, tailbone throbbing, and then something bites my ankle.

"Son of a . . ."

I look up to see the javelina fleeing.

"No good wild hogs," I says.

The stout creature snorts at me and then rejoins his small herd in devouring a cactus.

Thank goodness for my boots. If it weren't for the tough leather protecting my ankles, I'd probably be bleeding right now. I heave to my feet, still cursing the creatures, and hobble back to camp. I have my guard so low, I nearly miss the worse threat still.

"See? I told you we'd find his camp."

I freeze, crouching low behind a shrub.

"But where's the kid? Claude said he were headed this way."

"Why in tarnation would I know? Let's just scare his horses and take the gear."

"How we gonna get the bounty if we don't have a body?"

"He ain't gonna head nowhere but back to town on foot, you imbecile. Then we kill him and collect. Now get those reins untied."

"Hang on. There ain't even a rose burned into these saddles. Ain't that their mark?"

"Maybe there's no mark 'cus he's trying to keep it hush. 'Cus he knows Rose's head is worth a fortune and any of his riders's a nice purse too."

"I's got a bad feeling, Tom. Kid's probably watching us right now, ready to shoot us dead."

I don't wanna. Not if I don't have to. My bullets are meant to avenge Pa, but I still squeeze my pistol's grip.

"Go stand watch, then," Tom says to his partner.

"Stand watch? Watching ain't gonna do much 'gainst a Rose Rider." But he drifts up the ditch to where their horses wait and he can better survey my camp.

Tom yanks Libby's reins free of the tree. Just as fast, he draws his pistol and shoots a bullet into the ground behind her.

She rears, then takes off north.

Aw, hell.

I reach down near my feet and feel round till I find a rock the size of my palm. Then I throw it toward the trail. Soon as Tom's partner walks off to investigate the sound, I jump up from behind the shrub and sight Tom.

"I wouldn't do that," I says to him, cocking my pistol.

He lets go of Silver's reins and raises his hands.

"Walk back to yer horse and ride outta here," I says, "and we can forget this happened."

"And let you continue on and slaughter Abe's family?" he says. "I can't do that, son."

"Yer worried 'bout Abe? It don't got nothing to do with a bounty?"

"Well, you caught me. I guess it does."

He spins and draws his gun so quick, alls I can do is react. I pull my trigger. Tom goes flying into the mesquite tree and crumples still.

Jesus, he's dead.

I did that.

I didn't even mean to or want to, but he woulda got me. If my gun hadn't already been out, I know I'd be dead. My heart's pounding frantic in my chest.

"Tom?" his partner calls. "Was that the second horse? Can we get outta here now?"

I duck behind Silver and stretch my arms over her back so that when Tom's partner appears on the ridge he's already in my sights.

"I'll count to three, and if yer still here, I'm shooting," I says. "One, tw—"

He scrambles onto his horse and grabs the reins of the

second. I watch 'em flee north, the dust blowing up pale. Once he's gone, I whistle for Libby, knowing right well she's outta ear shot and ain't coming back. Pa had her nearly twenty years and I lose her in less than a day. It's like I'm failing him all over again. Like I can't get nothing right.

"You stupid idiot," I says to the dead man at the base of the tree. "I ain't a Rose Rider. I want 'em dead just like you, and alls you's done is lose me a horse and get yerself killed."

His wide eyes stare up at me, and my pistol starts in my grasp. I stuff it back in the holster. I gotta move. The other man'll be back, only I doubt by hisself.

I throw my saddle over Silver, then cinch my gear in place. One glance at the extra effects Libby was carrying and I know I can't afford to take them.

Abe, you better be worthwhile, I says to myself. Then Silver and I are moving again, a bullet streaking beneath the moon.

CHAPTER FOUR

Abe's appears on the horizon just after dawn. My stomach's growling and I ain't slowed once to quiet it or even take a drink. Neither of which is smart. I'm sweating so much, dirt's clinging to me like a gritty second skin, and the scent of last night's campfire lingers on my flannel, reminding me that I been up a long while without refilling my stomach.

Ahead, the homestead's quaint—a modest house resting in the corner of a fenced plot of land. What ain't quaint is the barn. It's massive, big enough that I start wondering if the place is a ranch. I thought everyone living round these parts stuck to mining—that's all Wickenburg's been good for since the first strike at Vulture Mine over a decade ago—but I reckon beef and dairy's gotta come from someplace. Could be Abe's got an arrangement with folk in town, supplies them with goods on a schedule more dependable than incoming freighting wagons.

I pull Silver to a halt 'longside the fence. A mangy-looking cattle dog lounges by the barn, where two boys — one round my age, the other a bit older — are saddling horses. They both pause to eye me. When I don't budge, they argue a moment, and finally the older one walks over.

He's squinting like the sun's in his eyes when it ain't, and he makes a show of tossing his jacket open so I can glimpse the pistol on his hip. The wine-colored handkerchief beneath his chin reminds me of one Pa used to wear. I feel my lip wanting to tremble, and I bite it.

Not here. Not now.

"You lost, friend?" the boy says. Up close, I wager he's round twenty. Dark stubble covers his jaw, and the only creases in his skin are the ones surrounding his eyes. Suppose he wouldn't even have those if he quit squinting so much.

"Wickenburg's just another few miles ahead. Keep right on following this trail." He points it out like I'm blind.

"I'm looking for Abe," I says.

"Abe's dead."

"What? He can't be."

"Sure he can. Got kicked in the temple by a horse two years back and died the same day."

"But I'm supposed to see him."

"That's gonna be a problem, then, ain't it?"

I'm 'bout to tell him he's a rotten pain when I spot a

flake of grief in his features. "I'm sorry for yer loss," I says dryly.

"You and everyone but God, it seems." He reaches a hand over the fence. "Jesse Colton. Abe was my father." I bend from Silver and we shake. "This is the part where you tell me yer name," Jesse adds.

"Nate," I says. It's the first thing to pop into my head. "Nate Thompson."

"Thompson?" Jesse's squinty eyes go even narrower.

"I were to come see Abe if anything happened to my pa. Well, something happened, so here I am."

But Jesse's not even listening no more. He's waving for the other boy in the field like a madman flagging down a stagecoach. "Leave the horses," he shouts to him. "Meet me inside."

What a waste of time. Abe dead, Wickenburg pointless. I click my tongue, and Jesse vaults over the fence, putting his hands up to stop me and Silver.

"What was yer pa's name?" he says.

"Henry."

"Henry *Thompson?*"

"That's what I said, weren't it?"

Jesse rubs his jaw. "Why don't you come in and sit awhile. Sarah's making biscuits and it won't be no trouble if you join."

"I ain't got time for biscuits or sitting," I says. "If Abe ain't here, I got places to be."

"Nate." Jesse grabs Silver's bridle and looks me dead in the eye. "Abe always said a young Thompson might come calling. We got something for you, something of yer pa's. We been holding it for ages."

Inside, the farmhouse smells of fresh bread and burnt coffee. The table's covered in mismatched plates and silverware, and I don't think there's a single mug that ain't chipped.

I smear honey on a biscuit and shovel it down 'longside some eggs. I know I'm eating like a heathen, but I can't tell if the quiet's 'cus of my lack of manners or just the very fact that I'm here.

"Yer real," says the boy 'cross the way. He's so small, his chin barely clears the table. Maybe five years old. "Will said it were all horseshit."

"Jake, you watch yer mouth," Sarah snaps, smacking the back of his head for added emphasis. She's pretty —pale hair and pale skin and a slender neck accented by the buttoned collar of her periwinkle dress. She looks like one of them porcelain dolls. I reckon she's Jesse's wife, but no one's introduced me proper, and frankly, I don't give two hoots. I'm eating, getting whatever they're holding for me, and making for town. Trails run cold pretty fast when you ain't riding 'em.

"You were mentioned by Abe nearly once a week when he were still alive," Sarah says to me by way of apology. "It was always, *Henry's kid'll come through one day, don't yous forget it,* but sometimes it were hard to believe. More coffee?"

She sloshes some into my mug before I can answer.

"And what do you know, Will?" Jesse says, elbowing the boy he was saddling horses with earlier. "I was right like always."

"And the day yer finally wrong, I'm gonna let you know it for a decade," Will mutters back. Theys got the same nose and jaw, only Will don't squint constantly.

Jake stuffs some biscuit in his mouth and keeps his eyes rooted on me.

"Didn't nobody tell you it's rude to stare?" I says.

The boy wipes his nose with his sleeve and keeps at it.

"Use a napkin, Jake," Jesse says.

"You don't gotta pretend to be his father," Sarah says to Jesse.

"Well, when's Roy getting back, Sarah? He were due two days ago, and we ain't heard a word. I told you I never trusted that miner. I don't know why you went and married him."

"You don't trust no one, Jesse. Not even yer own sister!"

Not married, then.

I keep my head down, eating while they argue 'bout Roy and someone named Clara. I ain't got the energy to try and figure the relationships or follow the argument.

When there's a brief lull, Will cuts in. "What happened to yer pa, Nate?"

"Got himself hanged."

"For horse thieving? High-grading?"

"My pa weren't no criminal," I says.

"So why a hanging?"

"It were a murder, and I'm fixing to find out why. Hopefully whatever Abe's been holding'll help." I drop my fork and wipe my face clean. "What was it you had for me?"

Jesse stands and motions for me to follow him. In a small bedroom, he pulls open a desk drawer and dumps the contents. Then he lifts away a piece of wood lining the bottom to reveal a hidden compartment. There ain't nothing in it but an envelope. He hands it to me.

"A letter?" I says, doubtful.

He shrugs. "I'll give you a moment."

I sink into the desk chair and turn the envelope over in my hands. It's yellowed with age, and there ain't a mark of ink on it. Not my name or nothing. I slide my finger beneath the wax and break the seal.

The pages I pull out are brittle and coarse. Pa's script is formal and elegant, so unlike his speaking voice.

If you're reading this, it means bad folk came for me, and I'm terribly sorry I never told you the truth, Kate. I always planned to, at the right time, but maybe time got away from me. Maybe I thought we were safe.

The short of it is, your mother and I found gold when we were very young. Not here in Wickenburg, but farther south, in the Salt River Valley. There's a mine and a couple caches sitting in the Superstition Mountains, and we only found our way to it because of the journal. We crossed two burro skeletons while prospecting, and a pair of human ones accompanying them. The saddlebags were still loaded up with gold, but the men had their skulls shot through, and the journal was sitting there among the bones. Leather bound, thick. The very one I keep under my bed. It had maps and directions. Instructions based on the sun and the cactuses and the canyon rock forms. It had everything, Kate, and we found one of the caches. Not the mine itself, but even still the cache was overflowing with ore.

I reckon it was someone's wealth, stored up. Probably the dead mens' or whoever shot 'em through the head, unless that were Indians. I didn't want to touch the stuff — I had a bad feeling — but Maria said we could live easy off it. We took as much as we could carry and never looked back.

The problem, see, is that gold tends to leave a trail. Back in Tucson, people wanted to know where we'd struck. They asked too many questions. Some even came to the house in the night, aiming to kill us for the prize. Once you were born, I knew we had to move.

In Wickenburg, I switched my name from Ross Henry Tompkins to Henry Ross Thompson. I prospected a few months until I got "lucky." Then we took the gold we'd had all along and moved to Prescott, claiming henceforth that our money was earned in a strike near Vulture Mine, though we never let on the true sum of our fortune. Not even Abe knows the full story, and he's a good, honest friend. He let us live in his barn those few months when we pretended to have no money or means to raise a shelter.

Abe might be the only person left I trust in this world, and you're to stay with him. He'll be a good father, and he promised me he'd look out for you. Take on his last name and don't look back to Prescott. Don't return to the house.

Don't ride after whoever came for me and the journal. Gold makes monsters of men, and they'll kill you for information, even a letter as simple as this.

Stay with Abe in Wickenburg. No matter how old you are when you read this, stay with Abe.

I love you, and I'm sorry.

I stuff the papers back in the envelope. *Stay,* he says. *Stay!*

Like he can command me round when he's dead and every bit of our past is a lie. My father's first name is Ross, not Henry. I ain't even truly a Thompson!

Morris's words return to me—Waylan Rose had asked after a Ross *Henry Tompkins* in Goldwaters. I grab my Stetson by the pinch and set it on my head. I wonder what else those bastards know 'bout my pa that I don't even know myself.

Outside the room I can hear Jesse arguing with Sarah 'bout Roy again. Jesse's aiming to head to Tucson with Will.

"And the boy?" Sarah says. "Nate?"

"What of him?"

"Yer gonna leave him with me and Jake? This place's hard enough to keep up when you and Will is here. Jerking the meat and tilling the land and milking the cows and—"

"So an extra set of hands should help," Jesse says.

"Why's you so sure Nate'll stay?"

"'Cus Abe always said once the kid came, he wouldn't

go. He'd be like family. That we were supposed to make room."

"I can barely feed the mouths already here."

"Well, which is it, Sarah? You want more people round or less?"

"Yer twisting everything I say."

"I got cattle to pick up in Tucson either way. If Roy ain't showing face, Will and I might as well meet Clara while we're there."

I's heard enough. Sarah don't need to worry 'bout me, 'cus I ain't staying. There's an obvious route now. The Rose Riders'll stick to the Hassayampa, following the trail south toward Phoenix. Then they'll ride east with the Salt River and into the mountains, where they'll use Pa's journal to hunt down the mine. 'Cus now I'm damn near certain it didn't burn in the fire.

Why'd the bastards have to hang him for it? Couldn't they have just beat him till he said where the journal were hid and then rode out with the prize? Couldn't they have left me my father?

Damn gold.

Pa's right—it does make monsters of men. And women. 'Cus while I don't want the riches, I want that gang dead, and I ain't quitting till each of 'em's as cold as that bastard in the outhouse. I know exactly where they're headed, and I'll see that their destination becomes their graves.

I tuck Pa's note into my pocket and drag the chair to the window, scrambling out without a backwards glance.

CHAPTER FIVE

I thought summers were hot in Prescott, but Wickenburg feels like hellfire burning my lungs.

When I ride into town at noon, the sun is high and angry, and with luck no one's followed me from the Colton ranch. Here, the streets are so hard and bone-white parched, I bet rain would just pool and puddle if it fell. I loosen the kerchief at my neck and twist round in the saddle. I'm sweating from every last pore, and while I'm used to that, I ain't used to it while pretending to be a boy. The wrap on my chest is growing damper by the moment, and I find myself wishing for a skirt more than ever in my life, if only to feel a bit of moving air on my legs.

The town is bustling. Women drift between shops, attending to errands. The few businessmen I spot are wearing vests and trimmed jackets, some even sporting walking canes. Most of the fellas are miners, though, looking worn out and beaten. I overhear a pair of Chinese men complaining 'bout wages, wondering if it's better to slave in the mines or to head to Yuma and lay tracks for the Southern Pacific. "Pay will be a fraction of the whites' either place," his friend grumbles.

I pass the stage stop, where a few grand-looking coaches—Concords—wait outside. Pa once said them carriages are built so sturdy, they never break down, only wear out. If these came all the way from New Hampshire and still look as pretty and solid as they do now on Wickenburg's streets, I don't doubt it.

Nearby is a general store, and I stop to replenish the supplies I had to desert after losing Libby. I splurge on a new shirt too, as the one I'm wearing's already starting to stink and I ain't sure when I'll be able to wash proper. I pay in gold from Pa's leather pouch.

"Where'd you get this, boy?" the clerk says. His teeth are stained dark.

"I didn't steal it, if that's what yer asking."

"Good. High-grading's a serious offense round here. Could find yerself swinging from the mine's hanging tree."

That there's an actual tree dedicated to the matter don't sit well with me. I snatch up my purchased effects. "Like I said, it ain't stolen."

He just eyes me wary, then spits into the spittoon. The dip dings the side. Of all the nasty, vile habits.

I force a closed-lip smile and leave, feeling his gaze on me the whole way. Makes me wonder if Tom's pal somehow sent word ahead to Wickenburg and people here are looking for an outlaw who matches my description. Tom's wide eyes flash before me. He coulda had a family, people relying on him. Somewhere in Walnut Grove, another girl might be without her father. Regret pinches in my stomach.

I hurry for Silver and load her up. As I ride outta town, a cloud billows up at the other end, two riders storming in. They're moving fast and shouting for someone, urgency on their tongues. I push Silver harder, not wanting to be caught in the middle of a shootout or whatever madness a mining town like Wickenburg tends to see.

When the first bullet is fired, it sounds sharp on my heels, and I realize it were meant for me. I draw my Colt and yank Silver's reins, but she ain't fond of turning to face the gunfire. I nearly fall off the saddle as she panics, and when I do get her to quit running, I twist over my shoulder, aiming my pistol.

The two riders chasing me rear up.

"Woah, woah, easy there," Jesse says.

"You gol-darn idiot! What are you shooting at me for?"

"Well, you weren't stopping. Didn't you hear us screaming yer name?"

"What?" I says.

"Nate. We were yelling *Nate* as we rode in, and you just left like you were deaf."

'Cus I didn't hear 'em, not that I'm sure I woulda responded anyway. It ain't like Nate's my name.

"Maybe he *is* deaf," Will says.

"You know I ain't." And to Jesse: "You coulda killed me."

"It were a warning shot into the sky," he says, "but I coulda stripped the hat from yer head without nicking you if I wanted."

"While riding a horse and me bouncing round on mine?" I says. "I doubt it."

I grab Silver's reins.

"Hang on." Jesse pulls up 'longside me. "Where the devil are you going?"

"Why's it matter?"

"'Cus yer supposed to stay at the ranch with Sarah."

"I ain't supposed to do nothing. It's a free country."

"What a grumpy loaf," Will says.

"Shut it, Will," Jesse says. And to me he adds, "You ran out and didn't tell nobody."

"I got places to be."

"Like where?"

"Oh, in tarnation." I stop Silver cold and glare. "If I tell you, will you leave me in peace?"

Will laughs, and Jesse squints those squinty eyes. "Maybe," he says.

"Well, *maybe* ain't good enough."

"Then I reckon we'll just keep riding 'longside you. We're headed to Tucson to pick up some cattle, and three men riding together's always safer than two."

Tucson! I'll be stuck with them on my tail the whole way to the Salt River Valley. I nudge Silver to action and nearly trample their cattle dog, which is apparently trailing them 'cross Arizona too. It's a blasted convoy on my heels.

"I'm going after the men that killed my pa," I says, hoping it will scare the boys off. "You might not want to stick too close."

"You know who did it?" Jesse asks.

"Yep. A gang goes by the Rose Riders."

"That's Waylan Rose and his boys! You can't be serious, Nate."

"More serious than a rattler shaking."

Jesse wobbles his head. "Nate, that man's the meanest hog in the Territory. He attacks coaches and cleans out treasure boxes. He don't leave no one alive, not even women or children. What the devil are you gonna do 'gainst him and a gang of grown men? Yer just a kid."

"I'm eighteen," I snap.

"Come off it."

"You calling me a liar?"

"Don't worry, Nate," Will says. "You'll fill out and get some whiskers on that baby-smooth chin. Maybe yer just a late bloomer."

"Shut it, Will," Jesse says. "Don't go making the kid feel bad."

"I ain't a kid, and I don't feel bad," I says, nearly screaming. "I don't feel nothing but soured that I ain't able to ride in peace."

"Sorry," Jesse says. "We'll talk less."

"Less?"

"Like I said, we're riding for Tucson. If you ain't turning

back to the ranch, I reckon we might as well keep each other company."

"I don't *want* company!"

"Sheesh he's wound tight," Will says. "Maybe we should go back to Wickenburg and buy him a poke."

I glare. "I don't want a poke neither."

"Every man wants a poke. And there ain't much but plains and creek beds here to Phoenix, kid, least of all gals."

"I said I don't want one."

"You ever had one?"

"I's . . . Course I . . ." God almighty, please strike me dead.

"Will, quit it," Jesse says. "If the kid don't want one, he don't want one."

"Suit yerself," Will says, shrugging.

"Why can't you both just shove off and leave me be?" I snap.

"Fine, we will—if'n you tell me yer plan," Jesse says.

"Plan? The plan's to track 'em, catch up, and put a bullet between Waylan's eyes. What more of a plan do I need?"

"So you'll follow the river the whole way? Stick to the trail?"

"It's the quickest route."

"Also the deadliest." Jesse folds his arms. "I reckon you got a plan for keeping watch at night, too. Maybe you's figured how to sleep with one eye open?"

I ain't got an answer for that and he knows it.

"Way I see it, we're heading the same way, and we're all better off riding together. There's safety in numbers, and yer pa sent you to mine so you'd be outta harm's way. Not so you could run off and get yerself killed within a fortnight."

The mishap outside Walnut Grove flashes—losing Libby, getting hunted for a bounty that don't even apply to me. I spend one blasted night alone and barely get through it. There's easily another three before Phoenix.

"Fine," I says, stifling my pride. "We can ride together, but only if you shut pan."

"It's like we ain't doing him a favor," Will complains.

Jesse just smiles and squints at the cattle dog. "What do you think, Mutt? Can we keep quiet?"

The dog yaps and runs ahead to lead.

I knew Abe's would be nothing but trouble.

Jesse keeps us on a southern-bound and well-traveled road that leads to Vulture Mine, then beyond.

We pass a few miners on horseback, reporting to or leaving work. We never see the mine entrance, but we do see the hanging tree. It's a massive mesquite, with branches so heavy, they's started to grow back toward the ground for a place to rest. There's an empty rope still swinging from one of the higher limbs, like the tree's proud of its work and wants to remind everyone of it.

Once we pass south of the mine, the land starts to

mellow, flattening out like it's been steamrolled. Ridges and rock forms vanish. Trees get scarcer and smaller. Soon I can see for what feels like forever, the Hassayampa plains spreading before me like a blanket. The sun beats down on my Stetson. I feel a bead of sweat drip between my breasts, and soon I'm fixating on it—wanting to tear off my flannel and wrap and go swim in the river. Not that there's likely anything left to swim in. It must be underground now.

Will spits dip at Mutt, trying to hit him, while Jesse checks our course with his compass. After peering at the land ahead through his binoculars, he gives us a nod.

"All clear."

There ain't dust puffing up anywhere round us, and I coulda told him the same just by using my naked eye, but I bite my tongue. The less talking, the better. I don't want 'em getting the idea I like 'em dogging me.

"So when are you gonna tell me?" Jesse says, riding 'longside me on Rebel. That's his horse's name. Will's is named Rio. Mutt used to be called Bailey, but he only responds to Mutt, so that's what he gets. I know alls this 'cus Jesse's told me even though I ain't asked. Heck, he ain't stopped talking since we left Wickenburg.

"Tell you what?" I says.

"Why Rose and his men hanged yer pa?"

"No idea."

"I think yer lying."

"I think yer nosy."

"It's just—what's the Rose Riders got to do up in

Prescott, hunting down one lone farmer? That don't sound like their typical job. 'Less of course yer pa was moving treasure boxes you ain't telling us 'bout."

I says nothing.

"You know, I lost my ma in a bad way. Not to a gang of outlaws but to a band of Indians. It were ages ago, and it hurt for a long, long while. Still does on occasion. But the hurt fades with time. You always feel it, but it becomes a duller sting, 'stead of sharp. Course, that's assuming you don't ride the road of vengeance. You got good intentions, Nate, but that path's like rubbing salt in the wound. Yer cut'll never scab over."

God almighty, it's like I'm sitting in the Sunday pews.

"Nate," he says, real serious when I don't respond. "Sometimes you gotta let the people you love go."

"Yeah, 'cus yer so good at that," Will mumbles.

"I mean it, Nate," Jesse says, ignoring his brother.

I glance over and find Jesse's giving me this real concerned look, like I'm a jackrabbit headed for a snare. His hat paints a line of shadow 'cross his eyes. Sure, sometimes you gotta let things go, but other times you can't till you set things right. And I know darn well it ain't worth arguing with a preacher. The only truths they believe are their own words.

So I just frown and carry on.

"You always this chatty?" Jesse says.

"Why should I bother talking? Yer jawing enough for the both of us."

I kick my heels into Silver and trot on ahead. Behind me, Will's laughing.

"Shut it, Will," Jesse says.

"Nah, I think that's what he wants *you* to do."

We ride on, Jesse now soured enough that the only thing coming outta his mouth is exhales. I listen to the wind in the brush and the scratch of tumbleweeds and dirt crunching beneath Silver's shoes.

Finally, peace.

CHAPTER SIX

We quit riding with an hour of sunlight remaining.

Jesse makes a big to-do 'bout picking a good camp and finally settles on a spot where we got a pair of shrubs and a bit of rock for shelter. It won't stop anyone from spotting us, though, so we'll take turns keeping watch throughout the night. "Just in case," Jesse says.

The Apache tend to stick to the mountains, and the Rose Riders are well ahead of us. I wager anyone else out is doing exactly what we're doing right now—making camp—but I don't carp. I'm tired and hungry and dripping sweat down my back. I'm as eager as any to call it a day. Plus, the sooner the boys eat, the sooner they'll close their eyes for the night, giving me a chance to relieve myself in private. A complication I didn't consider when deciding to pose as a boy. Then again, I never figured I'd be riding with real ones.

Jesse swipes a can of milk from my saddlebags and whips up some biscuits, baking 'em over our fire. They come out tough and plain and half charred, but we shovel 'em down 'longside some jerky and bacon while the horses graze nearby. I won't never admit it, but it's sorta nice to not be completely alone. When we're full, and after the sky paints us a mighty fine sunset, we tie the horses up to the shrubs and roll out our beds. My bladder's 'bout ready to burst, but there ain't much but flat plains surrounding us, nowhere I can sneak off to without looking suspicious.

"You riding to Tucson with us?" Will asks. "Or you peeling off early to track down men you ain't fit to hunt?"

"Phoenix area," I says. "That's where we split."

"Phoenix?" Jesse says from 'cross camp. He's sitting on his bedroll, a small notebook propped 'gainst his knee. "There's nothing there but a bunch of crazed homesteaders trying to create an oasis in the middle of the desert."

"That's where he's going—Rose and his boys," I says.

"How you know that?"

"I just do."

"We can't help you without details, Nate," Jesse says, and goes back to writing. Or maybe drawing. His pencil is making shapes too long and flowing to be just words.

"When did I ever say I wanted help?"

He shrugs and snaps the notebook closed, then settles into his bedroll and tips his hat low to cover his eyes.

"Jesse ain't fixing to pester you," Will says. "He frets over everybody; thinks it's his job. Plus, he's still crotchety 'cus I beat him at poker the other night. Hell, I always beat him. I'm good at counting cards," he explains, eyes sparkling. "You shoulda seen the brawl when he found out I'd been chiseling him all these years. I had one heckofa black eye. And yet he keeps playing with me." Will extends me his packet of tobacco, and I shake my head at the offering.

"I don't dip."

"Sure you do." Will jiggles the packet. "It's easy. You got teeth and a tongue, don't ya?"

"So does yer brother, but he don't seem keen on the habit."

"Jesse says it tastes bad and will make yer teeth rot."

I think back on the store clerk in Wickenburg. "I agree with Jesse."

"For once," Will says.

"Guess there's a first for everything."

"See, some of us are trying to sleep," Jesse says from his roll.

Will spits at a rock bordering the fire and hits it with dead-on accuracy. "You girls go on and get yer beauty rest, then. I'll take first watch."

Guess I'm gonna have to hold my business awhile longer.

Silver's anxious to move come dawn. I wake to her yanking on her reins and pounding a hoof into the dry earth, real stubborn-like.

"All right, all right," I says, stumbling over to her. "We're going."

The boys ain't stirring yet, and I relieve myself before waking 'em. I'm gonna get myself caught in a corner, I just know it. Ain't no way I'm gonna be able to hold a canteen's worth of water until my turn at watch tonight.

After a quick breakfast of more bacon, we break down camp and load the horses up. I cinch Silver's saddle and she gives me her usual nicker.

"We cutting east today?" I says. "Been off course too long."

"We ain't off course," Jesse says. "We're running parallel to the Hassayampa. That means—"

"I know what parallel means."

"Don't have to jump down my throat 'bout it." Jesse raises his hands like I pulled my pistol. "I didn't think they had a proper school up in Prescott."

"They got one proper enough."

What I don't mention is that the Prescott school weren't built till I were twelve, and at that point I'd already learned anything worth knowing. Pa taught me to read and write. He were the son of a schoolteacher in Charlotte before coming west. Even had a soft spot for poetry and used to make me read aloud from this small volume when I were younger. I never quite understood the purpose. Poetry don't make yer crops grow better or keep Apache from raiding yer land. It's just a bunch of flowery words that could mean any number of things depending on yer interpretation. I think it's a heck of a lot less trouble to just say what you mean.

"Why's you so anxious to get back to the river, anyways?" Jesse says.

"Water. For the horses. For a bath."

"Right you are on that last point, Nate," Will says. "I think you smell worse than me and Jesse put together."

"I been traveling longer!" I feel my cheeks growing hot and slip my hat on, hoping it'll hide my face. "You two don't exactly smell like roses neither."

Jesse gives Rebel a flank-side patting and climbs into the saddle. "The Hassayampa's long underground at this point, but I got something better than a river."

"Better?" I says.

"Don't tell him, Jesse," Will says. "A surprise like that'll shine after a long day of travel. Though I reckon it could be dry," he adds, mouth curling into a frown. "There ain't been rain in ages."

"Take it you's stopped here before?" I says.

He nods. "My favorite place between here and Tucson. Just you wait."

By midday there's a wind picking up, but it ain't doing nothing to battle the heat. We cross the Hassayampa beds at high noon, the sun beating down on us angry. The plains here are open and endless, sloping low only where the dry creek bed cuts south. Somewhere under all that dust, the river carves the same course. Due east, a small mountain range appears on the horizon, dark purple in the hazy heat.

Jesse's on edge, which ain't doing much but making Rebel anxious and Silver flighty by default. I urge her ahead, not wanting to stay too close. I don't know what's got Jesse wound so tight. Way to the north there's a small cropping of dust—a stagecoach or freighting wagon—but their dust's getting smaller, so they ain't heading our way. Otherwise, there ain't a soul to be seen and the land's flat enough that we'd be able to spot someone coming.

Course, there's nowhere to hide if we sensed trouble.

Maybe that's what's got him riled.

Behind us, clouds are starting to pocket the sky. A storm, maybe. It would explain the strengthening winds, though I'm still stumped by the odds. June don't bring much rain in Prescott, and if we don't get much there, I doubt these desert plains do neither.

We carry on, Jesse scouting through his binoculars every few minutes. A few hours later the mountain range's not looking so tiny as it had. But it ain't what's caught my focus.

There's a dark lump not more than a mile ahead. At first I figure it's a boulder sitting proud amid the flat earth, but it's smoking. Like campfire coals.

"You see that?" Jesse says, lowering the binoculars.

Me and Will nod.

We kick the horses into a faster clip and close in on the strange shape. Soon, it ain't much of a mystery.

The body of the carriage is black and smoking, its door facing the heavens as the charred wheels spin in the breeze. The scent of burnt leather mingles with wood;

thorough braces running 'cross the exposed belly of the coach are cracked and split, the heavy leather curtains used to keep out dust in a similar condition. A set of reins hangs limp from the driver box, but there ain't a horse in sight.

Meaning someone cut 'em free. Someone walked away.

The wind shifts and a new scent reaches me. Flesh. Singed hair. As sure as I am that someone walked away from this inferno, I'm sure another soul—or more— didn't.

And that's when I spot the body, sprawled out round the back of the carriage: a man round Pa's age, shot clear through the skull. The driver, I'd wager, only he ain't burned like I expect. That fate musta been reserved for the unlucky bastards inside the carriage. A knife's been taken to the driver's forehead, carving out a shallow coiling shape, like an onion bloom. Or flower petals.

There ain't even a rose burned into these saddles. Ain't that their mark?

I know who did this. Like the roses on their saddles, like the very same carving they left on Pa—it's their symbol.

This is the Rose Riders' work.

I draw rein and swing off Silver. The coach dumped its luggage when it tipped, and trunks lay scattered near the roof, clothing, books, and other worldly possessions spilling free. One of the smaller trunks is empty, and I'd bet it were filled with money before the Riders got their hands on it. A hunt for gold, the trek that comes with it . . . that ain't cheap. I doubt Rose went out of his way to rob this coach, but if'n he crossed it while traveling, he likcly regarded it a lucky find.

The heat coming off the still-smoking carriage becomes too much. I stagger away. My eyes catch something pale and small among the disheveled clothes. A child's dress. Then I spot a rag doll.

I gag on the singed hair filling my nostrils, the smell of burned flesh.

This weren't a freighter running goods, or a Pinkerton moving money. This was a family. I hold my breath and move closer, cringing 'gainst the heat. The drawn leather curtains are parched from the fire, 'bout ready to crack, so I use the barrel of my Colt to punch through the weak material.

There ain't nothing but charred corpses inside the coach, so black and flame eaten, they look more skeleton than flesh. One of 'em's small. No bigger than Jake.

I stumble away and vomit on the dust-caked earth.

"We gotta bury the driver," I says. I take another swig from my canteen and spit the bile from my mouth.

"It'll take all day to dig a grave here." Will stomps his heel into the desert.

"We gotta do something."

Jesse just keeps squinting at the carnage, like if he stares hard enough, the coach might right itself and the people walk out.

"This is what they do!" I says, practically screeching. "The Rose Riders don't care for nothing but money and riches. They burned a family alive, prolly right after shooting the driver." I point at the man spread-eagled near the luggage. "And I reckon they're wretched enough to have carved that symbol in his forehead long before he took his last breath. They did the same to my pa."

Jesse's face snaps toward mine. His lips are pressed in a thin line, but he don't say nothing.

Growling, I stride to the driver. Maybe I can't bury the man, but he deserves more than being food for vultures. I can add him to the still-smoldering carriage, set him free by flame.

When I grab the fella by his wrists and tug, his weight suddenly gets lighter. I glance up. Jesse's got the man by the ankles. He don't say nothing as we move the driver. Not even after he's kicked in the carriage door or helped haul the body inside and light it by match.

As the flames begin to devour the poor soul, Jesse looks east. "We been still too long," he says.

Like the rage brewing in my core, the wind roars as we ride out. The sky is angry with clouds. Nobody talks. We don't look back. We keep our gaze set on the horizon and the mountain range ahead.

The silence gives my mind too much time to wander. My thoughts keep drifting back to the coach, even as we put distance between us and it. I bet there weren't even much money to be earned from that robbery. It was prolly an honest, hardworking family, and still it hadn't mattered to the Rose Riders. Same as weary a homesteader like Pa hadn't mattered neither. I reckon nothing's too low for Waylan Rose.

Another strong wind whips, nearly lifting my Stetson off. I turn my head to avoid losing it, and catch something back the way we came that makes my stomach drop.

"Jesse?"

To the west, and crawling over the plains like it's chasing us, is dust. And not a plume caused by riders or coaches, but a whole rotten wall. It stretches wider than it is tall—nearly as wide as the mountains ahead—and it's moving unnaturally fast.

"Stay on my tail!" Jesse shouts, kicking Rebel into a gallop.

I don't need to be told twice.

We fly east, pushing the horses hard. Silver's moving faster than I's ever made her run, and I ain't sure how long she can hold the pace. Still, I urge her harder, faster, more, more, more. Mutt's lucky he were already exploring far ahead, 'cus we're catching up to him quick.

Every time I look over my shoulder, the dust's getting closer, easily moving twice the speed we are. I can hear it, a roar of a monster. Feel it on my neck, too, the heat and the wind.

The land's getting rougher. Cactuses I gotta weave between. Uneven dips in the dirt as shrubs sprout up again. But I don't let Silver slow. Not even when the wind starts screaming in my ears.

We ain't gonna make it.

We're at the base of the mountains but ain't got time to climb 'em. We're gonna be swallowed whole.

Ahead of me, Jesse passes Mutt and makes a sharp turn to the right, drilling into a narrow canyon you wouldn't spot 'less you knew it were there. Will follows, the dog right on his heels.

I tug Silver's reins, urging her to follow, but she's midleap, clearing a small batch of boulders, and my twitchy hands startle her. She whinnies and lands uneven. I nearly fall from the saddle.

We dart into the canyon just as the dust goes roaring by, but my balance is so off, I tip sideways. My shoulder slams into the rough rock wall, and pain rockets through me.

Silver pulls up, panting, and I press my hand to her neck. "That a girl, Silv," I tell her. "That a girl."

Jesse and Will are waiting just ahead, looking flushed atop their horses.

"What the devil was that?" I says, looking back at the mouth of the narrow canyon. The dust is still raging by, spreading only a small amount of dirt into our little haven.

"Dust storm," Jesse says. "Somewhere behind all that dirt there's rain and wind, and it kicked up the earth as it traveled."

"We ain't got those in Prescott."

"Nor in Wickenburg, but I seen one or two in the stretch between Phoenix and Tucson. Never one quite so big up this way, though. We got lucky. If we weren't nearing these mountains, it wouldn't've been pretty."

"Good thing yer so vigilant with those binoculars," Will

says to Jesse. "Woulda been a shame if Nate's naked eyes were the only thing we could count on to save us."

"Shut it, Will."

I manage to crack a smile. In the wake of all that's happened it feels like a small miracle.

"So now what?" I ask.

"Now we hang fire, wait for the storm to pass," Jesse says. "Might as well go for a dip while we're here too."

"I thought only Will dipped."

"I mean a bath, dunce. Come on. I'm gonna show you the prettiest tub you'll ever clean in."

CHAPTER SEVEN

Jesse turns Rebel round and leads. The canyon path widens and slopes up the side of one of the peaks, where we're still sheltered from the dust raging on the other side.

We gain elevation, and even get a quick rainstorm bearing down on us—likely the rain that stirred up all that blasted dust. It ain't more than a few minutes long, not even enough to thoroughly clean the dirt from my limbs or wet my hair through.

After a bit of a trek, we come upon a sight I can't hardly believe. Right smack in the middle of this rugged, mountainy land is a pool of water. It's being filled by rainwater from the storm, which streams down the steep, bone-white rock surrounding us to fill a shallow basin. In its deepest parts—right 'long the back wall—I'd say the water might be up to my knees.

Mutt prances in and laps some up, then comes out with his undercarriage dripping. He shakes, sprinkling us.

"Welcome to White Tank, Nate," Jesse says, waving an arm at the scene.

"How'd you two ever find a place like this?"

"Prospector by the name of Dee. Before he arrived in Wickenburg, he'd tried these mountains for gold and said he found nothing but a trickling waterfall and a series of 'white tanks' holding water. Then some Indians ran him out."

I immediately look over my shoulder.

"We've spent the night here a few times and ain't seen nobody," Will says, reading my unease. "Might be the tribe's moved elsewhere."

"Might be," I says, uncertain.

"Well I ain't getting any cleaner talking." Jesse hops from Rebel and kicks off his boots. "Last one in does dinner."

He starts unbuttoning his shirt before I truly realize what's happening. I blink, and Jesse and Will are down to their drawers. I turn away and a moment later hear 'em splashing into the water.

Dear Lord, I gotta find something else to do. I gotta bolt.

"Nate's cooking," Will says with a laugh.

I risk a glance. They're reclining with their backs 'gainst the far rock wall, water up past their navels. The waterfall splashes between 'em, rippling the surface so I can't see nothing else, thank God.

"I'm what?" I says, pretending I don't follow, and trying not to stare.

"Making dinner, you loaf. Didn't you hear us naming terms?"

"No, guess not."

"I think he really might be deaf," Will says to Jesse.

Jesse just smiles. They both got broad shoulders, and muscles I ain't seen when they were wearing them shirts. God, I'm staring.

Stop staring.

Jesse sinks into the water like he's trying to lie on the bottom of the pool. He's swallowed up, and when he reemerges, he shakes his hair out like Mutt. Something coils in my stomach that's got nothing to do with dinner or wanting food.

"Well," Jesse says, squinting my way, "are you gonna stand there sweating, or are you coming in?"

"I, uh . . . I ain't feeling well," I says, backing away. "I think I'm gonna walk."

"Walk?"

"Yeah," I says, tripping over a rock and barely managing to stay on my feet. "And maybe start that dinner I owe yous."

"Suit yerself," he says.

I don't go far, 'cus I ain't fond of being in these mountains alone, but I drift enough that I can relieve myself in private. Once light starts slipping from the sky and I spot tribal markings on a couple rock faces, I turn round and head for camp. I'll take an awkward exchange with the Colton brothers over Apache arrowheads.

When I get back, the boys are outta the pool and mostly clothed. Jesse's using his shirt to dry his hair, and the motion is making muscles twitch in his arms and torso. I don't mean to stare, but it were just me and Pa at the farm, and the only man round my age I ever spoke with often was Morris. I wonder if he looks like this under his shirt too.

I turn away and focus on starting a fire 'cus I don't care what Jesse looks like. Or Will or Morris or any boy for that matter. I ain't here to splash round in stupid mountain pools and waste time staring at something I don't want to begin with. I got a job to do, and the sooner we get back on the move, the sooner I can split ways and carry on alone. Track down Rose. Pull my trigger like I mean to.

Just me and Silver, no distractions.

Just me and revenge.

Once I get the fire roaring, I'm feeling more like myself. I grab my last bit of flour and open my final can of milk, adding a pinch of salt to the batter 'cus I want at least a little flavor tonight. When I's finished making the biscuits and have dished 'em out with more jerky, we all eat. Will makes a joke 'bout how I should be cook henceforth 'cus the biscuits ain't burned and rock hard like when Jesse made 'em.

I wonder if Will'd still make that joke knowing I'm a girl. Actually, if they knew, Jesse would prolly escort me back to Sarah straightaway.

I can't tell 'em. Not ever. They can't find out.

The horses wander round our makeshift camp as we eat, pausing to sip from the pool or nibble the grass tufts growing between boulders. The biscuits we don't finish, I wrap up in paper and stow back with my gear. They'll be stale in no time, but I ain't eating nothing but jerky for the next week.

Later, as I'm rolling out my bed, I catch Jesse staring at my hips. I go dead still, thinking I's been found out, that he knows somehow.

"That nickel plated?" he says.

"Huh?"

"Yer pistol. That's a mighty fine-looking six-shooter."

My hands go to the Colt on my hip. "Oh," I says, relieved. "Yeah, it is. It were part of a matching set—both my pa's—but he gave me this one after I mastered the rifle."

"How's a Prescott farmer afford a twin pair of nickel-plated Colts?"

With gold from a Superstitions cache, I think. But I stay quiet and just eye his guns.

"My Remingtons are just steel. No fancy work like yers," he says, "but they shoot straight and reload fast. Heck, I's even heard the Remington's preferred to yer Colt model when it comes to defense."

"I count on my rifle for defense."

"You do what?" he says.

"My Winchester. I count on—"

"No, no, I heard you. What I'm saying is, rifles are big and require room. What happens when the guy sitting next to you in a saloon turns murderous? How 'bout if someone pulls their pistol on you on the street?"

"I ain't had much experience with neither back in Prescott," I says. Tom from Walnut Grove comes to mind, though, how he nearly got the jump on me even with my pistol already drawn. I might be able to shoot bottles from a fence with my rifle when I kneel and squint and take my time aiming, but that ain't gonna do much good by way of quick draws.

"So how good are you with that Colt?" Jesse asks.

"Good enough," I says. I killed that Rose Rider in the outhouse, after all. And Tom. Poor Tom. I still can't get his wide eyes outta my mind, can't quit wishing there'd been another way.

"Good enough ain't never good enough," Jesse counters. "You gotta be quicker than quick, ace high, the *best*."

"And who are you—the Territory's authority on shots?"

Jesse frowns. "Nate, yer tracking down a gang of ruthless men for reasons you ain't shared in full, and you saw what they did back on those plains."

I also saw what they did to my own father, but I don't say nothing.

"You need to be able to fire yer pistol as easy as breathing," Jesse adds, "with aim sharper than an eagle's eye. I can help you as we ride. We can practice draws on cactuses and such."

The look he's giving me makes me want to kick a damn cactus. It's pity—pity all over his features. Like I can't be trusted to do nothing on my own. Like I'm a kid of eight, not eighteen.

"Will's right," I says low. "You think you gotta help everybody, but I'm fine, Jesse. I didn't ask for no lesson or chiding or even yer blasted opinion."

"Yeah, I reckon Will *is* right," Jesse says, nodding sullen. "You might be the deafest man I ever crossed."

Then he turns and slinks to his bedroll, not once showing me anything but his back again. I kick a bit of rubble into the fire and it hisses.

"You know," Will says, "you keep poking a bull like that and one day he'll turn round and charge."

I sit beside him and he offers me some dip. Like yesterday, I shake my head. "You saying I should be afraid of Jesse?"

"I'm saying you jaw like yer made of steel, and some men won't turn away—not no matter how tough you act. Some men think everything's a challenge and that backing down means yer weak."

"Don't it?" I says.

"I reckon it depends on the battle."

Will spits dip at a beetle climbing rocks 'longside the fire. I peer through the flames to where Jesse's lying. Mutt's curled into him like a baby, and for some reason that makes me angrier.

"It's just . . . I can take care of myself," I says to Will low. "I don't need nobody coddling me."

"And that's fine," he says. "Don't have him train ya. Be a lone wolf. But just try to act a sliver less ornery, huh? Jesse promised our pa he'd watch over me and Sarah when he were gone, and you, once you showed up at the ranch. This is more than a job for Jesse, and he's already let people down."

Whether he's aiming for it to or not, that piques my interest.

"Like who?"

"Our ma," Will says.

"I thought she were lost to Apache."

"She was."

I wait a long while, and Will don't say nothing. He spits at the fire and then glances at me. "Is this patient, heavenly silence a sign you want the story?"

"If yer willing to tell it."

He smiles. He's got the same grin as Jesse — tight-lipped, with the corners pulling down. Then right as he opens his mouth to begin, the expression goes stormy.

"When Wickenburg himself first struck gold in late sixty-three, Jesse were almost six, and Sarah and I were eight and three. Even though it were a bit of a haul from our ranch, Pa started going into town almost every day of the week, hoping he'd also strike lucky. Meanwhile, Ma was left with us three kids and a heapful of chores.

"Just a short year later, the town were booming with people. A businessman had bought the claim to what's now Vulture Mine, and men were working the earth for wages, swiping gold when they thought they might not be caught." Will shakes his head like those men were crazy. I remember the hanging tree and I think the same.

"Pa worked at the mine too—this was before we got into the ranching business—and Ma were pregnant again, 'bout six months large. One day she started getting terrible pains—so crippling, she could barely move. She thought it might be the labor come early. Pa were down at the mine, and Jesse were smart enough to know Ma needed the doctor but couldn't get there herself. So he put one of the horses to the cart, told Sarah to watch me, and rode Ma into town.

"The Apache raided that afternoon. Attacks were common in general back then, what with a war raging back east and so many of our soldiers off to fight. I think the tribes were starting to feel threatened by Wickenburg —how people were settling rather than moving through, digging round in their mountains. Or maybe they thought they were winning. We'd murdered and pillaged their kind plenty, and when the federal troops went east to repel the Confederates invading New Mexico, I bet it looked like a surrender. Like we'd given up and it were time for revenge. Whatever the reason, the Apache rode through town and destroyed everything they could that day."

Will pauses to spit and I shift on my mat, knowing right well what comes next but still scared to hear it.

"The way Jesse tells it, the cart turned in the panic and he got pinned to the street. I think the only reason he didn't die, or even break a bone, was 'cus he were so small. But he was trapped there, and he watched Ma get dragged off, watched her pull her derringer from her dress and shoot herself in the mouth."

Will's features go dark, his brows dipping. It's like he's reciting a story he's memorized, rather than feeling his own words. I wonder if that's the only way he can get them out.

"Even after it were all over with Ma, Jesse had to lie there and keep watching. Silent, afraid them Indians might hear him if he cried out. He watched 'em scour and kill. Watched 'em drag women off. Watched 'em disappear toward the horizon. Once they were gone, he still didn't call out for help, not even when survivors started combing the streets. I think his voice got scared straight outta him that day. He just lay there under the cart, rigid, staring at the blazing sun.

"When Pa came north from the mine and rode through Wickenburg, he found the madness, and then he found Jesse. He'd pissed himself, and he was still squinting— from the sun, or what he'd seen. Maybe both." Will's gaze drifts to his brother. "Jesse weren't the same after that. It took him a while to talk again, and he started practicing with one of Pa's pistols till he could shoot the branch of a sapling in half from a proud distance. He was a shot I'd never want to cross by the time he were twelve. After that, he holstered the gun and it was like it never happened. He were a new person. He told jokes again. He smiled. I'm pretty sure half of it's an act. He never forgave Pa for choosing the mine over the family. It didn't matter that Pa eventually quit Vulture and converted our place to a ranch, started finding other means of income so he'd be near us kids; Jesse's always blamed him for Ma's death. He's struggled to be the man of the house since that day, and I reckon pretending he's made peace with the past helps him cope. But it still haunts him. I'm sure of it. Hell, he never really has quit squinting."

Will spits again, and this time he nails the beetle so hard, it flips onto its back. The bug struggles, flailing, then scurries off once righted.

I glance at Jesse, asleep on the other side of the flames. I wonder what he saw earlier, looking at that overturned coach, if it reminded him of the cart, his ma's death, the bloodshed.

"I'm sorry," I says soft, though I ain't sure to who.

"Life don't care 'bout sorry's," Will says. "Bad things happen, and you can't let 'em harden you. Whatever happened to yer pa, it ain't yer fault, Nate, and you gotta let it go."

"You sound like yer brother."

"I ain't nothing like him. I wear everything on my sleeve and he hides half it. I's less of a pessimist too. Even after he lost Maggie last year, he still figured how to be some level of happy. He's a perfect example that living's what you make it. Or at least what you *pretend* to make it."

"Maggie?" I says.

"Our closest neighbor. They woulda married if she hadn't died, I swear it, and all from a bee sting. Unfair, ain't it? That something so small can kill a person?"

"Life ain't fair, Will. That's one of the only things I know for certain. And that's why I can't stop chasing Rose.

Maybe smiling and choosing peace and target shooting till he felt invincible worked for Jesse, but I ain't him, and this is gonna destroy me if I don't set things right."

Will leans back, settling into his mat.

"Yer deaf all right," he says. "But I like that. I'm deaf too. It's one of the reasons Jesse and I get on so well. He can't help but ride with stubborn asses who drive him crazy."

CHAPTER EIGHT

The sky's just beginning to lighten when I decide to abandon my watch. We'll be moving soon, and I gotta take advantage while the boys are still sleeping. I ease to my feet and pull a clean set of underthings from my pack, 'long with the fresh shirt I bought in Wickenburg. Then, with my blanket still slung over my shoulder, I creep for the pool.

Testing, I dip in a toe. It ain't very warm, but it could be worse.

I strip fast as possible, wade in, and drop to my knees. The water's like silk on my limbs. Sand and dirt float free. Where it's worked into the creases of my skin, I scrub at it with my knuckles. I lean back, dunking my head and running my fingers through my hair. Its shortness is still a shock, a length I ain't used to.

Once clean, I feel so smooth, it's like I'm a snake shed

its skin. More than anything, though, my chest is singing with relief. I eye the wrap lying with my clothes. It were starting to chafe below my armpits after all the travel, and the thought of putting it back on sours everything.

'Cross camp, one of the boys' snores sputters.

I dunk one last time and scramble outta the pool, drying myself fast with the blanket. Cringing and damn near whimpering, I wind the wrap back in place—over my chest, under my arms, cinching it down tight like I'm a horse being saddled. Then I cram my legs back into my pants and throw on the clean flannel.

I'm working on the buttons when I hear earth crunch behind me.

I yank the shirt tight and twist round. Jesse.

"You scared me half to death," I says.

"I thought something happened. You were supposed to be on watch."

"I'm fine," I says, turning away and finishing with the buttons. That was close. *Too* close. "I wanted a clean and figured I could watch camp just as easy from here as my bedroll."

Jesse yawns, and it makes me yawn too.

"You want coffee?" he says. "I'll start a fire."

"Jesse, wait. 'Bout yesterday—Sorry I was so . . ."

"Pigheaded?"

"I's gonna said rude."

He shrugs. "It weren't my place, I suppose. Yer gonna track down Rose. The fact that I don't think yer capable really ain't no one's business but mine."

I frown at the insult and wrestle on my boots. Then

I sling my pistol belt back round my hips and fasten it tight.

"Yer really eighteen?" Jesse says, squinting.

"Swear it on my father's grave."

He shakes his head. "You don't look it."

"I reckon everyone looks a bit more youthful when they ain't covered in days-old sweat."

I put my hat on over my wet hair. He's still staring all doubtful. I'm gonna get caught. They ain't dumb, and they're gonna figure it out in time.

"How fast are you really?" I says, changing the focus.

"What?"

I nod to his holstered Remingtons. "How fast?"

A devilish smile flickers 'cross his face. "Gimme a target."

"That flower," I says, pointing to a yellow bloom atop a prickly pear 'bout twenty paces off.

Before I even lower my arm, Jesse draws his pistol and fires.

"Come at me!" Will shouts, sitting bolt upright outta a dream. "Where are ya?" He twists, frazzled, weapon in hand.

Jesse laughs and I just stand there staring at the cactus, now flowerless as yellow petals float to its base.

"Yer turn," Jesse says. "Should I pick something in similar distance?"

"No use," I says. "I can't do that with a pistol, not even close. But I'm thinking maybe I should let you teach me after all."

"Will," Jesse calls over his shoulder. "I ain't sure who this is, but I think Nate drowned in the pool overnight."

"Good. Nate was a grump."

"And becoming one again right now," I says, raising my voice at Will.

He rolls onto his side, muttering.

"You better be up in ten," Jesse says. "We gotta move." Then he turns to me. "First lesson'll be quick. I don't wanna stall in one place much longer."

"Suits me fine," I says, 'cus I agree with him. That's twice now.

He points at the flower of another nearby cactus. "Picture shooting it."

"All right," I says, and glance back to him.

"Done already?"

"Well it weren't exactly a hard task."

"Fine, then. Tell me what you saw."

"I saw the flower, and then I imagined it blown to pieces."

He shakes his head. "No, see, yer approaching it all wrong. It ain't 'bout the flower or the cactus. It's 'bout *you*. The bullet ain't happening to the flower. *Yer* happening to the flower. You gotta feel it all—yer stance and the weight of the pistol in yer hand. The wind on yer limbs and if it's strong enough to tug the lead plum. Then you gotta picture every single movement, from reaching to drawing to aiming to squeezing. You gotta see yerself doing it before you do, and then when you act, you ain't gotta think 'bout it. You just . . . flow. Let yer limbs catch up to yer mind."

"So yer saying it's in yer head?"

"Ain't everything?"

I suck my bottom lip. It don't sound too different from how Pa taught me to fire my rifle. It's just everything's faster.

"But how'd you see it all so quick? You fired before I even finished pointing out the flower."

Jesse winks. "That's lesson number two—the final lesson: practice."

"Two lessons total?" I says. "And it's mostly all practice? What do I need a teacher for, then?"

"To come down on you when yer slacking."

"I don't slack."

"You did with yer watch duties this morning."

"Ugh, yer like a mesquite thorn, Jesse."

"Poisonous?" he says. "I'll take that as a compliment."

"I meant a nuisance. It's like yer trying to get me riled."

"I'm trying to motivate," he says, pointing at the prickly pear. "Now picture it."

I sigh heavier than necessary but turn my sights to the flower. There's the slightest breeze moving the petals from east to west, so my bullet might stray over a long distance, but prolly not one this close. Thinking 'bout the bullet moving through the air leads me to thinking 'bout pulling the trigger, which leads to the draw and the very weight of the Colt in my holster. I see it all in reverse, and in a flash I can imagine it happening. I got my weight pressed down through my left leg right now, and I change that, spreading it out even. I can see my hand going to the holster, drawing the gun, cocking the hammer, aiming the shot, exhaling just as I squeeze, like the bullet is part of my breathing. I image that same bullet flaring from my barrel and slicing through the flower, and I feel so in control, it's like it can't happen any other way. It ain't possible. I already seen the future.

I snap back to reality.

Reach, draw, cock, aim, fire.

"Dear Lord, what is yer problem!" Will says, leaping to his feet. Jesse laughs as his brother tramples 'cross camp to Rio.

"I missed," I says, looking at the prickly pear. The flower's gone, but so is the whole flat disc of cactus it were attached to. "I don't know why. I saw it crystal clear."

"A flower's a small target," Jesse says. "If that were a person, you woulda struck true. Maybe not to the heart if you'd been aiming there, but certainly somewhere on the torso."

I holster my Colt. "'Cept they'd've shot me first. I stood here gawking for ten hours."

"That's where the practice comes in," he says. "And besides, why do you think men stare at each other so much before a shootout? Everyone takes their time, pictures winning. It's just someone has to be brave enough to pull first, and that's when it comes down to who's quickest."

"Ace high," I says, remembering what he said yesterday. "The best."

"You might be an all-right student after all, Nate."

"I ain't nothing but a good listener," I says, teasing.

Jesse barks out a laugh. "You hear that, Will?"

"I heard it," he says. He heaves his saddle onto Rio

and looks at the sky, which is indigo directly overhead, a more violent pink closer to the horizon. "Time to ride?"

Jesse nods. "I reckon so."

Having cleaned seems a waste by midday. It's the hottest afternoon yet, and I'm dripping down my back well before noon. I ain't sure if my hair's still damp from my bath or if I'm just sweating from my scalp like a waterfall.

"Horses are gonna need a break at the river," Jesse says.

It'll be the Agua Fria. It runs nearly dead south, so we'll cross it and keep on a southeast route, not meeting up with another river till the Salt in Phoenix.

A break for the horses does make sense, and I been drinking so much water, I'm due to refill my canteen. But even in this heat, I hate the thought of stalled time. Yesterday's dust storm already cost us a few hours by forcing us to make camp early. Alls I can hope is it did the same to Waylan Rose and his boys.

As we ride I practice drawing and sighting cactuses. Jesse tails in my shadow, commenting on my form to Mutt. I think this is his way of critiquing me without being too overbearing. I sorta like it. I can hear what he's saying, but it ain't like he's breathing down my neck.

"Yer really picking up cattle?" I ask him when my arm's getting tired. "Yer not just tailing me 'cus Abe said I were to be in yer care?"

"We're headed to Tucson for cattle, I swear it."

"How's two cowboys gonna move a herd?"

"Very carefully," Will interjects.

"Yeah, sure," I says. *"How?"*

"With prayer and witchcraft and the real kicker: Mutt. He's a magic cattle dog."

"Shut it, Will," Jesse says.

"I ain't lying," he says to me.

"Course you are," Jesse says.

Will spits dip at Mutt, who skirts outta range.

"We ain't running 'em alone," Jesse explains. "It's a quick job from Tucson to Yuma, and we're hired hands. Benny's always threatening that he's got enough boys and won't have work for us if we don't come join his crew as steady wranglers, and yet the boss man calls time and time again when a herd needs moving." He smiles, sly. "If'n everything goes well, we'll take a half-dozen cattle home to the ranch. And a half dozen me, Will, and Mutt can handle."

"What 'bout Clara?"

"Clara?" Will echoes. "You sly dog, Nate. Are you deaf or ain't ya?"

"I think he's whatever suits him best at the moment," Jesse says.

"Well, what of her?" I says.

Jesse frowns and squints at the horizon. "Suppose it'll come down to if Roy's in Tucson when we get there. Clara's *his* sister, after all, and he were supposed to meet her. But last we saw him he was gambling away his earnings in Wickenburg, full as a tick with whiskey and muttering 'bout trying his luck in Yuma."

"Clara's traveled all this way from Philadelphia," Will says, waggling his eyebrows at me. "A real proper lady. Jesse's sure she'll faint at the sight of this land."

"I ain't never said that!" he snaps. "I said it weren't smart for her to be traveling alone, 'specially if she couldn't afford a coach past Tucson. Not that a coach did those poor souls any favors yesterday."

We fall quiet with the mention of the burned Concord, and I turn what I's learned over in my head. Roy is Sarah's husband, making Clara her sister-in-law. I wonder what Clara plans to do at the ranch and what the Colton boys make of it. It weren't a roomy homestead, but there sure was enough land to maintain. I try to picture a city gal with her bonnet and parasol beating rugs and milking cows. A grin tugs at my lips.

We crest a small rise in the plains, and there's the Agua Fria, carving through the valley before us and looking more stream than river. Her banks are sprawling and mostly dry, showing how wide she runs during the rainiest months. In her deepest areas, where the water's moving, patches of grass spring up and I can see the land heave and buckle with rocks and boulders.

Silver nods her head, excited-like.

"I know, girl," I says. "We'll be there soon."

"Hang fire," Jesse says, holding out an arm. "There's someone down there."

"Where?" I says, scanning.

He passes me the binoculars. "Not at the water. Dead ahead, halfway up the opposite bank."

I look and find what he's seen. Even with the binoculars, it's a keen spot—two riders hunkered down behind a boulder in a makeshift sorta camp. That is, I assume there's two of 'em. Alls I can see is their horses, both so tan in color, they blend right in with the dust.

"Maybe they got stranded in the storm yesterday and are hurt," Will says.

"Or they're looking to hurt us," Jesse responds.

"You think it's a trap?"

"I think it ain't right. If you were stopping to rest here, you'd do it 'long the water. And it's too early to be making camp for the night. 'Sides, who'd pick a sloped bit of ground like that to call the day quits? No protection at all."

"You'd be protected from people crossing the river and coming yer way," I says.

"Exactly," Jesse says. "That's all it's good for, that position—an ambush."

"So what do we do?" Will asks.

"I'm thinking on that," Jesse says.

I peer through the binoculars again, and this time I see something I ain't noticed on first glance. All the gear's been pulled off the horses 'cept for the saddles, and I can see an emblem in the leather. The same shape I's seen in two foreheads.

"It's them," I says. "It's the Rose Riders."

"No it ain't," Will says.

"They got the rose symbol on the saddles."

"It ain't them."

"Shut it, Will," Jesse says. And to me: "Yer certain?"

Another glance through the binoculars and I see one of the men standing, pulling a rifle into view. He leans on the boulder, setting up his shot, and there ain't no mistaking what he's aiming at.

Us.

CHAPTER NINE

"Get down," I says, swinging off Silver. "They's seen us, and they're aiming to fire."

I wrestle my mare to the ground, which ain't an easy task, but we got to be as small a target as possible. The boys do the same.

Not a second later, the first bullet flies, hitting several paces before us and exploding dust.

"I thought you said they were in Phoenix!" Will shouts from where he's hiding behind Rio.

"We're close to it, ain't we?" I shoot back.

But he's right. If the Rose Riders have the journal and are chasing the gold, they should be ahead, already in the town and fixing to head east into the mountains. How'd I catch 'em so fast, and why's they stopping an extra day here of all places? Maybe they got stuck in the storm like Jesse reckoned. There *is* only two of 'em. Could be the horses got hurt or they did. Or they were left behind as dead weight and now they're meaning to take out the next travelers passing through so they can catch up. It ain't like they know we're following them.

"I think they're after our horses," I says as another shot cracks.

I glance at Jesse, who's crouching behind Rebel. For once, he don't look like he has a plan. The narrowed state of his eyes is more fearful than stubborn, and I don't like it.

A few paces to our right there's a low, flat boulder, large enough to shelter one. I lean over Silver's flank and draw my rifle from the saddle scabbard, then let her up. As she stands, I scramble for the boulder, hoping the Riders' eyes are drawn to the movement of my horse and not me.

Resting the Winchester's barrel on the rock, I take aim.

"If you get him, I'll never give you a hard time again, Nate," Jesse says. I can hear the doubt in his voice, but this ain't a pistol shot. This is a shot only a long barrel can pull off. And me? I been practicing like this my whole life. That bastard 'cross the way is just another bottle on a fence, and after all he's taken from me, he ain't taking my horse, too.

I sight him steady. Feel the wind and ready my hands.

"Gotcha," I says at a whisper, and pull my trigger.

His head snaps back and he falls.

"Holy hell," Jesse mutters.

But I ain't even got time to relish his praise of the shot, 'cus the second Rider is fleeing. He's running up the opposite bank, arms flailing, fringe on his leather jacket flapping like a bird 'bout to take flight.

I jump to my feet, unwilling to let him slip outta range. *I'll get him for you, Pa. I'll strike him dead.*

"Nate, hold up!" I hear Jesse shout behind me.

But my feet are already flying. Down our side of the bank, racing for the boulders lining the trickling stream. I'm almost to the biggest of the lot when a gunshot sounds and water splashes a few paces to my right.

I look up, but the fool's still fleeing, his back to me. There were only two horses. Two horses and two men, unless—

Another gunshot, and this time water dances right near my feet.

"Get down, Nate!" Jesse's screaming. "Get the blazes down!"

I look over my shoulder and see Jesse racing toward me, drawing his pistols and aiming downriver at the same time. I follow his gaze, and that's when I see the third horse and the rider sitting in the saddle, rifle aimed. The fleeing man alerted him. This is the backup plan, the last defense.

There's two gunshots at once, and I ain't sure which is Jesse's and which is the Rose Rider's, but I know which hits me.

I stumble, tripping, then toppling backwards, and strike my head on a rock. Hard. The world goes blurry. My shoulder's flaming hotter than a poker, and I know how that feels, 'cus I was on the wrong side of one after running through the barn and tripping the day Pa branded our two cattle. I feel like I'm exploding and folding in on myself, and I ain't certain, but the sky seems to be collapsing.

The world's going white and it's raging of gunshots.

When it quiets, Jesse's shouting for Will, and then I feel hands lifting me.

"Watch his head," Jesse says. "Is it split?"

"No, but he's already got an egg. Where's the shot?"

"Shoulder, I think, but I can't see the damage." I feel his hand at my elbow, the other touching my shoulder, cautious. "We gotta get the shirt off, put a bandage down and slow the bleeding."

No, I want to say. *Don't.*

But his fingers are already moving. The buttons are being undone.

I feel the fabric rip open.

Will swears.

"Jesus, Nate," Jesse says. "Jesus Christ."

It's the last thing I hear before slipping into dark.

Hunched over our kitchen table, I'm rolling out dough for a pie. It's Pa's birthday. He said to surprise him, but I'm making apple. It's his favorite and he's a man of habit. He don't like surprises, not no matter what he says. When we eat it later, the filling warm and sugared sweet, I's still got flour coating my apron and speckled in my hair.

"You look like you got stuck in a snow dusting," Pa says.

"You look like a hog gone rolling in mud."

And he does. He were extending our irrigation line and brought half the creek bed home on his body.

"Well, this hog's in heaven," he says, eating his last bite of pie and slapping his gut. "Reckon I live in the prettiest pen, with the nicest hen, in all the southwest."

"Yer just saying that 'cus yer loaded with sugar."

"That don't mean it ain't true."

I crack a smile. "Happy birthday, Pa."

"Happy birthday indeed."

A sharp movement causes my head to loll into my bad shoulder. Pain flares. The world's pink and fleshy, but I ain't got the energy to open my eyes. The Coltons are arguing 'bout something, voices clipped and hard.

Another jolt, a shift.

I think we're moving.

I try to surface, but a fog pulls me under.

"It don't matter why it's important, it just is," Pa says.

We're sitting by the fireplace as winter winds blow outside and rattle the shutters.

"Say it back to me," Pa says.

"Abe," I says, but I'm more interested in my doll. I'm a few months past five, and Ma died a year and a half ago, but the doll tucked in the cradle reminds me of her. Trapped in bed. Never moving. Barely breathing. Pa always ordering

me clear of the room so I couldn't catch nothing. I gotta watch my doll. I gotta keep her warm and snug.

"Abe from where?" Pa says, not giving in.

"Wishenburg."

"Wickenburg."

"Yeah."

"Kate," he says stern. He don't use that tone often, and I know I'm in trouble. "This ain't a game."

"But *who* is Abe?" I whine. "What's gonna happen to you? You ain't sick like Ma."

"That don't matter, and it ain't the point." He shoves another log in the fire. It crackles, sending sparks flying. "Just promise you'll remember Abe from Wickenburg. If'n something happens to me, you go see Abe in Wickenburg. Say it again."

"Abe in Wickenburg," I says. "Wickenburg for Abe."

"Good," he says, setting down the poker. "Good."

I'm hotter than hot, burning up. I got a blanket over my middle, and every time I try to push it off, someone stops me.

"It'll break—the fever."

"I don't know, Jesse."

"It's just shock."

"She needs a doctor."

"And where're we gonna get one of those?" Jesse says. "We ain't exactly near civilization."

"We gotta keep moving."

"To Phoenix?" Jesse says.

"Yeah," Will says. "To Phoenix."

"With Nate's fever as high as it is? We gotta wait for it to break."

"I'm pretty sure her name ain't Nate."

"Shut it, Will. I ain't got nothing else to call her."

"And what if it don't break? What do we do then?"

"Gimme a minute," Jesse says. "I'm thinking."

Blankets are high above my chin—itching, dry. I got what feels like mesquite thorns lining my throat, and I can barely breathe. Pa says it's only a bad cold, but last I checked you can die from just 'bout anything left untreated.

It's March, three months to the day I'll turn eighteen, and I ain't been outta this bed in weeks. I don't know where I caught it. Worse than not knowing, though, is being so help-less in my own skin.

"I'm getting the doctor," Pa says from the doorway.

"I'm fine."

"You ain't. Yer breaking out red now, like a rash. A scar-let one."

I cough and shiver in one breath. I'm hot and cold, tired and restless.

"I thought scarlet fever liked kids."

"You ain't a kid, but you ain't exactly ancient, neither. You hang there, Kate. I'll get the doc."

"With what money?" I says.

His frown gets so deep, it draws a line between his brows. "Don't you worry 'bout that. I got my means."

I hear him rummaging in his room before the front door shuts. The doc shows up later, like I'm the most prized possession this side of the Mississippi. He fawns over me and don't leave the bedside. I get medicine I ain't heard of. I start feeling better a few days later, and when the doctor stops in one last time to visit, I'm ripe enough to crack jokes.

"What the devil did he pay you in, gold ore?" I says.

"Precisely," Doc answers. "Now you rest easy, young Kate. Don't try to do too much too soon."

I decide I like him. I ain't never met a doctor with such a sharp sense of humor. Gold ore! If Pa still had funds from Wickenburg, we'd've spent 'em last summer in the drought, or the year before that, when the creek flooded come spring and ruined half our crop. If Pa had that kinda money, Ma would still be alive, 'cus he'd've done for her what he just did for me. He'd've saved her. Ha! Gold ore . . .

My eyes flicker open, revealing a ceiling that ain't familiar. I press a hand down beside my hip. Unfamiliar sheets, too. A mattress. Mutt's curled up at my feet.

I sit up so fast, the room goes blurry.

"Easy there," Will says from his seat 'cross the way.

My hands go immediately to my shirt, but it's buttoned.

"We're in Phoenix," he says before I can ask. "Stopped a few miles outside yesterday, but you weren't doing too good. Jesse slung you over his horse and we rode to see Evelyn. She called the doc and he fixed you right up this morning with some stitching and a bit of alcohol. It were a bad graze, taking off a chunk of skin and muscle but never hitting bone." He points at my arm. "Doc said it were shock and the strike to yer head that did the worst damage. Evelyn swears you had a concussion."

"She a doctor too?" I says.

"A whore, but my favorite, so yer lucky I was kind enough to have her see to yer needs first and not mine." He cracks a smile, and I'm grateful for his humor, 'cus the longer I lie here with him knowing right well I ain't the boy I's been pretending, the crazier it's making me go.

"Where's Jesse?" I says.

"Just got back." Will sends dip into the spittoon at his feet. "He were tracking yer horse. She bolted during the shootout 'long the river, but he found her."

Silver, nearly lost. Relief comes flooding.

"I gotta thank him," I says, sitting taller. "I gotta see him right now."

I grab the blankets and Will shakes his head. "Ah-ah-ah, wait till I leave at least. Jesus."

I stretch my feet and understand his reaction. My legs are skin on skin. I spot my pants and boots sitting on a chest at the foot of the bed.

"You were burning up," he says.

My mouth falls open.

"Oh, hell, it were Evelyn who took 'em off. Don't go getting ideas."

God almighty I wanna disappear. I wanna undo the last few days.

"I think you should go," I says, feeling exposed.

He sighs heavy but don't argue. Soon as he's gone, I slide outta bed. I'm sore and tired and my balance don't feel quite right. When I roll my bad shoulder, it's tight and throbby. Least it ain't my shooting arm. What hurts worst, though, is my head. I reach back and find a heck of a lump. Damn, I hit that rock hard.

That stupid bastard on his horse.

I'll kill him. Him and all the others.

I snatch up my pants and stuff my legs in, relieved that the dull headache pulsing in my temples don't affect my balance. As I pull on my boots, there's a knocking.

"Yeah?" I says.

Jesse toes the door open.

"Yer up," he says, but I notice he's looking more at the bed than me.

"Thanks for not leaving me behind," I says.

"Couldn't. I made a promise to my pa." Then his expression goes stormy. "Damn it, Nate, you can't run forward in a gunfight like that. What the devil were you thinking? Coulda got yerself killed. Coulda gotten us *all* killed!"

"Kate," I says.

"What?"

"It's Kate."

"Right." He looks at me, and then his gaze instantly trails to the dresser. "Jesus Christ," he says.

I sit there on the bed. He stands staring at the dresser.

"You know, I had the vaguest memories of you and yer pa staying in our barn years back. I coulda sworn Henry's kid were a girl, but then you showed up and I figured I remembered it wrong. Guess I was off my rocker thinking you'd be honest with us when we're risking our skins riding 'longside you as you chase Rose Riders!"

"Jesse, I'm sorry."

"Sure you are."

"No, really," I says. "It's just . . . no one was gonna take me serious as a girl. I'd've had eyes on me everywhere, or been a target."

"You made one hell of a target down at that river, Na— Goddamn it—*Kate*."

"Well, you'd've sent me back to the ranch!" I says, nearly shouting. "You'd've ordered me to stay with Sarah if you knew. And I gotta do this, Jesse! I ain't never gonna breathe easy till every one of those bastards is as dead as the one I shot in Prescott."

"You what?"

If I'm coming clean, I might as well do it honest and true. He did save my life and all, track my horse, get me to Phoenix. So I break down and tell him 'bout the outhouse revenge and the letter Abe had been holding, 'bout the journal and the gold.

He don't speak for a long while.

"Jesse?" I says.

"Damn it, Kate. What the hell did you pull us into?"

"Nothing. It's my hunt, not yers."

"'Cept for that one Rider who got away. I shot the

saddled gun, but Will and I were too busy fussing over you to track the man on foot. Now he knows what all three of us look like, and that we're traveling together. You pulled us into a war over lost gold and spilled blood and you didn't even give us a choice!"

"Well, I said I never wanted company! I told you I were traveling alone, but you and Will forced yer way in. You never listened to a thing I said."

"What would it've mattered?" he roars. "You lied 'bout damn near everything!"

"Go on and get, then," I says. "Leave! It weren't like I wanted you round to begin with."

"Fine!" he says, yanking the door. "My pleasure!"

He slams it so hard, I'm shocked it don't crack.

CHAPTER TEN

I grab my effects from the chest, startling Mutt in the process. He gives me a low, throaty growl.

"Oh, don't you go taking that tone with me too," I says. I try to give him a pat and he nearly takes my fingers off with a well-placed nip. "I ain't the bad guy!"

But he just curls away, burying his nose in his fur. It's like he's got an allegiance to Jesse even when he ain't present.

I fasten on my pistol belt. Now that the chest wrap ain't crushing air from my lungs, bending and turning is a breeze. I snatch up my Stetson, plop it on my head, and storm outta the room.

Floorboards creak as I feel my way down the poorly lit hall. I can hear a couple tumbling in one of the rooms I pass, and below I can make out dulled chatter. While the words don't reach me, the scent of whiskey and wafting cigar smoke do. Rounding a corner, I nearly collide with one of the girls coming up the stairs. We do an awkward dance where I try to step outta her way, but she steps the same direction and we waltz like that till she manages to join me on the landing.

"Done with the room?" she says, eyeing my shoulder. She ain't got a fella with her, so I reckon she's come to check on me.

"Evelyn?" I says, testing the theory.

She nods, making her dark curls bounce. She's pretty. Bet she'd be even prettier outta this dingy dump.

"Thanks for all your help," I says. "And sorry 'bout using yer room, making it so you couldn't . . ."

She bats a hand. "Oh, it were nothing. Evening rush is just getting started. But if yer done and outta there, it'd be good to know."

"Oh, yeah," I says. "I'm done."

Done and racing after Rose.

"Swell," she says. "I got a Colton been pestering me since you rode in this morning."

Just then boots come clomping up the stairs, followed by Will's voice. "Ev?"

"Yeah, yeah," she says over her shoulder. "Come on up."

He climbs into view, and when he spots me standing there he winks. I think I make a face more revolting than necessary, 'cus he just says, "And I offered to buy you one once." Shaking his head, he turns to Evelyn. "Did I ever tell you yer the prettiest gal in Phoenix?"

"Those words'd be more convincing if there weren't

dollars behind 'em." But she's smiling as she says it, and there's something bright in her eyes. I don't know much 'bout painted ladies, but I never seen one look so genuinely pleased to take a client's hand.

I squeeze by Will and flee down the rickety stairs.

The parlor ain't big, and it's busting at the seams on account of the few folk spread throughout. Men lounging on fading couches, drinking whiskey and bourbon as girls in bright, frilly dresses dance about. An accordion's being played, the ivories tickled. Deep red curtains hang in the windows, looking rich and trying to distract from a mud-stained carpet.

Jesse's leaning 'gainst the sad excuse for a bar, a rolled cigarette pinched between his lips as he spins a whiskey glass with his free hand. He spots me coming down the stairs and straightens. I feel his eyes lingering on my flannel and can practically hear him chiding, *Ain't no reason to keep pretending yer a boy.*

He throws back his drink, then turns away from me, sliding the empty glass forward for a refill. I shove out the saloon without a backwards glance.

It's later than I expected. The sun's set, but a bit of light still stains the horizon. The lantern hanging from the parlor eaves is already lit and glowing scarlet.

Silver's waiting not far to my right with her reins wrapped round the hitching post. She stamps a hoof, tosses her head. Suddenly, not even the sight of her makes me feel better, 'cus alls I can see is Jesse tracking her for me. Finding her. Bringing her back.

Why's he gotta be so honorable? If he were more like

Will, he'd be easier to hate. But somehow I like Will just fine and can't stand Jesse.

Goddamn mess of a hunt. And now I can't even cut loose till morning.

I look at the darkening sky and curse under my breath. I hope Jesse drinks so much whiskey, he passes out. If I gotta see him squinting again when I get back, judging and glowering, I'm gonna go mad.

I stomp down the street, jiggling my fingers by my thighs like I can shake the prickling emotions outta my body. I pass a string of saloons and a bank, then finally find a general store looking like it could rival Goldwaters. Hancock's, according to the paint on the facade. The owner's closing soon, and he's sure to tell me it the moment I step through the doorway.

I shop quick, gathering up more cured meat, matches, ammo, and anything else I think I might need heading into the mountains come dawn. Then I dally on the general store's porch, groceries between my feet and back pressed 'gainst the wall. The last bit of light leaks from the sky. A few less-than-respectable-looking characters start wandering the streets, heading for the various saloons. I ain't ready to return to the parlor. If'n I stand here long enough, Jesse might be asleep when I get back. Maybe I can creep in extra late and sneak out come first light without so much as facing him.

It dawns on me that I don't know where we're staying for the night. Evelyn'll need her room. There were only so many couches on the main floor, and I reckon they'll be full of patrons. I should prolly see if there's a hotel round.

As I stoop to grab my groceries, two long coats drift by.

". . . shouldn't be stopping here," one man's saying.

"You know the boss man. He's got a weakness for cards," the second replies. I go rigid on the porch. "'Sides, he's only playing a few hands, and didn't Hank say the sheriff's gone on business till tomorrow?"

I strain my hearing, but they's already moved outta earshot, so I follow 'em, being sure to keep back a good distance. They walk fearless, like predators on the prowl. Finally, they head into the Tiger Saloon. It's a big place, two stories high. I hurry nearer, and sure enough, there's their horses. Seven of 'em. Waiting calm as ever at the hitching post, a rose burned into each saddle.

On the other side of the swinging doors I can hear music and rowdy men. Shouts and bets and a few girls carrying a tune. How's it folks in a town as small as Walnut Grove knew 'bout Waylan Rose, and here people don't seem to notice the demons they got stomping down their own streets?

Could be they *do* know and are too scared to do nothing 'bout it without the sheriff round. It ain't one man they're up 'gainst, but a whole gang.

Or, could be Rose and his boys ain't been recognized. When I's a kid, we had an outlaw squatting in Prescott a few weeks and not a soul noticed. There were wanted posters hung on every other town building too. Problem was, the illustration weren't very good—he were drawn too young and thin—and with the outlaw going by a different name and carrying himself all confident, no one batted an eye.

I step onto the porch and peer through the saloon window. A body's standing right 'gainst it, blocking any view I mightta had. For a moment I consider dropping my groceries and plowing inside anyway, pistol blazing. But I'm worried 'bout hitting innocent folks in the process, and besides, you can't gun down seven men unprovoked and walk away whistling. Assuming I can even make that many perfect shots, I'll still need Silver nearby so I can run when it's over.

I turn my pace brisk and head for my horse. Soon as she comes into view, I swear. My saddle's missing, swiped right off her back, and I'd bet all the gold left in Pa's pouch who took it.

I charge into the parlor.

Jesse's still at the bar—Will now drinking 'longside him—and he don't even look up as I march over.

"Where is it?" I says.

Jesse strikes a match and lights a new smoke. Then he exhales slow and runs his thumb 'long the rim of his whiskey glass like he ain't even heard me.

"Jesse, where's my damn saddle?"

"Why, you going somewhere?" His words are clipped, and I can't tell if it's on account of the smoke wedged between his teeth or how much he's drank.

"Jesse, I ain't kidding. I want my saddle back."

"And I want in."

"What?" I says.

Jesse straightens and squares to me so fast, I know for certain he ain't drunk.

"Will and me's been talking. We'll help you track down

Rose if'n we can have a share of what's waiting in those mountains."

"Oh, we're in agreement now?" Will cuts in. He's playing with a poker chip, letting it dance over his knuckles. "'Cus I recall arguing it weren't the smartest of plans."

"I'm sick of scraping by every day," Jesse says to him, "wondering if we're gonna have enough for Sarah to eat or the means to get a doctor for Jake next time he falls ill, leaving 'em alone and unprotected every time we need to take a job running cattle. We do this and we'll be set for life."

"It don't got nothing to do with the fact that yer gonna find gold when Pa never could? Yer gonna save the family where he failed?"

"Damn it, Will!" Jesse snaps, his hand curling into a fist.

"What, you gonna hit me for saying the truth?" Will shouts. "Go on and do it, then, Mister I Let Go of the Past. Do it!"

"Hey!" I shout as Jesse lunges at him. He pauses, lets his fist drop to his side. I ain't never wanted the Coltons on my tail, but suddenly they don't seem such a hindrance. Rose's gang is seven men strong, and two extra guns on my side certainly ain't gonna hurt things. We can all benefit, and this is a way to tip the odds in my favor.

"I ain't got no need for the gold," I says, "so if'n yer serious, we got a deal."

"Deal," Jesse echoes.

We shake on it. Will frowns.

"Rose is in town right now," I continue, "ready to play a few hands of cards at the Tiger. I reckon we can end everything tonight, and if we do, I'll hand over the journal and you boys can carry on yer way."

"Hang on," Jesse says. "Rose is in Phoenix?"

"I saw his men. The law ain't round and it sounded like they're fixing to enjoy themselves a few hours."

"So what are you aiming to do—barge into the Tiger and shoot Rose?"

"Not quite so recklessly, but yeah," I says. "Walk in, sit at a distance, watch and wait till I got a shot. This is a lucky break, catching up with him here. We got him in a room with four walls 'stead of in a mountain range. He can't dodge us."

"And we can't dodge him, neither. His men'll be spread throughout the room. He'll know we're on his tail if his buddy from the river caught up and warned him. He might even figure us to be bounty hunters. Either way, he could recognize us. It looks lucky, but it's a death trap, Kate."

I see his point, I do, but I can't stand here doing nothing. I might not get a chance like this again.

"I thought we had a deal," I says.

"A deal, yes. But not if we're gonna be dumb 'bout it."

"I reckon I'll just go alone and ride bareback, then," I says. As I turn to leave, Jesse grabs my wrist.

"Please, Kate, you ain't listening."

"Let go," I says. His grip only gets tighter. I writhe and squirm, but he's much stronger, and all of a sudden my heart kicks into a frenzy 'cus he's tugging me hard enough that I'm moving in a direction I don't want to go—away from the exit. "Damn it, Jesse, let me *go!*"

I throw my opposite fist into his chest. He drops my arm immediately, but I know it ain't 'cus I hurt him or convinced him with that one blow. My freed wrist sings with relief. Jesse watches me rub it, and I catch something shameful flicker in his eyes.

"Yer saddle's in Evelyn's room," he says finally. "But please don't be stupid 'bout this, Kate. I'll help, we both will. Only, let's have a plan . . . a smart one."

Evelyn comes down the stairs, smoothing the front of her dress. She gives Will a small smile and he beams back, his gaze never leaving her as the chip continues to pass effortlessly between his fingers. I remember his story 'bout cheating Jesse at cards, and the way's suddenly clear.

"I think I got an idea," I says.

They listen as I explain. If'n we're careful, we won't gotta shoot Rose. Everyone else in the saloon'll do that for us. Will can count cards, stack the deck on his turn to deal, set Rose up with a nice hand, but me or Jesse with an even better one. He can also plant a card or two on Rose's person so it looks like *he's* the cheater when we're the ones actually pulling aces from our sleeves. The other players'll turn on Rose in a flash.

"It ain't a bad idea," Jesse says. "'Cept for the fact that Rose might expect three men to be on his tail after that mess 'long the Agua Fria." His gaze lingers on my short-cropped hair and Stetson, then drifts to where Evelyn's mingling with the other girls and parlor guests. "But Rose ain't expecting a girl to walk into the Tiger."

Will seems to know what Jesse's driving at, 'cus

he shoves off the bar and pushes his way through the crowd. He says something hurriedly into Evelyn's ear. She touches the folds of her dress, glances at me.

"No," I says.

"Come on, Kate," Jesse argues. "You put on a borrowed dress and you'll be able to look Rose dead in the eye without him suspecting a thing. And Will and I'll be there watching yer back."

"Upstairs you said you wanted nothing to do with this."

"It don't matter what I want. I promised my father I'd watch out for you. That don't change if yer a girl on a vengeful road. It don't even change if yer a liar. *I* ain't one. I keep my promises, and seeing as yer bent on doing this no matter what I suggest, I'm stuck making sure you ain't dead before dawn. Plus," he adds with a smile, "the promise of gold sure don't hurt."

First he tells me not to go after Rose, to let the past be. Now that he knows there's a lost mine involved, he can't wait to chase down the bastard. Turns out Jesse ain't just a preacher, but a hypocritical one too. Lucky me.

I frown, and glance between him and Will.

"Fine" is all I says.

We work out the rest of the details, chatting till the plan seems foolproof. Then I follow Evelyn upstairs.

"I can't wear this."

"Why?" Evelyn says. "It fits you like a glove."

"'Cus it's . . ." I look back at the mirror above her dresser. "It shows too much."

It shows damn near everything. I's been hiding my breasts for so long, I half forgot I had 'em. The dress's neckline dips low enough to show off the little I have, then swings wide to expose the whole of my collarbones. And it don't even have proper sleeves—just short things that cover my shoulders and only a fraction of my upper arms.

I complain 'bout that too, but Evelyn says it's swell luck, how those few inches of fabric hide the dressing on my bad shoulder. She don't realize how much it hurts, though—having a confining sleeve 'stead of my roomy flannel. She gives me a shawl as if a sheer bit of cloth draped round my arms could make me feel less exposed. I reckon I don't have much of a choice. Proper ladies don't set foot in saloons, and I'll be posing as a gal in Evelyn's line of work for the evening.

She's right 'bout one thing, though—the dress do fit well. From shoulder to waist to hip, it hugs my frame like Evelyn and I are sisters. I just wish I didn't have to be in a blasted corset after finally being free of my wrap. I run a palm over the dress, tracing the dark rose pattern that covers the ivory fabric. The irony of the flowers ain't lost on me, though if they were blood red—not black—the stitching would be even more fitting. I'm gonna make 'em pay, those Rose Riders. I'm gonna watch 'em bleed out at my feet.

"Trust me. This dress shows just the right amount,"

Evelyn says. "Men don't need much for their imaginations to run wild."

"That ain't making me feel better."

She smiles so wide I worry a piece of me's broken, 'cus I don't think I'll ever smile like that again. Them Rose Riders taking Pa destroyed the only bright bits of me. I ain't been nothing but rage and black, bubbling anger since. Killing that bastard in the outhouse and the one 'long the river didn't bother me none. They both felt like nothing —bottles on a fence. It's like they weren't lives. Like I ain't got a conscience left to remind me that while they might deserve it, they were still men. They were still someone's baby once. If it weren't for Tom outside Walnut Grove— the regret that stings when I think of him—I'd worry I'm as crooked as the Riders I'm hunting.

"Ready?" Evelyn says.

No, but I weren't ready when they took Pa neither. I'm only doing what I gotta do.

I can feel my Colt strapped to my leg beneath the dress. I pull the shawl tight and look in the mirror one last time. My hair's been drawn back at my nape and pinned in place—Evelyn's work, and all she was able to do with the short length. Even now a few pieces hang free, framing my face. It's clean of dirt and sweat, my cheeks flushed. I don't recognize my reflection. This girl looks softer than the one I know, and older, too. She don't show the vengeance I feel burning in my core.

Evelyn pulls open the door. "I expect y'all back within a few hours, without a speck of blood on any of yer persons," she says. "'Specially that pretty dress."

I think this is her way of wishing us luck.

The Colton brothers are waiting at the bar, backs to me. Will spots me coming down the stairs first.

"By God, Kate," he says, grinning sly. "You make a much prettier girl than boy."

"Make another comment like that, and you'll regret it."

"It's like I ain't giving her a compliment," Will mutters to his brother. "I mean, don't she look nice?"

Jesse finishes paying for his drinks and turns. It takes only half a second, but his eyes burn a trail from my dress's neckline to its hem and back again.

"The dress'll do," he says.

It'll do?

It was his blasted idea! Least when I's pretending to be a boy, all he ever judged were my goal of tracking Rose and my less-than-stellar ability with a pistol. Now I ain't up to standards and I's done nothing but stand here drowning in fabric.

I can't wait to be done with this—Rose, the Riders, this *dress*. I'm regretting my deal with the Coltons already.

I wanna go home.

I wanna never see the Colton brothers again in my life.

"Are we going or not?" I says.

"We're going," Jesse says, and leads the way onto the street.

CHAPTER ELEVEN

Will goes in ahead of us as planned.

When Jesse and I enter, it's with me leading and him hollering after me loud enough for most to hear.

"I told you I ain't got time for this!"

He grabs me at the wrist hard enough to yank me to a stop. It hurts more than it should, only 'cus I feel the tug all the way up in my injured shoulder.

"I'll do what I please, thank you."

"You'll do what I say," he hollers back. "I'm a paying customer, and I asked for you."

"And I'm busy!" I snap. "There's other girls there now. I'm sure there's some here too if a walk to the parlor's too much on yer sorry legs."

"Why you . . ."

Jesse raises an arm like he means to backhand me,

then pretends to notice all the folks watching and considers otherwise.

"Yer outta yer damn mind," Jesse growls. "Playing casually with the other girls don't mean yer fit to sit at a table here."

These words catch the attention of a man nearby, who sits a little taller. One glance at his jacket—aged leather with a bit of fringe 'long the seams—and I recognize him as the Rider who got away at the Agua Fria. He sure don't seem to recognize us, though. Maybe 'cus I look very unlike a boy at the moment.

I tug my shawl tighter. Squaring my shoulders to Jesse, I jangle Pa's leather pouch, which me and the Coltons filled with nearly all the coins we got left between us.

"I wanna play," I says as the coins clink. "They wouldn't turn away a *man* with a loaded purse, so why's it matter that I'm a woman?"

"You should stick to what yer good at," Jesse mutters.

But the interested Rider's heard enough. His eyes sparkle as he stands. He thinks I'll be an easy match, a sure win for his boss. And more money in Rose's pocket prolly means more for the rest of the crew.

"Let the lady play," he says to Jesse. "I think you might have a problem if you don't." He puts his hand on the grip of his pistol. Behind him, and stretched through the room, a few others stand taller, shove off the wall, toss their jackets and coats open to show off their pieces. I look 'em over quick, counting five—six with the man right before us.

And just like that, we know where they're standing. Every last Rider 'cept Rose himself. Assuming he's already seated, playing cards. The saloon's too full of patrons to see the tables in the back. And I certainly can't sweep faces for one matching Rose's description without drawing suspicion.

Jesse holds a forefinger an inch from my nose. "A few hands, and that's it. Soon as you's lost a couple dollars, I want what I came for."

Even though it's part of our plan, my cheeks go hot at what his words imply. He don't see it, thankfully. He's already stalking off toward the bar.

It's a mighty regal one—all solid, shining oak. Instead of a mirror behind it, there's only more wood, but it's engraved with a roaring tiger and towering bears. The ceiling of the saloon is lofted, making the place feel too open. The upstairs rooms share a hallway that overlooks the tables. There's a bunch of girls up there now, leaning on the banister, shawls dangling and skin gleaming by the light of oil lamps.

"Lemme show you to an open table, miss," the Rider says. He touches my elbow, and for a moment I think real hard 'bout the satisfaction I'd get from drawing the pistol from beneath my dress and shooting him through the heart. But I force my face calm and let him lead me toward the game.

As we move away from the doors the stench of days-old sweat hits. It ain't regal folk in here, not no matter what the craftsmanship of the bar lets on. Tobacco smoke wafts in clouds between the shoulders of men from all walks of life—businessmen and farmers and miners and more. The only thing I don't see is any type of law, and that'd be useful on a night like this.

My boot toe catches on something and I go tumbling forward, jerked to a halt only 'cus the Rider's still holding my elbow. If it weren't for him, I'd've fallen flat on my face. Damn dress.

He turns and kicks what tripped me—an Apache girl on all fours scrubbing the floorboards. She hisses as his boot connects with her gut.

"*Clean* the floors," he snaps. "Don't trip people walking on 'em. Goddamn injun."

She mutters something in her language that I'm sure ain't kind. The Rider seems to think the same, 'cus he kicks her again. Men snigger throughout the saloon. Funny how folks here treat me like a lady—questionable honor and all—but don't give two hoots 'bout the Apache.

The man winds up a third time but I step a leg out at the last second, so his boot hits my shin 'stead of the girl.

"I reckon she'll scrub better if you ain't kicking her," I says.

He grumbles something but motions for me to follow. I catch the girl's eye as I pass by—confused and suspicious. I don't know why I did it. I wouldn't expect an ounce of kindness from an Apache if I was to fall into their hands and I reckon she don't expect much from us, neither. I walk on, trying not to cringe at my flaring leg. I bet it's already bruising. That's the last time I help an Indian who don't even thank me.

Ahead, the game table's waiting. Will's already made hisself comfortable, stretched out and chewing dip. He was aiming to scout out Rose and settle in next to him. If he didn't, the whole plan's shot.

I search Will's eyes, looking for a sign as to which man's Rose. Before Will can do nothing, the man to his left glances up and, as his face appears from beneath the brim of his hat, time freezes. My boots root into the floor-boards. I forget how to walk.

'Cus it's him. It's Waylan Rose.

The scar cuts his cheek in two, starting below his eye and carving a path down to the outer edge of his lip. It's a pale, pocked line on an otherwise leather-tanned face. He's wearing a long black coat over a blood-red shirt, and his dark hair hangs to his chin just like mine. He's older than I expect. Or maybe desert plains and a life of killing's just weathered his skin. There's a smile on his lips, appearing between the stubble covering his jaw, but what kills me most is his eyes. They're lively. Bright. Shining like he ain't got a care in the world. As blue and cheerful as a cloudless summer sky.

How can a man who's done so much evil have eyes the color of heaven? They should be dark and soiled. They should be rotten.

I force myself to keep moving, and by the time I reach the only open seat—directly 'cross from him—I's found my tongue again.

"This seat taken?"

Rose pulls a smoke from his coat. His gaze trailing over me feels like a knife. "How's a soiled dove come to be skilled at poker? Don't you gals have other games to play?" His voice matches his scar—scratchy and rough.

"I ain't never said I was skilled. Just that I know how to play and want to try my luck. But I's picked up enough here and there, if you must know."

"Hopefully from good teachers."

"I reckon we'll see," I says.

Waylan Rose lights his smoke and shakes out the match. "I reckon we will." Then he exhales in my direction, grinning so sly, my blood slows. "By all means, sit down, doll. The only thing more fun than stealing from men is stealing from women."

I pull out the chair, thankful the length of Evelyn's gown's hiding my unsteady knees.

The cards get cut. Chips are passed out. The first hand is dealt.

It ain't a large group playing—just me, Rose, Will, and three other men, one of which is the clerk from Hancock's. He's sitting on Rose's left and don't seem to recognize me now that I'm dressed like a girl. After a couple hands, it's obvious he bets bold too often. The men flanking me, however, are quiet and cautious players, and that suits me just fine. I only got one player to worry 'bout.

As planned, I make sure to lose a few hands early so no one sees me as a threat. I bet big on a poor hand. I fold on a hand that's actually good. I win one but leave it at that. I don't want no tell, and if I act rash and random, there ain't a way for the other players to get a read on my habits. Pa'd stressed that when teaching me how to play poker one winter. The long nights were filled with cards that season, and rifle cartridges that served as betting chips. I never thought knowing the game would be a skill I'd need, but I's thankful for it now.

Rose keeps his face blank, but his eyes twitch round the table like a hawk's. Watching the deals and the folds, flickering over the players' features, dancing over the chips. He thumbs his, which are stacked neat and precise.

As the game continues the Apache girl makes rounds, refilling whiskey glasses and emptying out ashtrays. The Rider who escorted me to the table is now standing 'gainst the bar, but every time the Apache slips behind it he spits dip at her back. When he ain't tormenting her, he's staring at our table. I can feel the eyes of the other Riders on us too. From all through the saloon, they're watching. Between them and Rose, this ain't gonna be breezy. Not that I ever thought it would be. But still.

Maybe a dozen hands in, the man to my left bets real big. He ain't done nothing of note yet, so I reckon he's got something good. I stay in till after the trade, just to throw people off. Then when he raises, I fold. Everyone does but Rose, who raises more. The guy to my left counts his chips, deliberating.

"Friend, you don't wanna test me on this hand," Rose says.

The man beside me looks at his five cards, then the pot, then his cards. Finally, he shoves all he's got left into the center of the table.

"All in," he says.

Rose's brows rise in amusement. He takes a long drag

on his smoke. Taps it 'gainst the ashtray one, two, three times. Exhales. Then he counts out what he needs to match the bet and slides the chips forward.

The man to my left flips his cards, grinning. He's got a full house. Three queens and two aces. It's a damn good hand.

"Ain't that a shame," Rose says.

He exhales slow and turns his hand over. Another full house—also a pair of aces, but with three kings.

"Sorry, partner," Rose says.

As Rose scoops up the pot, the losing man jumps to his feet and draws his gun. Somehow—even though Rose is bent over gathering his winnings—he manages to straighten, square, draw, and fire first.

Rose's mark flies back, toppling a chair, and is dead before he hits the floor.

The saloon goes stark silent. The last key plucked on the corner piano hangs in the air. The girls in the loft hush.

Everyone's staring, even the men at our table. The Hancock's clerk's mouth is frozen in a tiny O.

"I hate sore losers," Rose announces. He flicks his coat open and holsters his six-shooter, but not before I spot the grip of a second pistol on his hip. Shiny and pale. Engraved with a pattern I'd know anywhere.

The bastard is carrying my father's pistol like he owns it. Like he didn't steal my father's life and journal and even the contents of his belt.

Alls I can do is stare at my dwindling pile of chips, fearing our plan is bust. Rose were a faster shot than even

Jesse. I don't know how he did it, and even if everything unfolds like we got planned, I can't see anyone else in this saloon wanting to take a shot at him after he just unloaded on that other fella so fast.

But I also can't run. Not after that last hand. It's Will's turn to deal, and all those aces and kings and queens are in plain view on the table. This is our chance. We couldn't've asked for better luck or timing.

Will gathers up the cards, and he's so nonchalant 'bout it, you'd never guess he was counting 'em, stuffing the deck with purpose, setting up the deal.

The Apache girl comes back to refill drinks. It causes a nice distraction, making Will's deal a bit easier. Still, Rose's got his eyes sharp on the deck, and scared he's gonna spot a plant, I start talking.

"What brings you to Phoenix, sir?"

He takes a sip of his whiskey. "What makes you think I'm from elsewhere?"

"It's just I never seen you round here," I says, hoping it's a strong enough answer.

Rose eyes me a long moment, then says, "A job."

"And yet yer gambling, not working."

He sets his glass down hard. "Have we met before?" Rose cocks his head sideways, and I'm reminded of a coyote 'bout to pounce. "You look familiar."

I swear my heart's pounding loud enough for the other players to hear. Does he see Pa in my features? Are my eyes his?

"I been working in Phoenix most of my life," I says, "so I doubt it."

"Maybe in Prescott?" Rose takes Pa's pistol from his holster and lays her down on the table so I can see her in all her glory. My eyes lock on it. I can't stop staring. I swallow and force myself to look back at Rose. He's gotta recognize me. Or suspect. He knows something he shouldn't, or he wouldn't've brought Pa's gun into view.

"Prescott?" I says. "What's in Prescott?"

"Nothing, I guess." He tosses his blind in, nonchalant, and the man to his right follows suit. Will finishes the deal and I scoop up my cards.

I take a deep breath and force myself to focus.

Will's done me good. I got two aces, two kings, and a three. If Will's done the deal right through and through, Waylan's got the other two bullets.

I itch my collarbone with my left hand — our signal — and Jesse moves away from the bar.

Everyone calls, and when the bet turns to me I raise a hefty sum. Will folds. Rose sees me, as does Hancock's clerk and the man to my right.

I push my three toward Will, face-down. Waylan also trades a single card. I don't care what the others do, so I don't even bother making note.

Will deals out the trades. My three becomes a four.

Not that it matters . . . Jesse's coming.

"All right, that's quite enough of this," he says, bearing down on the table.

"I got a good hand."

"I don't care if you got a royal flush," Jesse argues. "Let's go. A man shot and dead! Who knows what else to come. I let you play and all you's done is lose my money."

"I won one hand."

"I don't care. It's my turn now." He grabs me by the wrist of my card hand and hauls me to my feet. With a yank I'm facing him, our chests pressed together with nothing but the cards squished between us. His face is so close, I can smell the tobacco on his breath.

"Yer making a scene," I says, yanking 'gainst his grip. In the fake struggle he slips a card from his sleeve and into my fanned five, swapping it with the one on the far edge—the four. Right where I promised I'd hold the card I didn't want. Now I's got a hand that'll best Rose, but he's still got one good enough that he thinks he can win. He ain't gonna fold.

"There won't be a scene if you just come like yer told," Jesse snarls, tugging me harder.

"I ain't going nowhere. I can win this."

"Listen, I already paid for you and I'm sick of waiting. If you don't come now, I swear to God I will—"

A weapon cocks.

Jesse steps away from me. We both look to Rose. He's sitting there calm as ever, his elbow resting on the table with his pistol aimed at Jesse.

"She already bet and has to play out the hand. Let her go."

Jesse drops my arm in disgust. I make a show of fixing my shawl and looking frazzled.

Rose motions toward the bar with his pistol. "Head back to the bar."

"Yer gonna pay for this later," Jesse says, pointing a finger at me. Then he sulks off.

Rose keeps his gun aimed at Jesse's back. "Should I shoot him for you?"

"No!" I says, prolly too forcefully.

Rose just shrugs and holsters his weapon. "It's yer funeral."

I feel like smiling. He's buying it. Every last bit of the act.

"All in." Rose shoves his pile of chips forward. "In fact, I'm gonna sweeten the deal some more. This is worth the pot and then some." He reaches inside his jacket, pulls something from the back of his pants, and tosses it onto the table. It lands with a thud, scattering some of the chips. My blood dries in my veins. The ribbing of Evelyn's dress is suddenly too tight. 'Cus it's the journal. Rose killed Pa for it, just like I suspected.

I can't stop staring. The journal's as worn and soft as I remember it. The cord wrapped round the middle, so tight, the leather puckers. The page edges worn and uneven. Pa's initials carved into the front.

"A journal?" I says, praying I sound unimpressed. "Worth more than the pot? How so?"

"You just gotta take my word for it."

"All right," I says after pretending to consider it a moment. "All in." I shove forward the little I got left.

Rose flips his cards. He has another full house. Two aces and three queens.

But I got me *three* aces, thanks to Jesse. I'm loaded and I'm winning back Pa's journal and then I'm shooting this bastard right between the eyes.

"Now, sir," I says in my sweetest voice. "How's it you

can have two aces"—I lay my cards down—"when I's got three?"

Everyone at the table goes rigid.

The Apache, approaching with fresh drinks, stops so abruptly that the glasses slide off the edge of her tray. As they hit the floor, shattering and chiming, everyone at the table lurches upright, pulling weapons. The men at my right ain't sure who cheated, but they know one of us is the reason they're losing money. Will's pretending to look just as mad. Rose's gun hasn't once trained away from me.

"Search her," he orders, and two of his men come forward from the wall. I stand there, frozen, trying not to grimace as foreign hands slap up and down my bodice and legs. They spend a bit too long on my chest, but I bite my lip. They don't find a thing 'cept the pistol strapped to my thigh, but it ain't unheard of for painted ladies to carry a piece for protection. They're only concerned 'bout cards.

"Maybe it's you who cheated," I says as my boots are pulled off and searched.

"I don't need to cheat," Rose scoffs.

"Then you won't mind turning yer pockets out for us," says the man to my right. He ain't had a good game. He's almost broke on account of losing several hands to Rose.

Sighing, Rose sets his pistol down and shakes out his coat, turns out his pockets.

"And yer boots," Will says.

Rose tugs 'em off, turns 'em over.

A single card floats free, landing face-down on the table. Rose stares at it, perplexed.

Will reaches forward, hesitant and confused-like, even though *he* planted it. He flips the card, revealing another ace. Its suit matches the diamond I already got in my hand.

Rose's face sours so fast, it's like he's a different person. Those blue eyes don't look like heaven no more. They look like ice and steel, like a demon ready to pounce. He knows it ain't him who cheated. He knows it, and yet everyone else don't. He's ready to kill, ready to carve another rose into the forehead of whichever player conned him.

"I'll take back the money you won from me," the man to my right says. "Right now."

"I ain't given you nothing," Rose says. "I been set up."

"You chiseled us," says Hancock's clerk.

"She did!" Rose says, pointing my way. "If I knew I had an ace in my boots, I'd've played it *this* hand, gone with a full house loaded with three bullets, not two. It's her who's chiseling."

"We all been here the whole time," Will says. "She ain't done nothing but lose most of her hands and get lucky this once. But you? Two full houses in a row? And another two earlier in the evening. What are the odds?"

"Yeah, what are the odds?" the man to my right repeats. "I think you owe us some money."

"Or else?"

"Or else I'm shooting you and taking it back."

"Not if I shoot you first."

Rose snatches up his pistol and sends a bullet into the man's chest. Then he turns on me. I dive to the side just before his gun flares, and in the time it takes me to hit the floor, the saloon erupts with gunfire.

CHAPTER TWELVE

I throw my hands over my head and crawl beneath a nearby table for shelter.

'Long the far wall, one of the Riders knocks a lamp onto the floor. The glass shatters, and when the flames find spilled whiskey, it sparks to life and snakes through the saloon. The place goes ablaze like hay.

"Will!" I shout. "Jesse!"

A body smacks the floor beside me, and I find myself staring into the lifeless eyes of the Hancock's clerk. Jesus, he's dead. Everything's gone to hell. This weren't the plan, weren't how it was gonna unfold.

"Jesse!" I try again.

But there's smoke everywhere. Fire raging. My skin's so hot, I think it might blister and peel clean off. Someone's shouting for me. One of the Colton brothers, I'm sure, but I can't see nothing, and all I can imagine is my father yelling my name as Rose beat him senseless. Calling for help as he was heaved high. Praying I'd show up from the creek to save him before his air stole out.

But I failed. I failed him then, and I'm failing him again now.

Waylan Rose were right before me, his chest a table's-width away, and I didn't put a bullet in him.

I pull my Colt from beneath my dress and squint through the smoke. The poker table's overturned, and though the wood's going up in flames it ain't caught the journal yet. It's just lying there 'longside the abandoned cards and scattered chips. I scramble for it, and right when my fingers close over the leather, Rose comes marching through the fire like a devil unable to burn. He kicks me so hard, I go end over end. I manage to keep hold of the journal, but my pistol bounces free, clattering outta reach. As I come to a harsh stop, the sleeve of Evelyn's dress catches on the floorboards, ripping to expose my bad shoulder. Rose sees the bandage, and his blue eyes blaze.

"I knew it," he roars over the flames. "Yer the same scum who shot my men!"

"And you hanged my father," I says, cringing through the pain. "We ain't even close to even."

He laughs—a deep, vicious cackle—and trains his gun on me. No, not his gun—*Pa's*. My father's Colt is gonna be what ends my life. Or maybe Rose'll take a knife to my skin first.

"And for a moment, I actually believed you a bounty hunter," he says.

Outta the corner of my eye, I spot my gun beneath a burning table. I reach for it, stretch. My fingers graze the barrel. Rose just thinks I'm trying to crawl to safety 'cus a flaming chair between us has filled the place with smoke.

Come on, just a little farther.

"Consider this a favor, girl," he says. "I'm ending yer suffering before you realize just how black that journal is. I'll even make it nice and quick, 'stead of stringing you up like yer Pa."

He cocks his weapon.

Aims.

And then, 'gainst all odds, he pauses. Confusion ripples over his features.

My fingers close over the steel of my pistol. I turn and shoot.

The gunshot is just another crack in the already roaring saloon. Rose grabs at his shoulder, cursing and hollering, but I don't wait to see much else. Scrambling to my feet, I fire blindly over my shoulder and dive for a table the flames ain't found yet. With a shove, I overturn it, then crouch down behind the surface so it shields me like a wall.

Through the smoke, I risk a glance back Rose's way. He's cringing—at the strength of the flames, the pain from my bullet—but his eyes are scanning the room for me. How'd I manage to even clip him? I know he's the faster shot, am certain he could've left me dead. It's like he hesitated, like he changed his mind. It don't make a lick of sense.

I duck back behind the table and try to steady my breathing. When I look again, Rose ain't there.

Cursing, I push to my feet and dart for the door.

A series of shots rings out, chasing at my heels, and I'm forced to turn away from the exit and head deeper into the saloon. I race past the bar, beyond the stairwell leading to the loft, where the air-hungry flames are snapping fierce, and into a narrow hall. Maybe there's a rear exit, another way out.

"Jesse?" I shout again through the smoke. "Will?"

"Help!" someone calls back.

But it ain't the Coltons. It's a female.

"In here!"

I move toward her voice, choking on smoke, and find a door—or what once was one. Now it's just a blazing frame. Through the tongues of fire, I can see her crouched and cowering a few steps down. The Apache. Only, she don't look so much like an Apache anymore, but just a scared girl.

This stairwell must lead to the cellar. She prolly ran in there for shelter when the shooting broke out, only now she ain't gonna do nothing but burn if she don't abandon post.

"Come on!" I shout to her, waving. "Run through it."

She shakes her head, frantic.

I reach an arm for her and snatch it back almost immediately. It's blazing stronger than hellfire.

"There ain't another way," I says.

She moves toward the flames, staggers away, tries again. The flames beat her back each time, and the hall-way's getting hotter and smokier by the minute. Bullets are still flying back in the saloon, some sounding like they're coming my way.

I glance back to the Apache. I ain't never seen eyes so wide and desperate. But the journal's gonna burn if I don't run. *I'm* gonna burn.

"I'm sorry," I says.

Her screams chase me as I shove out the rear exit. When my lungs get a gulp of fresh air, I drop to my knees, panting. I could cry in relief. I could sing.

I glance over my shoulder. No one's followed me. There ain't nothing in the hall but flames and smoke. She's gonna burn to a charred crisp in there—like those poor souls Rose murdered in the coach, like the card-playing townsfolk he shot just earlier. And she don't deserve it. None of 'em did. Only difference is, unlike the others, she ain't dead yet.

I heave upright, still coughing, and glance round. Blankets hang on a line behind the building to my right, flapping on the evening's warm breeze. There's barrels on the back porch too.

Please have water, I think, racing to 'em. *Please.*

I yank one of the blankets free and knock my hip into the barrels till one sloshes in response. I pull the plug and sniff. Not alcohol, that's for sure. Hell, there ain't a smell, period. I shove it over and roll it back to the saloon.

The flames are devouring the rear entrance now too. It's an inferno. She's prolly already dead.

But you can't leave her trapped in there. You can't, you worthless coward.

I toss the journal aside, to a place where it'll be safe from the flames. Then I drench a corner of the blanket with water, hold it over my mouth, and shove the barrel forward. After fighting to get it over the doorway's lip, I roll it down the hall and to the cellar. My lungs start heaving again in protest, my eyes burning. Every instinct in my body's screaming for me to leave, to turn round and run, but I kick the barrel over, letting the water pour into the stairwell. I drop the blanket, let it become a sopping mess. Then I smack at as many flames in the cellar doorway as I can. They muffle and hiss beneath the material. Smoke fills the air as the water kills most of the flames on the stairs themselves. My hands ache from the heat even with the blanket protecting them. My legs feel like they're blistering.

"Hello?" I shout through the clouds of gray.

Nothing.

"Hey, you still alive in there?"

And then . . . a cough.

I take a step into the stairwell, and the wood groans. I spot her slouched on the steps, barely conscious from all the smoke. I grab her at the wrist and sling her arm behind my neck, then wrap the blanket round the both of us. Before the stairs can give way beneath our weight, I heave her outta the cellar stairwell and down the hall.

My knees give out when we're a few feet from the saloon, and we both tumble forward. She lands face-down in the dirt, not moving. My dress is burning, the white material singed black at the hem. I slap at it with the blanket, muffling out the flames, then pull up the folds of the dress to check the damage. My skin's hot and red, but it ain't blistered. My boots've spared me a second time.

"You all right?" I says, checking on the Apache girl.

She coughs and hacks and coughs some more. The palms of her hands are blistered white, prolly from when she tried to reenter the saloon through that burning cellar door. She looks up at me. Her eyes are still wide, but there ain't so much fear and desperation in them no more. No, now it's a look of shock, of astonishment.

The thunder of cracking wood brings me to my feet. The Tiger's roof is failing, starting to buckle. The Coltons might still be in there. I take a step toward the saloon, and that's when a section of the roof folds in, showering down flame and beams. I stumble away, the dress heavy with water and nearly tripping me. *Goddamn ten-pound dress!* I draw my knife from my boot and hack at the skirt, cutting the material free. It were half burned and ruined anyway. Evelyn weren't getting back something she could wear.

Evelyn.

My head jerks toward the parlor.

We were supposed to regroup there if'n something went wrong. That was the plan. If'n the Coltons are still in the Tiger, there ain't nothing I can do for 'em now. It was dumb enough going back in the one time.

I kick the discarded section of dress aside and snatch up Pa's journal.

I can still hear the Apache coughing up a fit as I round the corner.

Even on the main street, the scene's crazed.

Smoke is billowing wild. People are running round, screaming for aid. Decent-looking folk wearing night-clothes are spilling from their homes to help, rolling barrels of reserved water nearer to battle the flames. It's good they're on hand, them barrels. The fire's already starting to flirt with the neighboring buildings, and in a town made of wood, the whole strip's fixing to go up like a book of matches.

I burst into the parlor, and Evelyn stops cold where she'd been pacing. Her eyes linger on the state of my dress, then my hair, which has all but come free from the pins and is hanging round my face in sweaty tendrils.

"Where is everybody?" I says, noting the empty state of the parlor—bare couches, deserted bar, quiet piano. Not even the other girls remain.

"Helping with the fire."

"And the Coltons?"

"They ain't back yet."

"They ain't . . . They . . ."

I can't bring myself to say much else. I don't know what it means, but it sure ain't good. This is my fault. The Coltons missing. The town burning. All those innocent folks caught in the Riders' crossfire.

I grab the half-shredded skirt of Evelyn's dress and

take the stairs two at a time. I gotta go back for the boys, but I know I ain't gonna get much done in this ridiculous dress.

"What happened?" Evelyn calls after me.

I race on without answering. When I burst into her room, Mutt bares his teeth.

"Yeah, it ain't like I fancy you, neither," I tell him.

I strip outta the dress and undo the blasted corset, throw my trousers on fast as I can. When I can't find my flannel in the messy room, I fish an undershirt from Evelyn's dresser, then grab my pistol belt. Before I got it fastened on proper, footsteps come pounding my way. The door bangs open.

"Jesus!" I snap, flustered. "Didn't nobody ever tell you to knock?" When I spin round, I find the Coltons standing there. Jesse's got soot on his cheeks and singes in his shirt and a black eye he didn't have before the Tiger. Will ain't looking much prettier, with a nasty gash on his forehead.

"See now, aren't you glad you were worried?" Jesse says to his brother. "Smart-mouthed and ungrateful and not even bothered to see we ain't dead."

"That ain't true. You just startled me," I says. "I was 'bout to go back looking for you."

"Ain't no bother," Jesse says, and whistles quick for Mutt. "You ready? We gotta ride."

"We're leaving?" I spot my flannel on a drying rack near the window; Evelyn must've washed it for me. "What 'bout Rose?" I ask, tugging it on. "Did either of you get a shot at him?"

"Missed my chance while the roof came down and I's dodging bullets," Jesse says real dry-like.

"But what if he's still in town? I could get him. I nearly got him earlier."

"Kate, the town's burning. Rose nearly killed you. We gotta leave before things get worse."

"I already heard people saying it was you two who started the fight," Will says. "If'n they give statements to the sheriff when he returns, the law'll be on our tail 'longside the Rose Riders."

"Precisely," Jesse says. "We can catch up with him later. But right now we gotta get somewhere safe."

Feet come pounding down the hall, and Evelyn bursts into the room, cutting off our argument.

"There's men downstairs asking for a girl in a flowered dress and the guy who paid for her."

Jesse swears, then moves the dresser in front of the door. "That'll be the Rose Riders."

I bolt to the window and throw it open. The scent of smoke hits me hard. Looking east, I can make out the flickering inferno that's devouring the Tiger. But straight ahead, Evelyn's window opens onto a lower section of roof—what covers the lounge wing of the parlor.

"Roof's clear," I announce.

"I'll take Evelyn and get her someplace safe," Will says. He's got an arm slung round her shoulder like he's a shield meant to protect her, and she leans into him like it's true. "You two run, then circle back. I'll have the horses ready."

Jesse nods just as feet come clomping up the stairs.

A door is kicked open farther down the hall. It bangs to a standstill, then another being forced open sounds. They're coming. Working their way down the hall to us.

I grab my Stetson and Pa's journal. Jesse watches me tuck it into the back of my pants, face serious, but he don't ask how I got it back. Will and Evelyn are climbing out the window when a thunderous impact strikes Evelyn's door. The dresser rattles. Deep voices curse and roar on the other side. I ain't sure if one of 'em's Rose, but I'm not waiting to find out.

Jesse clambers onto the roof and whistles for Mutt. When the dog leaps through the window, Jesse sends him after Will.

Another blow hits the door and this time the dresser gives a little.

"Kate!" Jesse whispers, reaching for me. I grab his wrist. Not a moment after he's pulled me through the window, the dresser falls over with a crash.

We don't turn to see if the Rose Riders have forced their way into the room.

We just run.

We run like hell.

CHAPTER THIRTEEN

Jesse leads, racing 'cross the roof and leaping the distance between the parlor and the neighboring house. I don't let myself pause or think on what I'm doing. I trust my legs to do as his do, and my balance ends up being sharper than I knew. Also helps that these buildings are built close.

As we soar 'cross the gap, gunshots rip out below—Riders who've spotted us and are shooting up from the street. And I reckon a new batch of bullets will be aiming for our backs soon as Rose's other men follow us onto the roof.

When I look over my shoulder, I can make out Will and Evelyn lowering themselves to the streets. A harsh order from Will telling Mutt to jump reaches my ears, but then I spot the dark frame of a man crawling out the parlor window and pointing our way.

I turn round and race after Jesse.

"Alley ahead!" he shouts, without slowing. He soars over it, landing on the opposite roof and skidding down the pitch a few feet before he catches himself.

I follow but land funny. One ankle rolls. Pain shoots from my heel to my hip. I go down on my rump hard and start sliding, jerked to a halt only when Jesse grabs me at the wrist. I push to my feet and a bullet tears through that section of roof, barely missing me.

I fire down where the shot came from. It's dark, but I hear someone curse me.

Still, their bullets ain't slowing.

"Faster," Jesse urges. But I can't go any quicker than this. The skin round my ankles—tender from the fire —screams with each step. My bad shoulder flares each time I check to see if there's Riders behind us and my head's aching like it's struck a rock all over again. Making things even worse still, I can barely see where I'm going. It's a cloudy night, the moon doing little to light our way.

Two more daring alley leaps later, and Jesse and me come to a building only one story tall. The drop to it ain't terrible, but it feels like thunder in my knees. Then Jesse and I are skidding to the edge of the roof, grabbing at the lip so we can swing down into the back alley.

I hear a whoosh, and Jesse goes flying off his feet, hitting his head hard 'gainst the building and crumpling still. I twist round, pistol out, and find myself face to face with a Rose Rider.

He's got gleaming, wild eyes and a shovel gripped in his hands. I don't know why his gun ain't drawn, why he didn't shoot Jesse 'stead of swinging.

I cock my Colt.

"Don't bother with that," he says, smiling. "Just hand over the journal."

My trigger finger is shaking from nerves. I wish I could see the Rider's waist, make out if there's another pistol on his hip. He's prolly faster than me. I bet any man riding with Rose draws like lightning. 'Less of course he lost his weapon in the chase or is outta ammo.

"Give me the journal," he says again.

I force down the fear, shove it deep inside where it can't own me. Then I lower my barrel a bit and don't think 'bout it. I just react, let my body catch up to what I already envisioned in my mind, exactly as Jesse taught me. Aim and pull. The Rose Rider goes down on his rump in the dirt, screaming at me and grabbing his now-ruined knee.

I aim for his chest this time, but when I pull the trigger my pistol just clicks. I'm empty.

The Rider reaches for his waist.

I don't wait to see if there's a pistol. I don't bother trying to reload my Colt. I just snatch up the shovel he's dropped and swing, bringing it 'gainst the back of his head with the fullest force I can muster. He hits the ground and stays still.

"Jesse?" I says, racing to him. "Jesse, you all right?" I shake his shoulder, praying he ain't dead.

He mumbles something.

"Oh, thank God. On your feet. Let's go."

I slide one of his arms behind my neck and push him upright. If he's trying to stand with me, he's doing a sorry job. I might as well be moving a bull. My rolled ankle burns in protest.

I shoulder my way into the building through the back door—thankfully unlocked—and we stumble into a confectionary shop. It's small and only feels more crowded on account of the endless rows of glass canisters. Ribbon candy, hard suckers, lollipops, and more glint by the firelight flicking through the glass windows.

I take a minute to reload my pistol, only then realizing that I ain't sure if the Rider outside is dead or just knocked out. But there's bullets screaming in the alley, more men on our tail. We gotta keep moving.

"Can you walk on yer own?" I ask Jesse.

He nods.

I peer out the front windows. I can't see much, but the constant shouting and cracks of wood suggest the Tiger's still everyone's focus on the main street.

"All right, let's go."

I heave open the door and we race back into the night. My heart is kicking wild in my chest, my eyes checking every alley we pass for a Rider. Jesse's keeping up all right, but he's got a hunch to his shoulders, like he's still feeling the blow of that shovel to his stomach.

Ahead, smoke from the Tiger billows, glowing silver-white by the moon as the townsfolk battle the fire with water. They's done a fair job. The flames are surrendering, and the worst of it seems to be contained. Still, the smell gets to me. The saloon ain't nothing like home, and yet so much is the same—the scent of burning wood and scorched blankets and thick, heavy smoke. Pa flashes before me. The rope creaking as he swings. His eyes wide and vacant. Then I'm seeing that charred stagecoach, the blackened bodies. Roses etched into skin. I buckle to my knees. Jesse grabs me at the elbow and hauls me upright.

When we get to the parlor, Will ain't there, and neither are our horses.

My heart sinks straight down to my boots, but then there's a whistle. I glance round and find Will waiting in an alley 'cross the way. He's atop Rio, and Rebel and Silver are standing there saddled as Mutt yaps anxious by their heels.

Jesse and me dart 'cross the street, but not stealthily enough.

"There! That's them!" someone shouts. Will fires over our heads as we run to our horses.

I step into Silver's stirrup and am urging her on before I's even swung my other leg over her back. Behind me, I hear pounding hooves and know the Coltons are with me. We tear up the main street and pass the Tiger. Water barrels are dropped as unsuspecting folk dive outta our way. Rose Riders I can't make out shoot and curse from the streets and the roofs. Their bullets chase us, but we don't even try to fire back no more. We just slap our reins and heel our horses and ride east, leaving Phoenix behind as fast as the devil can.

No more than a few yards beyond the outskirts of town, it's getting hard to see. The moon's stuck behind a lump of clouds, and there ain't much left to go by. The last lanterns lighting our way faded out when the streets did, and it took only a block before the dying fire at the Tiger didn't 'luminate the ground no more.

We cut southeast, racing through land I reckon belongs to some rancher. We don't never see the homestead, though, or his cattle or horses. A nearly blind mile or two later, we come upon the Salt River, and it's a blessing. Weak moonlight flickers and gleams off the water, bouncing where it trickles over pebbles and snakes between grass. It's just enough to show us the way. Here, the land 'long the bank is pitched and uneven, full of brush and brambles and rocks. I got a notion all three of us will be thrown from our horses any second on account of a poor step. But it ain't like we can stop, or even slow for that matter. Gunshots keep popping behind us, Rose's gang riding hard. I glance over my shoulder, but alls I can see is a gray plume of dirt a half mile back—a miniature dust storm.

"What do we do?" Will shouts from Rio.

Jesse don't say nothing, and I know as well as him that we can't ride endlessly. No horse can fly like this forever. I reckon Will knows it too and he's just talking to keep hisself busy. I's noticed he likes to do that.

Silver leaps a patch of brush, and at the crest of the jump I see something that lifts my heart: a ramshackle shanty of a home, roof half buckled, sitting 'cross the river where the bank rises a touch. It's abandoned for sure. If we get there first and set ourselves up right, we might have a chance. Six Riders 'gainst three of us. Maybe seven of 'em if that fella I clubbed lived through the blow and managed to get to his horse with a bad knee. It ain't the prettiest odds, but we'll have shelter and a perch. Them, low ground and open land. Riding atop their horses, they'll be like bottles on a fence.

"Abandoned home!" I point it out to the boys.

Jesse nods and guides Rebel into the river.

It's wide here, and looks to be deep so far as desert rivers go. I just hope it ain't deep enough that the horses need to swim. I don't reckon I can hold both my Colt and Winchester above my head *and* manage to stay in the saddle.

I give Silver a nudge in the flank, and she wades in after the others. It's slow going for everyone but Mutt, who leads the way easy. Not even halfway 'cross the river and I can sense Silver bracing 'gainst the current. Water's rising over her knees. When my boots flood, I reach down and pull my rifle from the saddle scabbard, holding it in my lap.

Please don't be much deeper. Please.

Silver trudges on. The current tugs at my stirrups. Water creeps toward Silver's ribs, then flank, and right when I'm certain all my gear and ammo's 'bout to be soaked, the water line starts retreating. We's crossed the worst of it.

"Good girl, Silv," I says, urging her on. As she climbs out on the opposite bank I kick her back into a gallop and chase after Mutt and the Coltons.

Unsure what kind of standoff we might find ourselves in, we can't risk letting the horses roam—they might get spooked and run off—so we lead 'em round back and secure their reins on fencing that once surrounded a chicken coop.

Staying low and quiet, the three of us grab our guns and ammo and slip into the house, taking Mutt with us. The place ain't been lived in for a good long while. There's a sorry-looking table 'gainst the back wall, and some failing chairs, but we don't got enough light to make out much more of the interior. Not that it matters. I'm only concerned with the windows, and when I examine the wooden shutters I nearly beam. There's a cross cut into the two that flank the door. Same goes for the window of each adjoining wall.

"Religious folk?" Will says when I point 'em out.

"It ain't got nothing to do with God." I bring my rifle up and aim her out the carved cross. "Up, down, side to side," I says, changing my aim to demonstrate. "We had 'em in our shutters too, case of Indian raids or bad men."

"Well, it's smart," Jesse says, "and I pray God's on our side tonight." He goes to the other front window with a rifle he'd had strapped to Rebel, and Will takes the west-facing side window with his six-shooters.

I make sure I got as many cartridges as possible jammed into my belt, plus extras nearby. I load up my Winchester and double-check my Colt. Then I lean 'gainst the musty wood wall and scan the Salt River Valley before us.

I don't got a perfect view from the confines of the cross port, but I should be able to see that damn cloud of dust.

"Here they come," Jesse says.

Scanning again, I spot 'em. There's no dust cloud, 'cus they ain't in dust to kick up. They're crossing the river. From here, they look like seven dark ducks paddling. Meaning that Rider I shot and clubbed somehow managed to rejoin the posse. I shoulda shot him dead.

I crank my Winchester's lever and take aim. I ain't making the same mistake twice.

"Not yet," Jesse whispers. "Maybe they ain't seen where we went."

But I'm pretty certain they did. Still, I don't think I could strike any of 'em from here. Not 'cus of my aim or nothing—it's just so far.

The gang's horses climb outta the Salt and onto the bank. One of the members raises a hand, stopping the lot of 'em beyond our guns' range.

"Tompkins!" Waylan Rose yells into the night.

My true name, Pa's name, coming from his mouth makes my knees knock. It sounds like fire and brimstone, like hell rising. Mutt growls beside me.

"Tompkins, you ride out to see me right now or this man dies!"

It's then I realize Rose's got the reins of the horse next to him clenched in his fist, and his pistol aimed directly at that rider's head.

"You want another innocent person dead 'cus of a family heirloom? Some dang journal? Bring it to me now and I'll let this man return to his wife and son in town. Otherwise he'll be dead on account of you."

My stomach clenches. That Rider I confronted must be in Phoenix after all. The seventh saddle holds an innocent man.

"I gotta do something," I mutter.

"It's a trap," Jesse says. "You think he'll let you ride back to us if you go meet him? You think he'll take the journal and just say *thanks?*"

"You got till the count of ten!" Rose shouts.

The men ain't more than dark shadows in the night, but the hostage is shaking something fierce atop his horse. Waylan Rose starts counting.

"I can't just stand here while he kills that man," I says. "I'll ride out a bit. Shoot soon as Rose's in my range. I'll—"

"Are you crazy?" Jesse roars. "You'll stay put."

"I'll decide what I do with my own person, Jesse."

The count's to five now. Four . . .

I lurch for the door.

Three . . .

My hand finds the latch.

Two . . .

And that's when Jesse collides with me like a bobcat tackling prey. We go crashing into the wall and his arms wrap round me, locking mine to my sides, where they're useless.

A single blast booms through the valley. Still holding me tight, Jesse moves to my window for a view out the cross port. I quit struggling 'gainst him and strain my neck till I can see too. The horse next to Waylan Rose is now riderless.

"Damn it, Jesse! He killed him. He killed him and that's our fault. We coulda done something. I coulda—"

His hand comes up, covering my mouth and cutting off my words.

"Shhhh," he says into my ear, and there's fear in his voice. So much fear.

I glance out the cross again and see the Rose Riders moving slow, guiding their horses toward the house. A few more steps and they'll finally be in range. Waylan Rose raises his weapon. A chorus of arms do the same.

Jesse seems to realize their intent the same moment I do, 'cus he shouts, "Will, get down!" and then dives to the floor, bringing me with him and using his body to cover me like a shield. The bullets tear into the house, cutting through the weak and rotting wood like spears. They zing overhead and find exit points through the rear wall. Our horses whinny and squeal out back. Gunfire screams. The bastards shoot till their pistols are unloaded.

When the world falls silent, Jesse raises his head, cautious, and I shove him off. Grabbing my rifle, I lunge for the window and stick the barrel through the cross port. I sight the first dark shadow I see and pull my trigger. A man flinches on his horse but don't fall. The Coltons join me at their windows, and that's when the Riders bolt. But it ain't on account of our bullets alone. On the opposite riverbank, back the way we came, a cloud of dust is billowing and moving fast. An angry mob from town, maybe, finally brave enough to face off with the gang.

I crank my lever action and keep shooting at the fleeing Riders. But they escape unscathed, riding east 'long the Salt River, which gleams black as oil beneath the slivered moon.

CHAPTER FOURTEEN

I'm shaking with so much rage, I don't even blink as Jesse checks on our horses—they're fine—or starts securing the house for the night. When I peer out the cross port, I can see the Phoenix mob lingering 'cross the way, making sure they's driven the Riders out for good. They don't seem concerned 'bout us though. Maybe they figure anyone shooting at the Riders ain't a threat. On our side of the Salt, a lump of a man lies on the riverbank —the poor bastard Rose shot when I didn't ride out to meet him.

That life's my fault. Another innocent soul gone and drained 'cus I sat here hiding.

Suddenly, I'm furious with Pa. It ain't my fault. It's *his.* For lying and withholding and spending all those years spinning me false yarns. Acting like our gold was from Wickenburg. Pretending our last name's Thompson 'stead of Tompkins. If'n he were honest, even 'bout half of it, we mighta been prepared. I'd never have left him alone or let him outta my sight, and he'd still be alive. We'd've watched each other's backs, been suspicious of every last rider approaching our homestead. But, no, he had to go and treat me like some helpless baby, keep the truth from me like I weren't tough enough to handle it. And look where it's got us both? Him in the ground and me caught in the middle of some bloody quest for gold, when alls I wanted was justice for his death.

Mutt weaves between my legs, frenzied, and I stop pacing.

"We'll keep watch till dawn," Jesse says, double-checking the door. "One set of eyes out the front, toward the Salt. Another to the east, watching the way the gang rode off. I don't think they'll double back with them men camping 'cross the way or the law rumored to be returning to Phoenix tomorrow, but it ain't worth taking chances. Only one person's sleeping at a time tonight."

"Whatever you say, boss," Will mutters.

"I ain't got a need for the attitude, Will."

"Oh, hang it all, Jesse! I'm sorry I ain't a peach right now. I'm sorry I ain't praising the Lord that we're in over our heads."

Jesse frowns. "You wanna translate that for me?"

"This damn hunt for gold. The Rose Riders. It ain't worth it. Let *her*"—he jabs a finger my way—"risk her life for revenge, but we ain't got no reason to die for some cache that might not even exist."

"You know damn well we need that money."

"No. *You* need that money. 'Cus yer still trying to do all the things Pa never could: find gold, keep everyone safe. Life ain't a breeze, but we get by. We keep doing what we do, and we'll be fine. We shoulda turned south toward Tucson right after arriving in Phoenix, not played cards. Might as well be sticking our necks in a noose."

"You wanna ride south on yer own? Go right ahead!" Jesse roars.

"And tell Benny what?"

"That I'll make it up to him in gold payment. He'll get over it."

"This is ridiculous," Will says. "You two are both outta yer minds. That guy out there's dead. And all those folks at the poker game. Those lives are on us."

"You think I don't know that?" I erupt. I can't stay quiet no more, can't sit here letting 'em go on and on like I ain't even in the room. "I feel so awful, I can't even find the right word for it. But there are lives that ain't on my conscience neither—my father, that family in the coach. Those souls deserve justice, and there's only gonna be more like 'em if I don't go after Rose."

"Yer deaf all right," Will says. "Deaf *and* dumb."

"Say that again," I says.

"I said yer dumb."

I lunge at him. Jesse hauls me away, but not before I manage to get in one good shove. When Will moves to retaliate, Jesse pushes him back.

"Cool off, Will. Sleep and try to get yer head straight. If'n you still think running cattle with Benny is the best thing we can do for the family come dawn, I won't stop you from riding south."

Will curses God and kicks at one of the failing chairs. Then he glares between us before settling onto the floor.

I look over at Jesse. "Thank y—"

"Don't," he snaps. "You ain't got the slightest . . . This whole thing is so . . ." He bites his lip and turns away from me. "Just don't talk." He snatches up his rifle and moves to the other window.

For a good long while, we keep watch in silence, the only sound in the shanty Will's snores. Moonlight winks off the Salt. Shrubs sway in the summer breeze. The mob's camp is still and there's no sign of the Rose Riders. No sign of nothing, not even the coyotes wailing somewhere in the distance.

It gives me too much time to think. 'Bout those poor souls who died in the Tiger. 'Bout Evelyn and if she's safe. 'Bout that wide-eyed Apache girl and if she ever made it outta the alley.

I shift my weight and roll my bad ankle in circles. It's tight and achy, but hopefully it won't swell much if I keep it moving.

"Quit with the racket," Jesse whispers from his window.

"My rustling clothes is a racket?"

"And creaking floorboards. How's we supposed to hear someone approaching if yer covering their noise?"

I sigh heavy and gaze back out the cross port. Plain's still as calm as ever, river still rippling only on account of the current.

"Why do you hate me, Jesse? We were getting on well enough before our deal . . . when you still thought I were Nate."

He grunts. "I don't hate you."

"Yeah, you do."

"I don't even know you," he says.

"I told you plenty—'bout my pa and his twin Colts and Prescott and how I like my rifle over a six-shooter."

"See, anything said by a person pretending to be some-one else is kinda hard to believe." He shifts his footing, and it causes just as much a "racket" as I did. "Just shut pan and keep watch," he adds. "All right?"

Pa's journal in the waistband of my pants feels heavy suddenly—like a chestful of deception I been lugging round. If'n I'm perfectly honest, I know what Jesse's driving at. It's the very reason I can't think on Pa the same no more. Once I learned all the lies he kept, even the truth-ful, happy moments seemed tainted.

"I never went to school in Prescott," I tell Jesse. "The schoolhouse weren't built till I were twelve, but Pa taught me good. My letters ain't bad, and I can read just fine. Whole books and everything. He bought me *Little Women* when the first copies made it to our bookstore.

"It were a gorgeous book, prettiest I ever seen—leather bound and thick. I always wondered how Pa parted with the money for something so . . . useless. Libby needed a new saddle that year, and we were always running low on salt or flour, and yet he went and bought a *book* for my birthday. Now I know right well his finances were fine. It were all a show: the struggling, the act that we were barely getting by. That or he just didn't like spending the gold too often—was worried someone would talk and his demons would catch up with him just like they did. Still, I'm glad he splurged. It's the best damn story I ever read, Jesse. I swear. When I were sick with scarlet fever earlier this year, I just kept thinking, *Beth survived it and you can too.* Course, she heals pretty weak and ends up dying young, but I reckon I'm more like Jo than Beth anyway. And Jo does herself just fine."

I realize I been talking to my feet this whole time, and I look up. Jesse's staring out the cross port and I ain't even sure he's been listening. But then, without so much as altering his gaze, he asks, "What's it about?"

"*Little Women*? Life. Sisters. Ordinary days, but there were something magic 'bout that. My copy burned in the fire. Couldn't even find a single page when I dug through the house."

Jesse finally glances my way. Moonlight shines through the shutter, painting a brilliant cross over his heart.

"What?" I says.

He shakes his head. "Yer just so violent and vexed half the time. I'm having trouble picturing you nose-deep in a book, reading all calm-like."

"Maybe if I had that ten-pound dress on again, looked more like a civilized lady?"

"Nah," he says. "I like you better like this." He nods at my flannel. "You didn't look like *you* in that dress."

"What's that mean?" I says, defensive.

Jesse frowns. "Means it's time for you to wake Will and take yer turn sleeping."

I shake my head and push off the wall. "Fine," I says. "Yer the boss."

I know my tone ain't nice and that I'm getting short with him like Will did, but how damn hard is it to just say what you mean? Evelyn's dress ain't got nothing to do with changing shifts. Halfway to Will, Jesse calls after me.

"Thanks, though," he says. "For sharing something true."

"Like I said, the other stuff were true too."

"You know what I mean."

And I do. Pa and I can't start over. He can't prove hisself to me again, rebuild the trust that were shattered when I read that letter in Wickenburg. But I can rebuild things with Jesse if I want, and as I shake Will awake I realize that, 'gainst all odds, I want to be a person Jesse Colton trusts. I really do. Whatever the devil that means.

CHAPTER FIFTEEN

When dawn gleams down on the Salt River, we find ourselves blessedly safe. The men from Phoenix cleared out and drifted home sometime during the night, and the Rose Riders never reappeared. I ain't sure what to make of it.

As the boys scarf down some breakfast, I change the dressing on my shoulder. It's still sore, but the wound's healing well. Then I flip through the journal. Maps are sketched here and there, and other pages are filled with clues and instructions. A good lot of it's in Spanish, but the words I don't know from my early years when the language were still used in our household, Pa's translated in the margins. His handwriting stands out to me easy, and I can almost imagine a young version of him hunched over the journal, scribbling notes onto the pages while he schemed of gold. Maybe Ma was sitting nearby, helping him translate. Funny how finding the journal and getting rich ruined everything for them. Money's supposed to fix problems, not give you more, but I guess life ain't that straightforward.

I trace a canyon pass with my forefinger. Waylan Rose must've already seen enough of this journal to not need to come back for it, angry mob and all. Maybe he's copied the most important pages. I wrap the cord back round the journal and head outside to join the Coltons. My rolled ankle is tight but bearable, though I'm still glad Silver'll do the walking today.

It's shaping up to be a good morning, with a cheery sky and a steady breeze blowing from the southeast. I load up Silver, and she gives me an anxious nudge in the shoulder. She don't like sitting still long—damn horse's got too much energy for her own good—and I doubt she's happy after all those roaring bullets last night.

I give her a pat or two and climb into the saddle. That's when the guilt hits.

"We gotta bury him," I announce. "That guy Rose murdered last night."

"With what shovels?" Will says.

"We at least gotta close his eyes," I says.

"That we can manage," Jesse agrees.

We ride to the Salt, where the poor fella lies face-down on the bank. I swing off Silver and drop to my knees beside the corpse. Heaving with all my strength, I roll the man onto his back. When I see his face, I shoot to my feet.

"Aw, hell," I says.

It's the man who attacked me and Jesse outside the

confectionary in Phoenix—the guy I hit with the shovel and musta only knocked out. Waylan Rose killed one of his own men last night, an execution that likely would've happened whether I'd brought the journal forward or not. I doubt the boss man was happy this Rider let me and Jesse slip free.

"Still think you shoulda rode out to meet him?" Jesse says from atop Rebel.

I turn round and glare.

Will spits dip at Mutt, then checks the sun. "Jesse, we got a herd to drive the day after tomorrow and a long way to Tucson still."

"Someone's anxious to see a chuck wagon," Jesse teases. Then he frowns and shrugs, reconsidering. "Hell, it *would* be nice. I don't think we've had a proper meal in almost a week."

Will glares at Jesse. "You know that ain't what I'm driving at. This really the right thing to do?"

"You don't think so, go on and ride south. I told you last night I wouldn't stop you."

"Jesse, you know I ain't gonna go somewhere you ain't. We stick together, that way when plans blow up in yer face, I can rub it in and say 'I told you.' Gosh yer thick sometimes."

"Not as thick as Kate," he says. "She was gonna go after them Rose Riders completely alone."

"Could be the jury's still deciding on the both of us," I says to Jesse.

He don't look amused. Turning his face to the east, he observes the horizon. The Superstition Mountains are barely visible, just small mounds of purple and gray in the morning haze. It's another two days' travel, easy, 'specially 'cus I know that land ain't gonna be flat like here in Phoenix. We'll be traversing rocks and hills and rugged mountain foothills soon enough.

"So what's the plan, Kate?" Jesse says.

"The Salt cuts straight through them mountains," I says, nodding at 'em in the distance. "We could follow the river and then turn south into the Superstitions. Or there's a pass that cuts north into the mountains— Peralta Trail according to the journal—but we'd have to travel southeast a bit before meeting up with it. And we'd be far from water."

"Still don't think this is smart," Will mutters. "What 'bout the ghost shooter, Jesse?"

"That's a fool's tale and you know it," his brother snaps.

"Well, *something's* been killing folk, and it ain't Apache, according to Waltz's last letter."

"I don't care what some old mining buddy of Pa's has to say 'bout those mountains. But I do care that Waltz has a seasonal place 'long the Salt and prospecting equipment we can borrow, since he'll be back in Phoenix this time of year." Jesse turns to me. "Forget the Peralta Trail. Let's follow the river."

"What's this nonsense 'bout a ghost?" I says. I don't point out that I can take any blasted route I want. I don't need mining gear, just the means to trek the land.

"There's some sharpshooter been firing from high in the mountains," Will says. "Only, Waltz's never seen him and reckons it could be a ghost, or an Apache spirit protecting their land."

"Waltz is getting on in age," Jesse scoffs.

I nearly laugh with him. There ain't no such thing as ghosts. I gave up on believing in such nonsense when God took my mother from me for no apparent reason. And now my father, too. Seems pretty darn clear that the greatest evil in this world walks on two feet right beside us, in the form of men like Waylan Rose and his boys.

"It's called the Superstition Mountains," I says to Will firmly. "Course it's a land of legend. Now, are we going or are we gonna sit here jawing 'bout ghosts?" I gather Silver's reins. "You wanna beat Rose to that gold still, don't you?"

Jesse clicks Rebel to action, but Will spits dip with extra force. "Goddamn reckless. We ain't gonna make it out alive."

And this is where we differ, me and the Coltons, 'cus for them, walking out of those mountains matters. But I only want to avenge my father's blood. It ain't like I gotta live through it to be successful. Besides, what do I got to go home to anyway—a burned house and no family? I just gotta keep my heart beating long enough to fire my pistol six times. Once for Waylan Rose, and once for each of his remaining crew.

So long as they go down, I don't much care if I go with 'em.

We follow the Salt River in silence most of the morning. Where the occasional Rose Rider stayed close to the water, hoof marks sink into the damp dirt, marking their trail. But soon I can't see no sign of 'em, and I ain't sure if it's 'cus they turned off to take the Peralta Trail and approach the mountains from the south or if the wind simply erased their tracks.

Despite the breeze, it's turning into another scorcher of a day, sun beating down overhead. Least we're on water, able to refill our canteens whenever necessary and stop to let the horses sip at their leisure. As we carry on, the river wanes and swells, sometimes no more than a dry bed with a trickle running down the middle, sometimes wide enough that we'd need to ford it on our horses to cross. It don't look as deep as the place we crossed last night, though. Hasn't since we left that shanty.

Mutt sneezes and I jolt in my saddle. I don't like the quiet. I's gotten so used to Jesse rambling and jawing all the time that the stillness now seems a distress. Every time I glance his way, thinking of starting a conversation, I end up biting my tongue. I don't got nothing to say. And besides, Jesse ain't looked at me normal since last night. I open up and tell him one true thing and he takes to squinting at me like he don't got a clue who I am.

"We's got a shadow," he announces, breaking the silence.

I follow his gaze back the way we came, and see a lone rider in the distance. "One of Rose's men?"

Jesse pulls out his binoculars and takes a look. "Definitely not. I think it's a girl." He passes 'em over, and I squint through the eyepiece.

"Aw, hell," I says. It's the Apache. She's riding a stout pony and wearing the same smocklike dress she had on at the Tiger, only now it's bunched up 'bout her waist and she's got trousers on beneath it. Her hair's parted into two long braids, and they hang over her shoulders looking like suspenders from this distance. Her pony is a sad-looking thing—saddleless, with a shabby rope bridle —and I wonder how he even made the journey so far. He looks 'bout ready to collapse.

"Friend of yers?" Jesse says.

"No."

"That's right. You ain't the type to have friends."

I glare. "I helped her outta the Tiger," I says. "I'll take care of it."

I kick Silver into a gallop and ride out to meet the girl. I come up on her fast, but she don't seem startled or concerned. She folds her arms in her lap and just waits for me to pull Silver to a halt.

"Morning," she says simple. I notice her palms are wrapped in cloth, protecting the skin that burned last night.

"Yer following us," I says back.

"I am traveling the same path. It just happens you are before me. I could ride with you instead of behind," she offers.

"With me? We ain't looking for a caboose."

She cocks her head at me, then says, as if it's already decided, "I will ride with you."

"You will not," I snap. "Go back to the Tiger."

"I'm never going back to that saloon. I used to have family and purpose and hope. White Eyes came and took it. They marched my people to camps like a herd, commanded my life like they were my god. You helped me in town, so I figure you might be fair to ride with; that when I turn off the path and head home, you won't shoot me in the back."

"You don't know nothing 'bout me," I says. "I's shot plenty of men."

"And women?"

I frown.

"You head for the mountains," she says, regarding the growing Superstitions. "It is sacred land, not to be tampered with. Angry land. A guide might be useful."

I never even wanted the Coltons round, and yet here I am seriously considering the girl's offer. As though I actually need another flea on my hide. I's got the journal. We know where we're heading. But what if she really do know the area well? What if we run into her kind in the canyons or get lost or can't find water? She'd be good for that, or so it seems. I can't figure why else Fort Whipple keeps scouts hired on otherwise. And I know Prescott's armed division ain't the only one working with 'em. *Use the enemy to fight the enemy,* Pa always said. Makes me wonder who's crazier, the Indians who desert their own kind or the ones fighting an endless supply of uniforms.

I return my attention to the Apache. "You know the mountains well?"

She nods. "My people move when it suits us. When

White Eyes came, the men had gone west to what you call Fort McDowell, along the Verde, to retaliate against a recent raid. Us women and children stayed behind only to be rounded up by the very men ours went to fight. The lucky ones got away, the rest walked to a prison White Eyes called a reserve. I was fortunate to escape the march but was picked up and taken to that saloon to work." Her eyes drift toward the mountains. "I will go back to our stronghold. If what remains of my tribe has not reassembled, I will search for signs of their movement, and I will follow."

"And yer willing to serve as my guide 'long the way?"

She nods again, then asks, "What do you seek in the mountains?"

"Justice."

"The mountains are sacred. If you wish to pray to Ussen, there is no better place."

"Ussen?" I says.

"The creator of life."

"Right." Heaven forbid she just call him God.

"And what do you seek justice for?" she asks.

"You always this nosey?"

"If I'm to help you find what you seek, it is only fair that I know your story."

"A bunch of men hanged my pa," I says, feeling something harden in my gut. I grab my Colt and sight a cactus several paces to my right, then stuff the gun back into my belt. Draw and sight again. Put it back.

"Sounds like revenge. A personal raid in response to theirs."

"Revenge, justice, raid. It don't matter what you call it. I'm only doing what I need to do to set things right."

"How will you find them?" she asks.

"They're after a gold mine mapped out in my father's journal, so that's where I'm headed."

"Gold? The yellow iron?"

"Yeah."

She frowns, looking cross. "It is one thing to pick up gold scattered on the ground and another to dig in Mother Earth's body for it. To do so will bring Ussen's wrath and awaken the Mountain Spirits. They will stomp and stampede, causing the ground to heave and destroying everything near."

"A quake?" I says. "You think all mining'll cause earthquakes?"

"The Mountain Spirits serve Ussen," she says, her voice as serious as ever. "They will bring ruin upon those who dig for gold. I cannot help you. Not if gold is what you seek."

"It ain't," I snap. "Haven't you been listening? I don't care 'bout the gold. I'm just trying to find the mine 'cus I know that's where the Rose Riders'll head. Now, you said it ain't an offense to pick up gold already lying in plain sight, so surely it ain't a crime to visit a mine that already exists. It ain't like I wanna dig round in it."

"And them?" She jerks her head toward Jesse and Will. "What do they seek?"

"They're family friends," I says. "They're helping me track the gang." And it's the truth. I ain't lied. I's just left out the bits she don't want to hear. I feel a twinge of guilt and push it aside. I saved her damn life, and a scout could save us precious time in the mountains. She owes me this. I'll just have to warn the Coltons not to mention their goals or the full nature of our deal round her.

The girl lifts her chin high, like she's trying to gauge the sincerity of my words. I reckon it might be an intimidating gaze if she weren't on that sad pony. It's so small, and I'm sitting far taller on Silver.

Finally, she says, "If you promise you will not dig in Mother Earth, I will help you."

"I promise. I only want justice."

"Revenge," she corrects.

"Yeah, that."

"Then I will help, at least until I locate my people. But if we come to the mine and the men you seek are already violating the earth, I will turn away and not help further." She tips her flat-brimmed hat down to shield her eyes from the sun and says again, "It is sacred land, not to be tampered with."

"Yeah, yeah, let's get to it. We're wasting time."

"I am Liluye," the girl says. "I won't work like a nameless mule."

"Fine," I says.

"Li-luw-yee," she says, emphasizing every last beat when I don't address her proper. "Or Hawk Singing if Liluye is too much on your tongue."

"That's two names," I says. I glance over my shoulder. Jesse and Will are starting to look restless. "Look, I ain't got time for dallying. You coming with me or not?"

She sits a bit taller in her saddle. "What is your name?"

"Kate," I says. "Kate Thompson."

"Thank you, Kate, for what you did for me at the Tiger."

"It were nothing, Lil. Now let's ride." I turn Silver round and trot off toward the Coltons.

"My name is not Lil," I hear her say to her pony, "but it's a start." Hoofbeats follow, staying close.

Guess I got myself a scout.

CHAPTER SIXTEEN

"*She's Apache,*" *Jesse says* when we join back up. He's squinting again, only it ain't his normal squint. Everything 'bout his face has gone narrow. His lips are thin and pinched. Even his brow seems somehow tighter. "She ain't riding with us."

"She's gonna help us out in the mountains," I says.

"She ain't riding with us!" He bats a hand at Lil like she's dust he can banish back the way we came. "Get outta here," he snarls at her. "You ain't welcome."

"Jesse!" His face snaps to mine and his features are caught somewhere between hate and fear. I remember the story Will told me 'bout their mother, and understand. "Look, I'm sorry 'bout what happened to yer ma, Jesse, I am, but it was years ago," I says. "And it weren't Lil who did it."

"It was her people," he barks back.

"But not *her*."

"I don't care. I won't have no blasted Apache riding with us. Not over my dead body!"

"Oh, in tarnation!" I snap. "Will's right. You preach 'bout letting the past be, 'bout moving on and not letting yer demons eat you whole, but yer holding on to the past more than any of us here—harping on things happened well over a decade ago! You spout all this shiny advice and can't even figure how to follow it yerself!"

He bites his bottom lip and glares at Lil. She's just sitting there atop her pony, gazing up at the sky like she ain't got a care in the world.

"You don't gotta be her best friend, you just—"

"We'll *never* be friends," Jesse snarls.

"Ugh, you make me livid!" I snap. "You just gotta *ride* with her, I was trying to say. You and me and Will and her. That's all. Don't talk to her. Don't even look at her if you can't bear it. But she knows the mountains, and I ain't turning my back on that sorta resource 'cus yer too damn proud, or maybe yellow-bellied"—he glares at that —"to set aside yer prejudices a few days."

"Oh, and you like Apache?" he says. "Yer fond of Indians now?"

"I like people who make my life easier."

Jesse folds his arms over his chest. "I thought that's what me and Will were doing. We help you with Rose, you help us get the—"

"I know what the deal is," I says, cutting him off before his words send Lil running.

Jesse gnaws on his bottom lip a moment. "Still don't

see why we gotta make things more complicated by adding a fourth to the group."

"Safety in numbers. Ain't that what you's said before?"

"Well, I'll be," he responds. "Guess you ain't deaf after
all."

"You got a shine for everything, don't you Jesse?"

He eyes me, frowning. "Not everything." Then clicks
his tongue and nudges Rebel east. I sit there on Silver
a moment, watching him ride off 'longside Will as Mutt
streaks ahead like a bullet.

"He likes you," Liluye says.

"What?" I says, turning toward her. "No he don't."

"Tarak used to always speak to me in riddles. It was
only after he died in a raid and his sister confessed that
he wanted to marry me that I understood."

"Yeah, well, Jesse ain't Apache, so that riddle logic
don't apply."

"He listened to you," she insists. "He gave up his fight."

'Cus he wants the gold more than he wants to split
ways. Staying ain't got nothing to do with me or what I
said 'bout his bias 'gainst Apache. I'd bet good money on
it. We're using each other, me and the Coltons. Ain't nothing more to it than that.

I remind myself to tell 'em to stay hushed 'bout the
gold as soon as possible, then flick Silver's reins.

"Come on, Lil. We're falling behind."

"Liluye," she says.

I ride on and she follows.

We make good time 'long the river. The land is mostly flat and we don't got to pause to check our course—the Salt's guiding us just fine. But by late afternoon, all that's changing.

Everything's getting greener, but not in the way Prescott's mountains do. There ain't any pines to be seen here, just ancient saguaro cactuses that tower like they think they're trees, breaking up the horizon. Between 'em, shrubs and brambles crop up in abundance, surrounded by prickly pear and woody cholla. The vegetation slows us plenty, and I know it's only the start of it. Ahead, the terrain's getting angrier. Boulders and rocks lift outta the earth; heaving hills and miniature plateaus stand proud. If this is just the foothills, I ain't sure the horses are gonna be able to take us far. Definitely not into the thickest parts of the mountains. We'll be forced to travel in the shallows of the Salt soon, taking the path it carves through the wilderness.

Beyond Silver's perky ears, I watch Jesse riding. He keeps whistling for Mutt even though the dog ain't wandered outta the river once, and his hips rock side to side with Rebel's movements, a standard horseback sway. My cheeks go hot. Feeling flighty and skittish, I reach for my six-shooter and start practicing draws. I pretend each cactus I sight is Waylan Rose, imagine shooting him over and over again. I won't miss next time. I'm gonna hit his heart, not his damn shoulder. Soon I'm feeling much more like myself—sturdy and tight and focused. I stuff the pistol back in its holster and keep my gaze on the destination 'stead of Jesse's back.

The Salt bows ahead of us, disappearing behind a section of rocky terrain. I picture the maps I examined this morning, calling up the river's course. It will curve round that rough land ahead, then cut east again, driving straight through the Superstitions. Most of the clues leading to the mines gave directions approaching by way of Peralta Trail, as I'd told the Coltons, almost as if the original gold seeker had come from Tucson or farther south. Seeing how many of the pages were written in Spanish, it wouldn't surprise me if the journal once belonged to a Mexican. But with our current course, following the river to Waltz's and then turning into the mountain canyons once we're north of the mine . . . I'll have to reverse all them clues, use other landmarks mentioned among the pages to find our way. Least I got Lil to help.

If the Rose Riders are following the journal's clues sure and precise, it means they'll be coming from the south, riding their steeds north into the canyons, and this'd be ideal. We won't be coming up on their heels; we'll be cutting 'em off, taking 'em by complete surprise. But if they're ahead of us . . . I don't want to think 'bout the sort of race we'll end up in.

We decide to call the day quits when we reach the bow in the river. The day's fading and we're all beat and covered in sweat and dust. The spot'll make a fair camp — water nearby. But there's upheaved rocks at our backs and 'cross the way, making me feel trapped. There's four of us, though, and we'll keep watch like always.

While Jesse sketches in his notebook and Will muses aloud 'bout how much farther it is to Waltz's, I catch Lil wandering from camp. Worried she's 'bout to run off, I chase after her.

"Where you going?"

"To find dinner," she says.

"We got some cured meat already. And biscuits." I don't mention they're hard and stale.

"To find *fresh* meat," she amends. My mouth waters at the thought of it.

"Hang on, I'll come with you."

By the time I's raced back to Silver and grabbed my rifle, Lil's already disappeared among the dense vegetation. "Thanks for waiting," I mutter to myself, and take to tracking her between shrubs and cactuses. When I finally catch up, she's crouched low behind a boulder, some sort of net clenched in her grasp.

She puts a finger to her lips and nudges her head toward the other side of the boulder. It's then I see the quail—maybe a dozen of 'em, pecking at the dry earth for what I reckon must be insects. I creep forward, but gravelly earth crunches beneath my heel. There's a flutter of feathers and a chorus of squawks, and the birds go scampering deeper into the thickets of shrub.

Lil glares. "You walk like your feet are made of stone."

"Oh, is that something else Tarak taught you? Not just riddles but how to float above the ground?"

"You have to look where you put your feet, not just charge forward blind."

"There ain't nothing but dirt and rubble here," I says, pointing to the earth.

"Lead with your toes—stay light. Keep throwing all

your weight into your heels and even the grub will hear you coming."

"Grub don't have ears."

She raises her brows as if to say, *Precisely.*

Frowning, I load my Winchester and crank the action so I'm ready next time. I ain't 'bout to scare them birds away twice.

"We will not need that," Lil says, nodding at the rifle. "They stay in groups, quail. Shoot and you may hit one, but the rest will scatter. But this . . ." She raises the net. "Come."

I follow her round the boulder and past a thicket of prickers, between cactuses and beneath the limbs of a rather large palo verde tree. She points out the quail's tracks as we go. I don't know how she's doing it—tracking 'em, stepping sure and quick, not making a single sound. Every time I look where to put my feet, I feel like I'm 'bout to run headlong into a cactus. And when I stay on my toes, my balance feels shoddy, 'specially with my sore ankle. I like my heels. They're sturdy and firm. I ain't never noticed how much noise my clothing makes as I move, how my trousers scratch when I walk and my flannel brushes beneath my underarms.

But then there's Lil. Silent, like she's made of mist. Like she ain't even really here.

When we finally close in on the quail, I'm sweating something fierce, every muscle in my body tense. I realize I's been holding my breath to try to make less sound, and exhale quiet.

We crouch behind a low and sprawling cholla cactus.

My calves are already tired from all the tiptoeing, and they don't fancy this position at all. Lil quietly unfurls the woven net. It's made like a giant cobweb, with stones secured round the exterior so the edges will be weighted to the ground once thrown. She must've had it packed on her pony all this time.

Lil extends the net toward me, as if I should make the toss.

"I don't wanna scare 'em off again," I says at a whisper.

"Then throw well." She demonstrates. Net held at her side and stretched wide, then to be released like yer tossing a basket over the birds. I still ain't sure why she's trusting the job to me, and decide its 'cus her burned and bandaged hands ain't up to the task. I take the net and give her my rifle.

When I stand, I do it so slow, it seems to take a year. I don't wanna startle the quail, and if I pop up fast, or too loudly, I know they'll bolt. And I gotta be able to clear the cholla cactus with my throw.

The birds don't seem to see me, or if they do, I'm unthreatening enough that they don't care. They go on pecking at the earth, beaks nipping, brown heads bobbing. Slowly—painfully slowly—I unfurl the net, position my arms for the toss.

And then, just like during my shooting lessons with Jesse, I picture it all: the extension of my arms, the point of release, the path the net will take. Before I can lose my nerve or doubt my injured shoulder or think too hard on how soured Lil'll be if I mess this up again, I throw.

A dull pain throbs where that bullet grazed my arm,

but the net flies out and over the cholla cactus, propelled by its weighted edges.

The quail hear it coming, or maybe sense the shadow. They scatter, but not before the net comes thumping to the earth, trapping three of the birds beneath its webbing.

"Ha!" I says, leaping upright. Lil walks calmly to the birds and wrings their necks, then scoops them up in the net and slings it over her shoulder.

"Time to eat." She hands me my Winchester and heads for camp.

She's silent as we walk. She don't congratulate me or smile or say I done good. And I don't care. I'm too busy staring at my rifle, wondering how in my right mind I turned my back on an Apache who was holding a loaded weapon.

We cook the meat over a small fire and dish it out evenly, 'long with a bit of jerky and the stale biscuits.

Jesse makes some comment 'bout the quail being poisoned and I answer him by taking a huge bite and chewing while looking at him.

He mumbles something I can't make out—unkind, I'm sure—but after I swallow and don't drop dead, he tears in. Even Jesse ain't so proud he'd pass up this meal. We ain't had variety since leaving Wickenburg, and the quail tastes like heaven.

We got another day's worth of travel to Waltz's, according to Will. He goes on talking 'bout a temporary home built into the nook of a hillside, right 'long a deep, flowing section of river. It sounds like a fool's wish. The Salt ain't running very wide here, and when I look at the parched and rugged land surrounding us, it's hard to imagine her opening into anything substantial. But he swears it's true, and Jesse nods in agreement, though he don't take his eyes off Lil. He's been scowling at her all night, but she don't seem to mind. She licks her fingers clean, hums a tune, pretends like he ain't even there.

I finish off my last few bites of quail and set my mess plate down. "God bless you, Lil. That's the best meal I had all week." But she's drifted off again. I spot her down by the water, washing her hands. "Girl's quieter than snowfall," I says.

"Apache are good at sneaking," Jesse says.

I shoot him a look.

"It's true. They're murderous and bloodthirsty and sneaky."

"Maybe we're just noisy and clumsy. Besides, both kinds've been attacking each other long as I can remember, so it ain't like we're the more virtuous people." I don't know why I'm sticking up for Lil so fiercely. She ain't a friend. Hell, she ain't much but a stranger. I reckon I just ain't fond of this side of Jesse—the hate and the grudge and the anger. I liked him better when he were nagging me at White Tank, when he thought he knew everything but there was still a bit of laughter in his squinty eyes.

"We should let the fire die out," Jesse says, standing.

"Who knows where them Riders are at, and we don't need to be announcing our location come dusk. Help me with the horses, won't you, Will?" He stalks away from camp and don't look back.

CHAPTER SEVENTEEN

After I's cleared my plate and skillet and cleaned my weapons of dust, I roll out my bedroll. Then, propped up 'gainst my saddle and using it like a backrest, I pull out Pa's journal.

Getting to the mine sounds so easy on paper: Head south into Boulder Canyon and pass the three pines. Find the rock form shaped like a horse's head and wait for the sunrise from a specified bluff. When the light shines over the horse's neck in late summer, it will fall on the location of the mine. On one of the maps, the location is also marked by a small *x,* supposedly within the shadow of Weavers Needle. But this is where things no longer sound so simple.

Pa made a whole page of notes on Weavers Needle, the massive column of rock that rises outta the mountains like a spire. He reckons the summit is a couple thousand feet high. I gaze beyond the foothills to the dark shadows of the Superstitions. I can't see the Needle from camp, but the journal claims it's visible from many vantage points within the mountains, and if it's as massive as Pa says, knowing the mine lies in its shadow don't help much. Early or late in the day, that shadow could stretch forever. I reckon it's good there's the horse-head clue, then. That is, assuming I can find the rock form. The boulders 'long this bow in the Salt are so mangled, I bet I could see any number of creatures in 'em if'n I stared hard enough.

Supposing the whole light-over-a-rock-form method fails, there's still a few other clues. One haphazard map drawing shows a large palo verde tree noted to be a few hundred paces from the mine. Scrawled at the bottom of the page is a note claiming that a few saguaro cactuses west of the mine shaft have been altered by knife so the limbs point the way toward the gold.

I keep reading after the fire dies, till the sky's lost most of its light and my eyes are starting to smart. Snapping the journal shut, I tuck it into the back of my pants. Ain't no use obsessing over details and landmarks now. I reckon they'll all make more sense when I can see 'em. And besides, I got something Rose don't: a scout.

Lil's down at the Salt now, enjoying a bath. 'Cus she ordered the Coltons far outta peeping view, and 'cus Jesse decided to be agreeable for once, the boys're on the other end of camp, observing the mountains and having a smoke. I figure now's as good a time as any to tell 'em 'bout Lil's issue with gold. I push to my feet and make my way over. They don't say nothing when I tell 'em not to mention their side of our deal round Lil, which is a relief. I half expected Jesse to shout it to the heavens in hopes that she'd leave. Maybe he thinks she'll slit their throats while they sleep if she knew the truth. Either way, the boys both agree to keep quiet.

When I head back to my bedroll, they follow, only Jesse don't stop at his. He trails me clear 'cross camp and plops down at my side.

"I's been wondering," he says, a rolled cigarette still stuck between his lips, "how a deaf gal like you coulda heard something I ain't said."

"Huh?"

"'Bout my ma," he clarifies. "That raid in Wickenburg and how she died."

"Will told me back at White Tank, while you were sleeping."

He exhales and nods, not looking at me.

"I'm sorry. It ain't right when we lose folks before we're ready."

"That ain't what's bothering me," he says. "It's just . . . maybe I ain't the best at letting the past be. Maybe I *don't* heed my own advice. But either way, I don't like digging up what's already done—speaking on it, reliving it. And I certainly don't like my brother doing it for me. 'Specially with someone we barely know."

I frown at that. Uncertain what to say, I look 'cross camp to where Will's playing with Mutt. The hair on my neck goes all prickly, and when I glance back to Jesse he's looking dead at me, features serious.

"You were right earlier, 'bout how I was blaming yer scout for crimes that ain't her doing," he says.

"It ain't me you gotta apologize to, Jesse."

Lil's back from her wash now and rolling out her bedroll, but Jesse don't make an effort to go talk to her.

"You can tell me you were wrong, but not her?" I says.

He shrugs and plucks the smoke from his mouth, rolling it between his thumb and forefinger. "Guess I'd rather've told you 'bout my ma and my prejudices myself. When I were ready to share it."

"So tell me something else," I says, knowing I ain't gonna win this battle and get him to apologize to Lil tonight. "Something true, like I did back in that shanty."

Jesse raises an eyebrow. "I ain't never told you a lie."

"You ain't shared much neither. Yer awful good at judging everyone, Jesse, and dishing out advice, but you don't say heaps 'bout yerself. Hell, the only things I know I heard from Will, or picked up while at yer ranch. So tell me something. Tell me something you ain't told no one else."

In the growing darkness, his squinty eyes are gleaming like a coyote's. They flick over my features—nose, lips, neck, back up to meet my eyes.

"I think yer something," he says.

I'm hot again, skittish. "What's that mean?"

"Ain't sure. Still trying to figure it out myself."

"Then it don't count. Tell me something you got an understanding of."

He looks to the dying embers of our fire. Opens his mouth, closes it, takes a long drag on the smoke.

"I ain't the best reader," he says finally. "I know how just fine—I's written correspondences, can read the letters Clara sends to Wickenburg or the notices posted outside the sheriff's—but I ain't never gotten through a whole book. Hell, I don't think I's ever read more than a couple pages."

"That ain't nothing to be ashamed 'bout," I says. "Who's got time for reading when there's crops to tend and herds to drive? It's a luxury, Jesse. It ain't nothing worthwhile."

"Yeah, but you went on and on the other night 'bout that novel . . ."

"*Little Women*?"

"Yeah. It were so obvious those words got inside you, and I thought, *By God, there's a girl with more determination than I'll ever have.* 'Cus I don't think I could do it, Kate. I don't think I could finish something that thick without dying of boredom."

"Then you ain't found the right book yet," I says. "There's something for everyone. My pa had this thing for poetry—most flowery, ridiculous nonsense I's ever heard in my life, but he loved it. If novels are a luxury, poetry's another thing entirely. Folks who got the time for it have something wrong upstairs if you ask me."

Jesse takes one last drag on his cigarette and puts it out in the dust between us. "Figures you'd think that."

"Why?"

"I's gonna say that's the only type of reading I ever had any patience for. Sarah has a book of poems she reads to Jake sometimes. It's like a song, that stuff. Like an escape."

"Oh, I'm sorry. I didn't mean it."

"You did, but that's fine. People don't gotta like the same stuff. If they did, life would be pretty boring."

His gaze drifts over toward Lil, and I wonder if this is his way of telling me he won't ever approve of her or apologize to her face. That we're just not going to agree on this point.

"I don't think you got something off upstairs," I says. "That were an exaggeration. I mean, my pa were one of the smartest men I know."

Jesse just smiles and shoves to his feet. He takes a step toward his bedroll, then pauses and turns back to me. "Kate," he says. "That short for Katherine?"

I nod. "I don't go by nothing but Kate, though."

"It suits you. See you in the morning, Kate." He winks, and something flutters in my gut. Then, without another word, Jesse walks 'cross camp to where his bedroll's laid out near Will's. I lean back and turn onto my side like I gotta hide my smile from the sky. I catch Lil grinning knowingly from where she's settled in for the night.

He likes you.

I flop in the other direction and tug my blanket tighter beneath my chin. One blasted wink and I got knots in my stomach? A wink from eyes that ain't never open properly to begin with! Maybe it were a twitch, a squinty flinch or something. Maybe a bug flew in his eye.

I think up more theories as I try to find sleep, 'cus I ain't fond of it. I talked with Morris plenty in Prescott and never felt like my stomach were in my boots. Something's wrong with me. I gotta drink more water tomorrow, watch how much sun I get. This rough land's doing something to my head.

For once, Silver ain't fixing to move come dawn. I think she fancied this camp, what with its plentiful water and vegetation. When she were grazing last night, I swear I heard her whinnying all playful with the Coltons' horses. Or maybe she's getting on well with Lil's pony. Something 'bout the creature's stooped form and worn coat reminds me of Libby. Poor horse.

Silver nickers at me when I cinch her saddle in place, then nips in my general direction as I secure my bedroll and gear to her back.

"If'n yer grumpy already, it's gonna be a long day," I says to her.

She *hmphs* like she understands my words, but quits being a pest. Sometimes I wonder how keen her ears are when it comes to picking up my tone.

Once we get camp broke down and fill our canteens, we're back to riding. The brothers lead—or rather, Mutt does—while I bring up the rear with Lil. As the land gets rougher we're forced to slow our pace and take to guiding our horses into the Salt, where she's already done the work cutting a path through the heaving land.

Early in the morning, the Salt begins to widen a little. It's a beauty of a sight, vibrant blue 'gainst the dust and rock shades we been used to. Mutt charges into the water, jumping in all limb-spread like he thinks he can fly. We pause to refill our canteens and splash our faces clean of sweat, but then we're moving again. There's several miles to cover before we reach Waltz's, and I'm anxious to get there. It sounds like he's settled near Boulder Canyon, the route I reckon we should take as we head for the mine. Least that's what the maps suggest.

The Salt's getting all sorts of crooked as the day wears on, weaving and turning nonstop. I find myself wishing for dry plains again, just so I can cut a straight line to my destination. But we got rugged mountains cropping up every which way now, and where there ain't mountains there's hills large enough to be a nuisance. I can't see over 'em, and I don't want to have Silver climb 'em only to realize the land on the other side ain't the way we need to trek. So we stick to the river, guiding the horses through the shallows when the land gives us nowhere else to walk.

We don't see no one. No sign of life beyond the hawks soaring and the lizards sunbathing on rocks 'long the shore. It's eerily empty, this land. My mind starts drifting to Lil's tales, 'bout mountain spirits and angry gods; to the ghost shooter Will mentioned, preying on folks from his perch in the ridges.

As we guide the horses through a narrow pass where rust-red rock climbs high to either side of the Salt, goose flesh dances up my arms despite the heat. These rocks do look angry—like tombstones and corpses and giant, blood-drenched blades. Like men frozen by vengeful spirits, cursed for all eternity. Darn Apache folklore and tales 'bout ghosts. Like I don't got enough to worry 'bout already.

A few hours before sunset, we happen upon a sight: burnt-red rocks and buttes that tower tall, the river cutting a deep blue slash between 'em. It's running fairly wide here, just like Will promised. Even looks deep enough to swim in. Short trees and brambly shrubs and tall, wild grass sprouts up 'long the shore.

We carry on with the river, riding 'gainst the mild current.

"Not much farther and we should find Waltz," Will says.

"Should?" I echo.

"We never actually been to the place ourselves. We's only visited him at his home in Phoenix. Once."

"So how in the hell we gonna find him here?" I says, batting a hand at the rugged land.

"No faith," Will says, shaking his head.

"Shut it, Will." Jesse angles toward me in his saddle. "Waltz said so long as you follow the river and keep looking to the south, you couldn't miss him. It ain't like this is well-traveled land and he needs to hide from strangers."

"Someone lives beyond that rise," Lil says, pointing to a small butte ahead that borders the Salt.

"How do you figure?" Jesse says, squinting.

"The dirt path curving round the rock is worn, but not

from the water. It is from travel there. Feet and hooves. See how the grass and shrubs are beaten back?"

Now that she's pointed it out, it do look like an obvious man-made path.

"Huh," Jesse says.

"Well in that case, I'm washing before we call the day quits," Will says, dismounting Rio.

A devilish smile breaks over Jesse's face, and he swings offa Rebel to join. "We'll keep our drawers on this time," he adds, smirking at me over his shoulder as he unbuttons his shirt.

"Darn right, you will," I says.

A moment later and he's nearly all pale skin, charging into the shallows and diving under. My stomach does a thing that feels like hunger when I know it ain't. Will and Mutt join Jesse in the river, rowdy and playful, and suddenly the water looks divine.

I toss my Stetson down with my gear.

"You like him too," Lil says.

"What?"

"The older one. You like him."

"Christ, Lil, do you ever mind yer own business?"

"Liluye," she says.

"I ain't . . . I don't . . ." I exhale hard. "I'm going in, that's all. I ain't had a proper wash in days, and I want one before we head into the canyons."

I pull off my boots. Lil just shrugs and pats her pony on the rump. I don't gotta defend myself to her. I want a wash, and gosh darn it I'll have one. I start undoing my pants and realize I'll have to swim in my underwear and the undershirt I swiped from Evelyn back in Phoenix. It's completely indecent, and I can't believe I'm doing it, but it's hot and I stink and Lord knows when I'll get another chance to bathe. Plus, I got a shoulder wound needing cleaning.

I strip off my flannel and drop it with the rest of my gear. "You coming?" I ask Lil.

"I washed last night. I will walk."

"Walk where?"

"White Eyes always need a destination," she mutters. "They do not know how to simply be."

I watch her go, then wade into the water. It ain't cold, but it's still a brutal shock after a full day riding beneath the blistering sun.

"By God do I know why you didn't clean with us at White Tank," Jesse says. His eyes linger somewhere 'long my middle, and I fold my hands over my chest, thinking the undershirt mighty thin all of a sudden.

"Now that you know she's a girl, you'd think you'd have manners round her," Will says. It's an expected jab, but there's something awful sharp in the tone of Will's voice. If I didn't know better, I'd think he were fussed 'bout something.

As Jesse lunges for his brother, shouting playful curses, I run forward and dive in. It ain't terribly deep, maybe to my hips, but plenty easy enough to get a good clean. The boys go on wrestling and I take a moment to scrub my scalp and limbs and see to my shoulder, then float on my back and admire the endless blue sky. It's so big and calm, it almost looks like a lake hovering overhead. I breathe easy, and right as I'm about to fold outta my float, something grabs hold of my ankle, yanking down. I barely get in a gasp before going full under. For a moment, I think a water snake's got me, but this is too strong. Before I get a chance to kick or lash out, it releases me, and I resurface in a coughing fit.

Jesse's paddling an arm's length from me, grinning. "Sorry, couldn't help it."

"You damn rascal!" I shove water his way. "Yer lucky that weren't my sore ankle. What happened to having manners?"

Will rolls his eyes. "He don't got none. He just pretends otherwise."

"Shut it, Will."

"You shut it, Jess."

"Shut it all, y'all!" a voice barks from the shore. It's followed by the unmistakable clank of a shotgun being pumped.

CHAPTER EIGHTEEN

I turn slowly.

Standing on the riverbank is a haggard-looking man wearing a mean snarl.

"Out," he orders, emphasizing with the shotgun. "Outta the water right now." He's got a slight accent, only I can't place from where.

"Waltz, put that blasted thing away," Jesse says. "It's me, Jesse Colton. From Wickenburg."

"Jesse?" Waltz echoes. "Abe's boy? Gosh, you's grown. Last I saw you, you didn't have so much muscle. And Will were still a scrawny thing."

"That were over three years back."

"Was it really? Time's gone a-flying, I guess."

Waltz lowers the shotgun. He's older than I expected. Gray sideburns and faded beard and wrinkles stretching over his skin like cracks in parched desert earth. When

Jesse said Waltz and Abe were mining buddies, I pictured someone closer to my pa's age, somewhere round forty. But Waltz looks easily twenty years past that.

"How *is* old Abe?" the man asks.

"Dead," Jesse says.

"I'm sorry to hear that. Abe were a good man."

Jesse grunts. "So why the firearm and threats, Waltz?"

"Heard shouting from the house and thought you might be looking to cause mischief. Can't be too careful, you know. These mountains ain't been nothing but trouble lately—endless gunshots from the range, vultures flying in circles. I keep hearing hoofbeats in the night too, like an outfit of ghost riders passing through, but every time I crawl outta bed and light the lantern for a look, there ain't a sign of nothing."

"Well, apologies for startling you," Jesse says as we climb outta the river, wring our undergarments, and start pulling on dry layers. "We had a notion you'd be back in Phoenix this time of year."

"Usually am, but I's feeling lucky. Decided to stay longer this season." Waltz pauses and squints at the boys. "Which means you didn't come all this way just for a visit."

"We're passing through," I says. "I'm Kate Thompson. My pa were friends with Abe too."

Waltz gives me a little hat tip. "*Passing through* just means *planning to squat in my house,* don't it?"

Jesse smiles. "Guilty."

"Well, yer lucky you caught me. I'm heading back to Phoenix in a few days. I ain't got a roof big enough for the lot of you, but yer welcome to stay the night outside. Rest and have a bite to eat. Just trapped a beaver this morning." His gaze trails to our mounts. "Say, where's yer fourth?"

"Behind you," Lil says, stepping silent as a deer through the tall grass.

Waltz yelps, jumping damn near outta his skin. "You don't go sneaking up on a man like that!" he snaps. "'Specially one with a loaded gun."

"Apache are good at sneaking," she says. There's a hint of a smile on her lips, and I catch her eyes darting to Jesse. There and back. So fast, it's like it barely happened. She heard him last night, what he said to me as she cleaned in the Salt. It's like she's everywhere, that girl. In the earth and the sky and the dry Arizona air.

I remind myself to never cross her.

Waltz don't seem too pleased 'bout the fact that an Indian's part of our group, but he shows us to his place after a bit of grumbling. His house, if it can be called that, sits beyond the small butte, just as Lil suspected. The whole thing don't look much larger than Silver's stall; a one-room home for sure, made of rock and packed mud, with a shoddy roof that tilts uneven, almost like it wants to rest 'gainst the rocky alcove the house is set into.

Inside, things look just as weary. A grass-stuffed

mattress 'gainst the far wall. One window and a lone table and chair. Prospecting gear seems to fill every last inch of the place.

"You ever find anything in these mountains?" I ask him.

"Nah, but I's heard talk these parts are rich with gold. Can't help coming back every season."

I look at his leathered skin and stern features, the stubborn light in his pale eyes. "Ain't you a little old to be prospecting?"

"Age is just a number, and old's in yer head. I's mined all over this damn Territory. California, too. The work ain't killed me yet, nor the Indians, so I figure that means I ain't supposed to quit."

There's that odd lilt to his voice again—certain words pronounced different than how I'd say 'em.

"Say, Waltz?"

"Jacob," he corrects. "Jacob Waltz."

"You ain't from round here, are you?"

"Germany," he answers. "I been on American soil thirty-eight years now, and been a citizen for sixteen. But don't let my youthful looks fool you. I'm as old as yer guessing."

He gets a smile outta me with that.

As Lil starts a fire and the men prep the meat for dinner, I step away to tend to the horses. They're down near the water, grazing where Waltz's mare is kept company by a stout gray burro. Mutt's there too, lounging round like the lazy oaf he is. At this hour, Waltz's temporary homestead is draped in shadow, the sun having dipped behind the butte, and there's something peaceful 'bout the place.

I gather up Silver's reins and lead her over to a short tree. I secure her for the night and pull off her saddle, then repeat the process with the others. I reckon we'll be sleeping where Lil's making the fire, and the thought of lugging the saddles there—even though it ain't terribly far—smarts. I'm starting to feel all this travel in my lower back and rump. My hips are achy too, my thighs weary from sitting in a saddle day after day. And even though the wound on my shoulder's nearly healed, I feel the weight of the gear there more than in my ankle.

Grumbling to myself, I turn for the house and find Will blocking my way. I'm so startled, I nearly drop the saddle.

"Damn, you scared me," I says, bracing it 'gainst my thigh. "You practicing sneaking like Lil?"

His mouth don't even twitch outta its current scowl. "Whatever's going on with you and Jesse's gotta stop," he says.

"There ain't nothing going on."

"Don't play with me, Kate. I ain't in the mood."

"And neither am I. This saddle ain't made of feathers." I try to walk past him and he sidesteps, blocking my way again. "Will, I ain't got time for this."

"Don't act like you don't know what I'm talking 'bout," he growls.

"Well, I *don't!*"

"He ain't thinking straight," Will says, waving an arm toward the house. "It's bad enough he's set on going after the same gold a gang of outlaws wants, that we struck this deal with you, but now—"

"Oh, in tarnation, you two are both adults. You wanna walk, convince yer brother you both should walk. We can break the deal. I got Lil to help me now. I'll find Rose with or without yous. But you ain't getting those maps from me if you back out."

"We ain't gonna back out. I hate it, but Jesse's right. We need the money, even if half his reason for going after it is tied up in the past. But now *this*." He jerks his chin at me. "You getting in his head . . . It's too much. It's complicating things and it ain't gonna go smooth."

"I ain't done nothing, Will."

"See, but you did. Jesse's focused. He's smart. He don't spend time on things that are distractions. He ain't like me in that regard. But once Jesse's heart starts drifting —even the tiniest bit—he goes and gets himself blessedly in over his head, cobweb tangled, lost without a compass. I seen it before with Maggie, and I sure as hell can recognize it when it starts up again."

The saddle's beginning to feel like it's bearing a rider in my hands. I can't hold it no more. Not with what Will's implying.

His glare at Jesse while swimming makes sense now. Will's picked up on a change in Jesse. He's seeing exactly what Lil's already told me, only Will don't seem to find it amusing.

"I ain't got no control over what Jesse thinks," I says as evenly as possible. "If'n you got issues with where his head's at, maybe you should talk to him 'stead of jawing to me."

I try to shove by Will again, and he grabs the meaty part of my arm, stopping me cold. "Don't encourage it, Kate. Don't smile or joke or ask him for another shooting lesson. I can see you ain't interested—you been on a mission that ain't had nothing to do with us since day one—so how's 'bout you make that clear to Jesse before he goes sinking any deeper."

He drops my arm and walks off toward the others, whistling, like our exchange were over the weather.

By the time we's finished dinner, I'm in a foul mood. I's found a mostly level pitch of ground and rolled out my bed. I's cleaned my Colt and buffed my boots and smacked all the dust possible from my hat. It don't matter how much I keep my hands busy; Will's words are ringing strong in my ears.

He's sitting on the other side of the dying fire, chipper as all can be, spitting dip and acting like he didn't just accuse me of things I ain't got no control over to begin with. It ain't my fault if Jesse's head's in the wrong place, if he's seeing Maggie in me somehow. Hell, I got the notion Jesse didn't even like me much. He were furious after the ordeal 'long the Agua Fria and could barely look at me in Phoenix. Guess I did lie 'bout everything, and that mighta sat poorly with him, but still.

Jesse sits with his notebook propped 'gainst his knee again, blissfully unaware of my argument with Will. I follow his gaze and reckon he's sketching Mutt, who's sprawled out by the warmth of the fire.

As Jesse's pencil scratches over paper, Waltz tries to convince us not to enter the mountains. He won't let up. It dawns on me that he might think we're after his beloved gold, so I tell him 'bout Pa and the Rose Riders.

"Even more reason to not go in there," he says. "Those mountains are dangerous enough as it is. Last thing you need is a gang of outlaws complicating yer trip."

"My mind's made up and ain't changing," I says firm.

He sighs and shakes his head. "Then you lot should at least take my donkey. Leave yer horses with me a few days. It ain't like they'd make it far in them canyons anyway, and my mare could use a little company. And take some of my prospecting equipment too. I noticed you ain't got much by way of mining gear."

"I told you, Waltz," I says. "We ain't after any gold. I'm just searching out a mine 'cus I know it's where them Riders will go."

"Still, you can't be too prepared. Never know when you'll need a pickaxe or shovel or a length of rope."

Jesse closes his notebook, smiling through the smoke pinched between his teeth. "First you nearly shoot us in the river. Now yer fixing to send us off right."

"You think I'm joking," Waltz says. "It ain't safe in them canyons."

"Perhaps you angered the Mountain Spirits," Lil offers.

She's sitting cross-legged on her bedroll, stitching a tear in the hem of her smock dress. "It is wrong to dig for the yellow iron and destroy Mother Earth's body."

"Indian lore ain't the problem," Waltz says. "Last time I were in Boulder Canyon, bullets chased me out. I weren't even doing nothing offensive, just gathering some water. And the shooter coulda got me if he wanted. Blew my wooden bucket to splinters. I scanned the ranges and saw nothing, but when I reached for my shotgun another blast went off and dirt exploded right near my feet. I got the heck outta there after that. If'n that gun could get my bucket and nearly my feet from that distance, I was damn sure he could get my heart."

"The ghost shooter," Will says.

"That's a laughable legend," Jesse says. "How many times I gotta say it? Spirits can't pull triggers."

"Then who was shooting?" Will argues.

Waltz rubs at his gray beard. "Apache, maybe."

"White Eyes are always blaming us for their troubles," Lil says. "You were not pulling gold from the earth, and so my people would not have bothered you. One lone man? He is no threat. Sounds like you faced your own kind."

"Don't matter who it were," Waltz counters. "All I'm saying is, it ain't safe and you gotta be ready for anything. Those shots have been ringing for as long as I's been coming here—years now—and no one stays in them canyons that long. It ain't prosperous land—little water, jagged earth. Might not even be human, that shooter. I'm certain these parts are haunted. Ghosts and demons. Spirits unable to rest 'cus of their lust for blood and gold."

"Superstitious tales," Jesse says with a shrug.

A gunshot cracks somewhere deep in the mountains, and the skin on my arms goes prickly. As the blast echoes beneath the purple-bruised sky, I start wondering if all them tales 'bout the ghost shooter might hold water. That, or it's just Waylan Rose, slowly killing off his own crew so there'll be more riches for him when he gets to the mine.

"Superstitious tales in the Superstition Mountains," Waltz repeats, nodding. "Sounds fitting to me."

He retires to bed soon after, leaving us uneasy and anxious. Me, Jesse, and Will, at least. Lil don't seem fazed one bit. Heck, she's already dozing with her nose pointed at the stars.

"You mind company?"

I jerk toward Jesse's voice and find him holding his saddle and bedroll. He nods at the level patch of sandy dirt beside me. I glance through the flames to where he'd been set up originally. Will's cleaning his pistols and glaring back something fierce.

"What's wrong with yer side of the fire?" I ask.

"Uneven and rocky," Jesse says. "Plus, Will's being a grumpy pest."

"And here I thought I were the grumpy one. Least that's what you lot said back at White Tank."

"Yeah, well, when Will's mood turns, it goes 'bout as sour as yers." He drops the saddle and starts rolling out his bed.

I can feel Will's eyes on us, sense his scowl.

"I didn't say I wanted company," I says to Jesse.

But he's already flopping down and stretching out. "Neither does Will. He insulted me enough times in the last ten minutes to last a month."

"Jesse, I ain't sure what yer looking for, but I don't think I got whatever it is."

He glances my way so I can see those squinty eyes. "I want a peaceful night's sleep. Why? What do you want?"

Something goes tight between my ribs.

Just tell him to leave. Tell him he can't sleep here.

But my mouth's dry and my tongue feels swollen.

Jesse shrugs and looks back to the sky. "Sleep well, Kate," he says, then tips his hat down to shield his face.

He don't see my eyes well up or my lip start to tremble. I ain't heard those words since Pa died. I were certain I'd never hear 'em again, and now here I am in the middle of Arizona wilderness, an orphan and a loner, feeling not so alone after all. I don't know what to make of it. Or of the tear that trails down my cheek and settles into the corner of my smile.

CHAPTER NINETEEN

Jacob Waltz sees us off come dawn. We's got the bulk of our gear loaded up on the burro he's loaning us, and he promises to take good care of our horses till we return.

"Still think yer crazy," he says.

"I don't got much of a choice," I says. I'm starting to wonder if that's a guarantee with revenge: yer brain ignores all sorts of logic till you see justice achieved with yer own two eyes.

"Yeah, but these lot do." Waltz points at the boys. "They don't got no need to follow you into those cursed canyons."

"We got an arrangement," Will says, "but I still think the whole thing's reckless."

"More like a deal," Jesse explains. "Family friends helping each other out."

"Fine, I won't pry," Waltz says. "I can tell when the details ain't meant for my ears. And what 'bout you, girl?"

"Liluye," she says.

"Huh?"

"My name is not *girl*."

"She's going home," I answer for her.

Waltz frowns. I get the feeling he ain't too fond of Apache. Last night, he mentioned a few run-ins with Lil's lot, instances where he barely escaped with his life. The stories seemed too dramatic to be completely honest, like he enjoyed building 'em up for a fresh audience.

"If you or the boys ain't back within a week, I'm selling yer horses and heading home for Phoenix," Waltz says. "Ain't no reason to stay out here half starving and poor when gold don't want to be found, and gunshots and gangs terrorize the landscape."

"Sounds fair," I says. "Say, you wouldn't be able to point us to Boulder Canyon, would you?"

He motions east, toward land obscured by the rock buttes surrounding his house. "Follow the river till she comes to a sharp bow and you'll see the canyon to the south. Some of the Salt drains right into Boulder Canyon, but fill up yer canteens before heading far on foot. Water ain't easy to come by once yer in those mountains."

"Thanks, Waltz," I says. We shake and the boys tip their hats and Lil gives the old man a curt nod. He watches us go, but soon we're skirting round rocks and outta view.

We find the start of the canyon easy enough—prolly woulda been damn near impossible to miss. The Salt comes to a sharp bend before continuing northeast, but some of it do indeed leave course here, drilling into the mountains and carving out Boulder Canyon. It were definitely smart to leave the horses. Silver had nickered something sorrowful this morning when I patted her farewell, but the land before me ain't made for a mare. The canyon walls are ragged and heaving, the ground pocked with holes and craters. Besides the burro Waltz lent us, only the pony's making the trip, and that's 'cus Lil ain't coming back out.

We fill up on water as suggested and then head into the canyon. Soon as we're in its belly I feel trapped — prey in a corner, fowl already snared. Rust- and dirt-colored rock rise up round us. I ain't never had such little sky overhead. After days on the plains, the thin strip of blue above feels like a knife, a reckoning 'bout to come crashing down on my back. I try to keep calm, but I ain't fond of this path — narrow and getting skinnier still, with nowhere to run. Prime land for an ambush. How Apache feel at home in this sorta world is a mystery.

It don't take long before the runoff from the Salt's dried up and swallowed by the canyon floor. Cactuses and shrubs grow where they can find purchase, but the earth looks brittle and bare and parched. Lil leads on her pony and I stay on her heels with the burro. Will's arguing with Jesse behind us, but I don't bother trying to eavesdrop. It'll be over things I don't wanna hear anyway. Something 'bout me or this trek or where Jesse's head's at.

We hike all day, but I don't think we get more than three miles. Too often we gotta slow to pick our way through a cactus-strewn gully or round a particularly vicious section of uneven rock. Long before sunset, the canyon starts slipping into shadow. Count that as another thing I ain't fond of—losing light to a ridge 'stead of the horizon like's natural.

Relatively speaking, it ain't awful, though. Boulder Canyon's forking ahead, and according to the journal, we gotta stay to the left for Needle Canyon. There'll be a good place to camp for the night up ahead if Pa's notes are accurate.

"This way," I says, pointing the group in the right direction. "We're looking for a marker: three pines."

"Pines?" Lil echoes.

"Yeah, pine trees. Tall and straight with needles green all year."

"I know what they are," she says. "But they do not grow in these mountains."

"They grow in the Bradshaws."

"Well, we ain't in the Bradshaws now, are we?" Will says.

I pull Pa's journal from the back of my trousers and flip to the map. "It says three pines. They're drawn here and everything."

"Swell. One landmark in, and the course's already shot. Why are we trusting this map again?"

"The Rose Riders killed my pa for it, Will. They murdered him!"

"And maybe they're as dense as him for believing it held any water."

"You no-good son of a bitch, you take that back!" I

shove him in the chest, and he's so startled, he nearly topples over. When he catches his footing, he straightens, glaring as he adjusts the pale, paisley-print kerchief at his neck.

"I ain't saying nothing other than what the rest of the group's thinking," he says slow.

"My pa weren't crazy," I snarl.

"Yeah," Will says, "maybe that's just *you.*"

I lunge at him again, only this time I ain't aiming to shove. If it weren't for Jesse launching himself between us and pulling me back, I'd've clocked Will square 'cross the jaw.

"Jesus, Kate," Jesse says, struggling to keep me still. "Stop it. Cool down."

"Just like I'm sure you'd keep cool if'n someone went insulting yer deceased."

Jesse frowns but knows I got a point. He turns toward his brother. "Why you trying to cause trouble?"

Will spits dip at a sickly looking cactus. "You know damn well why."

"Aw, Christ," Jesse growls. "That's enough. From the both of yous. I reckon noise carries in this canyon, and I ain't fond of our voices reaching any Rose Riders. So shut pan and get along. I don't care what you gotta do to make it so, just quit the bickering." He stoops and picks up his hat, which got knocked off in the tussle. After smacking dust from the brim, Jesse sets it back on his head. "Now, maybe the maps've got a few flaws. But this is just one landmark outta many, right, Kate?"

I nod.

"So we stay left like you said and hope the next one shows true. It ain't like the pines marked nothing we didn't already know."

"'Cept water," I says.

"Huh?"

"Water. Only bit for the next few miles."

"Aw, hell." Jesse exhales heavy. Suddenly, I got a fearsome thirst and scratchy throat. The canteen slung over my shoulder feels mighty light.

"White Eyes are hopeless," Lil says. "There is always water if you know where to look."

"Sass," Jesse mutters. "How helpful."

Lil inclines her chin and points up Needle Canyon. "I see a cottonwood." She walks ahead a ways and then calls over her shoulder, "I see three."

"So?" Jesse says.

"Three pines, three cottonwoods. Could be the same marker, only the mapmaker did not know his trees." When no one reacts, she sighs. "The cottonwood drinks much from the earth. Where their roots dive, water can be found."

I perk up. "See that, boys? Precisely why I got myself a scout." I head after Lil, smiling, not caring that Will mutters something rude at my back, or that Jesse's complaining 'bout all-knowing, overbearing Apache.

The cottonwoods ain't much to look at. Struggling to grow in a well-shaded area of Needle Canyon, the poor things ain't much taller than me. Their trunks are wide enough to suggest they ain't young, but they look days away from dying. Mangled, cracking bark. Limbs that grow like broken arms.

As me and the boys pick a spot to make camp for the night, Lil takes to digging round the cottonwood trunks with a sharp rock. Once she gets past the hard surface dirt, the earth goes darker and wetter, till suddenly water's pooling in the shallow hole she's carved.

"They drink plenty, cottonwoods," she says, smacking her hands clean on her smock dress. "During the rainy season, water trickles through these canyons. When the sun dries the creek, the trees still drink from below."

I dip my cupped hands into the small pool and splash some water on my face. It's warm and slightly clouded. We'll have to run it through a makeshift sieve of some sort—a shirt, maybe—and boil it. But we's got ourselves drinking water. I'm so darn pleased, I don't bother pointing out the hypocrisy of it all: Lil can dig round in Mother Earth for water, but not gold? Prolly 'cus this is the ground and not the mountains, so the spirits don't care. Or maybe 'cus if the tree roots dig for it, human hands can too. I ain't interested enough to ask.

We're back to our typical meal of cured meat and stale biscuits. The meat ain't awful after having variety the past two nights, but the biscuits taste like ash. We finish off our water, washing down the meal and knowing we'll be able to refill our canteens come morning.

The sky ain't fully dark after dinner, but our little camp is already overrun with shadow. I still feel trapped, and the way the firelight dances over the canyon walls ain't comforting in the same way it flickers over flat plains. I keep seeing shadowy figures in the folds of the rock —monsters and murderers. No wonder legends like the ghost shooter exist.

"Tell us a story, Lil," I says.

"Why? 'Cus I'm Apache and in this moment our folklore might appease you rather than annoy?"

"'Cus I don't know any good stories—how 'bout that?" I says with a glare.

She pulls her knees to her chest and considers this a moment. Jesse quits sketching in his notebook to stoke the fire, which is lit more to keep away any hungry coyotes than it is to provide warmth. Sparks go dancing.

"I think I know of the mine you seek," Lil says finally.

That gets all our attention.

"The Needle, Black Top Mesa—they are all within distance of a mine I know."

"Those are landmarks from Pa's journal," I says, surprised. "You been poking yer nose in things, Lil?"

"Only once. I asked to look, but you did not answer. I figured you'd have said no if it were important."

"Asked? You never asked."

"Yesterday morning, while you slept."

"Damn it, Lil. Course I didn't answer if I were sleeping. You don't do that. You don't just take things that ain't yers."

She inclines her chin. "White Eyes take our land and Ussen's gold. They take it as though it were always theirs. Least I put the journal back after looking."

"I still—"

"Hang fire," Jesse says. "Who cares if she read the journal or not." He turns to Lil. "Do you know how to find the mine?"

Lil sits a little taller and adjusts her smock dress. "Before I came unto this earth, my tribe faced conflict three moons into my mother's fifteenth year. A group of Mexicans rode into the canyons from the south and traveled beyond what the journal calls Weavers Needle, and into a gorge east of a black-topped mesa.

"They came to retrieve gold from a family mine. A treaty was to be signed soon and the mountains would then belong to White Eyes. The leader of the Mexicans, Miguel Peralta, feared his family grant would be ignored and that he would lose his mine forever. He told us this when our tribe warned them to leave the yellow iron be."

I feel a chill spread over my limbs. *Peralta.* Like the trail approaching the mines from the south, the very route I reckon Rose is taking.

"Our men warned the Peraltas to pack their mules and ride home. The gold belonged to no man, and words on a bit of paper could not make it so. But the Peraltas dug there, pulling the yellow iron from a deep pit for days.

"We tried to discourage them. Our warriors entered their camp as they worked, slaying mules but no men. Still the Mexicans would not take heed. So our tribe gathered among the ridges, hundreds strong, and when the Peraltas left for Sonora our arrows flew like rain. I do not know if any survived, but gold lay scattered there for years to come. The story has been told at our stronghold many moons since, and I have walked the trails on the hottest days to show my gratitude to the warriors who defended Ussen."

"So you know where it is?" Jesse says, sitting straighter.

"I do not. I have never seen the mine."

"But the trail. If yous walked the trail where yer people ambushed the Mexicans, you at least know the proper canyon, and points near the mine."

She shakes her head. "I cannot take you there."

"What! Why not?" His voice is getting too loud, the veins in his neck too defined. "You can save us time and guesswork deciphering map clues. You can take us clear to the right canyon."

"You have no more claim to the mine than the Peraltas," Lil says.

"Goddamn it!" Jesse snarls, jumping to his feet and pacing. "What in the hell is the point of having a scout when she don't show you the way nowhere?" He turns on me. "You get her to see reason, Kate. She's yer scout and we had a deal. We help you get Rose if'n the gold can be ours."

"Gold?" Lil says, turning toward me. "You said you did not want the gold, that you would not touch it."

"I *don't* want it," I says. "I don't want nothing but Rose and his men dead."

"And your deal with them?" Lil glances 'cross the fire at the boys. "It conflicts with ours. You lied."

"I didn't."

"I cannot help you," she says, standing. "I *will* not help you."

"Lil, come on."

But she goes on marching for her bedroll, her shoulders held back firm, her dark braids swinging.

"Where's the blasted mine?" Jesse shouts after her. "Goddamn it, tell us. Tell us you worthless, no-good—"

"Jesse!"

"She knows, Kate." He throws an arm after Lil. "She knows everything! We could hike straight to the damned thing and she won't help. Yer scout is worthless, and I ain't gonna apologize for something that's true."

There's a glint in his eyes I ain't never seen before—an angry fire. I remember Pa's note to me in Wickenburg, that warning. *Gold makes monsters of men.* The promise of riches is turning Jesse into someone I don't recognize.

"It's yer own damn fault," I says to him.

He glowers. "Pardon?"

"I told you not to mention the gold round her, or our deal, and you did. So don't go cursing me or Lil for something that's yer own error. And don't you dare try to preach to me 'bout lying to her by omission, or how I'm the villain here. I'm just trying to avenge my father so his soul can rest. But you? Yous got this lust for gold, this burning desire to do whatever yer father couldn't, and yer so damn drunk on the thought of success, you can't even realize how selfish it is. *And* you lost me my scout."

"Yer . . . I could . . ." Jesse takes a step toward me, away, back at me again. "Christ almighty!" he roars, and stomps off toward his bedroll.

Will's still sitting there on the other side of the fire, watching with interest as he cleans his pistols.

"Thanks for backing me up," I says to him.

He shrugs. "I ain't the one who struck a deal that conflicts with another I already got going."

I'm so mad, I could throw something. Lurching to my feet, I storm away from the fire and pace round a cactus till my blood ain't boiling so hot.

I can't change that the truth's out there, that Jesse spilled everything and Lil's prolly gonna walk at first light. Alls I can do now is focus on getting to the mine and them Rose Riders on my own.

My mind races back through Lil's story. I remember Pa talking 'bout his first days in the Territory. He'd been in his early teens, heading west with his father and damn near half the country, hoping to get rich on gold in California. The land they traveled 'cross was all considered Yankee soil back then. I remember him saying so. But just a year prior, it had belonged to the Mexicans, and war had raged over borders. I reckon the treaty Lil mentioned is that of Guadalupe Hidalgo, the agreement that named much of the southwest American soil. In Arizona, everything north of the Gila River—the Superstitions included —was no longer part of Mexico.

A few years later and after gold were a bust, Pa and his father were back in Arizona, running cattle with a small crew. It were an even bigger Territory then. I remember Pa saying something 'bout a purchase that extended Arizona south in the hopes a transcontinental railroad could be built through the area. Well, that train still's barely reached Yuma, let alone Tucson, where Pa's pa took ill and never recovered, and Pa went on to meet and marry Ma.

I touch the journal, still tucked in the back of my pants, and silently curse Jesse. He'll blame this on me somehow. Tomorrow it'll be my fault Lil's gone, I just know it.

When I make my way back to camp, Lil's already asleep and the Coltons are getting ready to retire. I grab my bedroll, and as I'm unfurling it Jesse steps up behind me.

"I'm sorry," he says. "I lost my temper. It weren't like me."

I grunt and go on spreading out my bed.

"Want one?" he says, offering me a rolled cigarette.

I straighten. "Is it half as vile as dip?"

"Not even."

Pa used to fancy a pipe, and it always left his shirts smelling like cedar and musk. Something 'bout the memory makes me want to smoke with Jesse now. Not 'cus I'm forgiving him but 'cus the thought of having those scents on my clothes is as close to Pa as I'm ever gonna get. I never got to smoke with him, and even though he told me it weren't fitting behavior for a lady, I think he'd like the thought of me enjoying one now in his memory. 'Sides, I ain't never been much of a lady to begin with.

I take the cigarette from Jesse and hold it between my lips. He strikes a match and steps close to light the smoke for me, using his spare hand to shield the flame from any wind. I puff on it like I seen him do. There's the subtle taste of oak and spices, then I start coughing.

"Jesus," I says, buckled over and nearly losing a lung.

"You'll get the hang of it," he says, smiling.

"Maybe I don't want to."

"Say, Kate." His voice is real serious. I straighten, the cigarette forgotten in my grasp and dangling near my knee. When I meet Jesse's gaze, his eyes are narrow like always, but there's something pained there too. He's gonna apologize and mean it. He's gonna promise to stop being such an ass.

"You wouldn't mind letting me look at that journal of yers, would you?"

I bring the smoke back to my lips, trying to mask my disappointment. I manage an inhale and exhale with only the slightest muffled cough.

"Look, it's just . . ." Jesse gazes in the direction of the cottonwoods. "I never thought this trip were smart to begin with, but I couldn't pass it up, and now we're here at the very first landmark, only it don't match the journal clues quite right. It ain't a good sign. 'Specially if yer scout cuts and runs. Will thinks the mine might be a hoax, despite her story. He said Waltz spent summer after summer in here and didn't find nothing, and we're just gonna get ourselves lost or killed or hunted by Apache."

"And what do you think, Jesse?"

"I think Will's got a point."

"Really?" I says, glaring. "You ain't just siding with him 'cus it's easier than standing on yer own two feet?"

"I don't do what's easiest, Kate, I do what's *right*. That's all I's ever done, and it's all I'm trying to do now. I wanna get gold for our family, the ranch, but I wanna be smart 'bout it." He sighs heavy. "Look, I'm asking to see the journal 'cus I care 'bout you, and heck, I care 'bout myself quite a bit too and don't feel like dying in these mountains. Just 'cus yer pa said the mine exists don't make it law. I know how you can glorify a person after they's passed. I done it before myself. But did it ever dawn on you that yer pa had an awful lot of secrets? That he lied to you constantly? That maybe he didn't have everything exactly right upstairs?"

And there it is: that damn sermon. I flick my cigarette into the dirt.

"You wanna look?" I yank Pa's journal out and shove it into Jesse's chest. "Go right ahead! Be sure to let me know what you think 'bout my own sanity when yer finished."

I turn and stalk off toward the cottonwoods, taking my bedroll with me.

"Kate, that came out wrong," Jesse calls after me. "Hey, where are you going? Come on, Kate."

I just walk faster.

I set up my bed beneath the sad trees and spit till the taste of tobacco's outta my mouth. When I risk a glance back, Jesse's already stretched out and reading with Will, looking anything but sorry as the fire glow plays over their features.

CHAPTER TWENTY

That night, I dream 'bout my mother, which is to say my dreams are a tangled web of clouded, foggy memories.

First I'm standing at the entrance to her and Pa's bedroom, my hand pressed 'gainst the knot-strewn door. I ain't brave enough to push it open and step through — Pa would have me by the ear — but it's cracked today, and I find the courage to peer through the slender gap.

Sun's streaming in their one window, lighting up the space. I'm young and short still and can barely see over the foot of the bed. The quilt's disheveled and lumpy. I ain't seen her in over six months. I ain't seen her in so long, I'm starting to forget what she looks like or even where we stood the last time we were together.

A memory of a kitchen that ain't ours surfaces, and a table that wobbled 'cus one leg were too short. A basket sat on it, woven with bits of brightly dyed wicker. I remember a lot of color in that house. Colors and shapes that felt like Ma. We don't got none of that stuff no more. It's like she got sick and Pa threw it all out.

Ma ain't moving in her sleep. I wonder if she might already be dead and Pa just ain't noticed. His hand reaches over my shoulder, startling me as he yanks the door shut.

"What'd I tell you 'bout staying clear of this room, Kate?"

I tilt my head back. He's towering overhead and looking mighty displeased.

"I wanna see Ma. I miss her."

"I know you do. But I don't want you getting sick."

"*You* get to go in the room," I says, pouting. "You go in there every night."

"'Cus I'm big and grown and strong. Yer little and can catch what she's got too easy. Now how's 'bout you help me with dinner while Ma sleeps?"

The memory dissolves, blowing like sand till it settles on a new moment.

Our neighbor Joe Benton is bringing me home in his cart. His dog had a litter that morning, and Pa took me over to see the pups. I watched 'em so long, he left to tend to our land. All day I stared at those tiny creatures, so plump and pudgy that they looked like rolls of dough. They couldn't even open their eyes yet.

I get a bad feeling during the ride home—a prickling sensation on my skin, a sense of dread. Something ain't right, only I got no idea how I know it.

When Joe's cart bumps over the rise separating our claim of land from his, Pa's in the distance, standing beneath our mesquite tree. It ain't till we're nearer that I can make out the shovel in his hand, the hunch to his back, the dirt he's throwing into a hole.

I scramble outta the cart and go racing toward him. It takes my little legs forever to get there, and when I do, I can see there ain't no bottom to the grave. It's already filled in, the dirt fresh and dark and nearly level with the grass. I only know what I'm looking at 'cus I helped him bury our barn cat not a week back.

"I wanted to see her!" I scream at Pa, pounding his thighs with my fists. "I hate you, I hate you, I hate you!"

"She didn't look like herself no more," he says when I'm through attacking. "I thought this would be best. She'll rest easy beneath this tree—sheltered in the winter and shaded in the summer. We can visit her together."

"I wanted to see her," I says again.

"I know. But remember her like this: healthy, smiling." He passes me a photograph taken when I were still a baby. I's seen one just like it in a lunch box Pa uses to store important papers.

I don't take the picture from him.

I get up and stomp to the barn and cry by myself in Libby's stall.

Later that night, I find Pa's put the photograph under my pillow. I keep it there for years, till Pa buys me a copy of *Little Women* and the photo starts serving as a bookmark. It stays tucked between those pages till it burns up in the fire, and I swipe Pa's copy from his lunch box, 'long with all that remains of his life.

When I wake, back turned to camp and last night's dreams still fogging my head, the sun's already up. For how long, I ain't sure, but the sky sure is light enough. I reckon I woulda woken earlier if it weren't for the canyon walls leaving our camp in shadow.

I shove to my feet and stumble farther beyond the cottonwoods, till I find a private spot to relieve myself. As I'm fastening my trousers I notice footprints in the dry dust. The toe of a boot, the gouge of a heel. My heart goes a thumping in my chest. Someone were here, this close to camp. Definitely one man. Maybe even two. Apache? No, not with those pointed boot toes. Maybe Rose himself. Or the ghost shooter.

I follow the tracks best I can, but they're half scattered by the wind and disappear where the canyon floor becomes mostly rock.

Rounding a bend, I come to an abrupt halt.

Far to the south and climbing toward the sky like a church steeple is Weavers Needle. It's a beacon among the ragged terrain, a marker you couldn't miss if you tried. I hold up my hand, gauging its size 'gainst my fingers. I reckon it's another three or four miles off still, but that would mean the horse-head landmark is within our grasp. If'n we get to it tonight, we'll be in position to watch the sun rise tomorrow morning and mark the mine's location when it shines over the rock steed's neck.

It should make me happy, this progress, but every hair on my person is suddenly standing on end. I get the feeling I'm being watched, that I ain't alone. I turn the way I came, expecting Lil to be sneaking up on me, but the canyon's empty. When I turn back toward Weavers Needle, there ain't nothing but wilderness as far as I can see.

Still, something ain't right. The tracks, the stillness, this feeling in my chest. Just like that time with Ma, I can sense something foul.

I spin round and race back to the cottonwoods.

I stumble into camp. Lil's there, loading up her pony, and Waltz's burro grazes nearby, but otherwise she's alone. Their beds, their pistol belts, their gear—all gone. There ain't a sign of 'em.

My hands go to my lower back, but no—I gave Jesse the journal last night, let him look. I scramble for my bedroll, digging frantically through my gear, hoping in vain he put it back after reading it. But it ain't there.

The journal's gone, and the Coltons went with it.

"They left early," Lil says. "The stars still shone."

"Why the hell didn't you stop 'em?"

"I want them far from me. They seek to destroy everything I value."

"Damn it, Lil, they took my journal!"

It shouldn't be a shock. We were using each other, the Coltons and me. That's all it ever were, our deal, and the boys ran when they no longer needed my help, when they secured the means to their end. They got the maps now. They don't gotta put up with me or Lil. If they travel swift, they might not even have to face the Rose Riders. They could beat 'em to the gold and leave these mountains rich men without raising their pistols once.

Lil swings a makeshift sack over her shoulder and nudges her pony to action.

"Where are you going?" I ask.

"Home."

"And our arrangement? Yer supposed to be my scout!"

"You lied to me. Our arrangement no longer has worth."

"Lil, you can't leave me here. You can't leave me alone."

The canyon walls seem to be closing in on me, collapsing and tumbling. I won't last by myself in this place. Plains are one thing, but I ain't prepared for this.

"I have a little farther to go before I leave this canyon," Lil says. "Will you continue or turn back?"

For one dark moment, I consider giving up, just hiking back to Waltz's and riding Silver home. But then I catch the scent of tobacco smoke on my flannel, feel a shiver of a breeze curl round my neck, and it's like Pa's right here. Like his ghost has followed me all the way to these blasted mountains and is whispering in my ear. I can't go home. There ain't nothing to go home to anyway, and I didn't come all this way to fail him. I didn't come all this way to quit. I know my way to the horse-head marker, and if I find that, maybe I don't need the journal. Maybe I can make do on my own. And if I can't, I'd rather die out here trying to do something honorable than crawl back to Prescott with my tail between my legs.

I check Waltz's burro. The Coltons've taken the bulk

of their gear, but I'm glad they left me the creature. Not that I'm daft enough to think it were an act of kindness. Those boot prints beyond camp are theirs. They crept out on foot, didn't want to risk waking me as they passed by.

I load up my gear fast and don't bother with eating. I got two scores to settle now. I'll find Rose with or without the journal, and if I find the Coltons 'long the way, I'll have some choice words for the both of 'em. They'll be lucky bulls if the only thing I throw their way is curses.

With the sun spilling over the ridgeline, we leave camp. I guide Waltz's burro on foot. Lil rides the pony but stays close on my heels.

There ain't much of a breeze today, and by midmorning the heat's getting unbearable. Sun-basking lizards scamper outta our way as we wind through the canyon. I tip my hat lower so my skin don't roast in the sun, and scan for signs of the Coltons, fantasizing 'bout what I might say if'n I catch up with 'em. Should I shoot first and holler second, or the other way round? I reckon cocking my pistol and aiming might be enough of a threat. I don't actually wanna kill 'em, and I'll prolly be shaking with so much rage, my barrel'll be as twitchy as a jackrabbit.

Spineless cowards, sneaking off like that in the middle of the night. *Stealing* from me. By God I could . . . I will . . . I bite down so hard, my teeth grind.

The mountains surrounding us seem endless. At every curve or crest in the trail, I think they might start leveling out, despite what the journal maps have told me. When I start hearing things on the air, I consider the possibility that the canyon leads straight to hell. Some of the noise is natural, like screeching hawks, or weak wind whistling over rocks. But then there's the stuff that makes my skin crawl: men screaming and shouting, bloodcurdling yelps. These cries are so faint, so distant, I worry they might be in my head.

This is cursed land for sure. Haunted. Unnatural. Waltz were right.

I take a long swig of water, concerned the heat's getting to me.

Another scream reaches my ears, no louder than a whisper.

"You hear that, Lil?"

She regards me quiet, then turns her attention back to the path.

"Now you ain't talking to me? Well that just shines. What'd I ever do to you, other than save you from a burning saloon, huh? What'd I do to deserve this?"

Nothing.

"Come on, Lil. I'm going crazy out here—the heat and the Riders and the Coltons running off. Say something. Say anything."

It's silent awhile. Finally, without bothering to look at me, she says, "I want to tell you a tale."

"I'm sure that'll fix everything."

She continues in an even tone, as though she ain't heard my grumbling.

"Long ago, only those called Fireflies possessed fire.

One night, Flies held a ceremony and Coyote came there. He danced at the edge of their fire and poked his tail into the flames. 'Friend, your tail will burn,' the Flies warned. But Coyote laughed. 'Let it burn!' he said, and put his tail in until it flared up.

"The Flies tried to stop Coyote, but he jumped up and over them and ran far away with the fire. He scattered it among the mountains and gave fire to Eagle to spread. Everywhere, the world burned. The Flies tried to put out the fire, but the wind helped Coyote, blowing it until it became impossible to control. In this way, fire came to exist in the world."

"Pretty dumb fireflies," I mutter.

"But as the fire spread," Lil continues, "the Flies asked the stones and earth and water to all become hot for Coyote. And so they did. Wanting relief from the burning earth, Coyote jumped into a pond and, right there, he was boiled."

She stops, looks at me stern.

"That's it? What the devil does that got to do with anything?"

Lil frowns. "If you cannot see, nothing I say will help."

"What's to say? The poor coyote gets us fire—a thing we'd be lost without—and dies for it."

"Coyote the Trickster stole, and there were consequences," Liluye says. "He will never make use of fire himself." Her gaze trails to the back of my trousers, where the journal's usually tucked.

"You saying the boys are the coyote, Lil? That they

stole from me and it's my job to make sure they ain't able to reap the benefits of having those maps?"

Her brows raise high. "You said that, not me. I only told a tale."

A landmass Lil refers to as Black Top Mesa looms into view at midafternoon. It looks done up by a painter—rings of color marking it from base to flat, broad summit. At the top, ashy black to suit its name, then shades of cactus and shrub mixed with layers of sand-tan and rust. I remember it from the journals. We're still cutting south, running almost parallel to the mesa. By the time we manage to pass its southern edge, it'll likely be dusk. I wonder if Lil'll have turned off by then.

I ain't heard no more yelps or screams from the mountains. I ain't heard much wildlife, neither, and the vast stillness of the afternoon's making me anxious. Lil might as well be mute for how much she's said since her tale 'bout fire. I draw my Colt and sight a cactus, practice the act till my arm gets weary.

Lil keeps letting her gaze drift to the east. The journals said the mine's farther south, and in the opposite direction from where she's looking, so she must be thinking on home, searching for familiar paths. It stings in my side again—the realization that she's ditching soon. She might be a pain, but she's the only thing left between me and the dark quiet of my own thoughts.

"Say, Lil . . ."

"Liluye," she corrects.

"Who told you that tale 'bout the coyote?"

"I do not remember. It is old. When I think of my child-hood, I have always known it." She pauses briefly. "It was Tarak's favorite."

"Did you like him?"

She nods. "He made me angry. All those riddles. I hated him."

"But you just said—"

"It is funny how the things we hate are the things we miss most when they are gone." She holds her chin higher and looks into the sun. "He'd have made a good husband. He was stubborn, but fair. And honest."

She gives me a sideways glance at that last word. How many exchanges today is she gonna try to wrangle into a jab 'bout Jesse? I know she don't like him. It ain't like she needs to keep reminding me. Hell, I ain't too fond of him neither at the moment.

"Weren't you furious when he were killed?" I says, try-ing to take the focus offa me. "Didn't you want revenge?"

"Tarak died a warrior's death. If Ussen meant for him to live, it would have been so, but instead he is in the Happy Place. There is nothing to be done. Revenge will not bring him back, and my Spirit Guide agrees."

I reckon the Happy Place is heaven and a Spirit Guide is a guardian of some sort, but I don't ask, 'cus some-thing's caught my attention. We's come upon the mouth of a small valley, and a dead ironwood tree looms just ahead, knobby and twisted and bare. Prickly pear and saguaro cactuses crop up in abundance beyond it, and given the amount of wild shrubs and small trees, I reckon there's water nearby. But I can't tear my eyes away from that ironwood, 'cus there's something hanging from it. Swinging slightly. Its shape so familiar.

I drop the burro's reins and force my legs into a run. When I come upon the tree, I sink to my knees. Bile claws at my throat.

Hanging from a noose, eyes wide like he's seen the devil, is Will.

CHAPTER TWENTY-ONE

I pull my knife from my boot and cut him down.

He crumples like Pa did. Scratches mark Will's neck, gouges made by his own nails as he clawed at the rope beneath his chin. The rose emblem is carved shallow in his forehead. Enough blood trails into his eyes and down his cheeks for me to know it were done while he were still breathing.

I turn away and lose what little there is in my stomach.

That bastard. That goddamn heartless bastard.

Rose shouldn't even be here. He were supposed to be coming from the opposite direction, taking the Peralta Trail. Unless he followed the Salt just like us. Unless those hooves Waltz claimed to hear during the night belonged to the gang riding by, and them screams I been hearing in the canyons were actually the Coltons falling into Rose's hands, Jesse yelling himself hoarse as they strung up Will.

I see the note next, pinned to the ironwood with a meaty knife. I yank it free. It's a page torn from a Bible. With trembling hands, I read the words written atop a psalm.

Stay right at the fork. Bring the journal or the other dies too. You have till dawn.

The only signature is a hastily sketched rose.

I take a step backwards, the world seeming to tilt on its side.

He's here and he's got Jesse. And the journal . . . He wants the journal, which means the boys musta had time to stash it or throw it away. Before they were ambushed and taken hostage, the Coltons got rid of it. But Rose still thinks it's in my care and now Jesse's gonna hang if I don't turn it over. They're gonna string him up. Just like Will, like Pa.

I turn away and heave again, only my stomach's good and empty now. I stay buckled over, an arm clutched to my middle as I cough and hack.

"Water."

I glance up and see Lil standing there, my canteen held in offering. I take it and down a few gulps. My throat is raw and ragged. Dust cakes my lips.

"Lil, you gotta help me."

"Liluye," she corrects.

"He's got Jesse and he's gonna kill him."

"I do not care about Jesse. See there?" She points

ahead to the far end of the valley, where it goes slender, then divides into two new canyon passes. "If I go left, I will find a spring and then a marsh and then a trail that leads up the ridge to a broad, flat mesa. Our stronghold is there. I'm leaving."

"No, please, Lil. *Please.* I got till dawn. Maybe yer people can help. Maybe we can do something together."

"My people do not help White Eyes looking to rape Mother Earth," she snaps, eyes flashing. It's the first thing she's ever said with ferocity, and it chills my blood.

"Please, Lil. I'm begging here."

"He stole from you."

"To help his family, to try to gain a better life for Will and his sister and her son." I see it now, know exactly why Jesse's done what he did. "You gotta understand. Gold don't mean nothing to yer people, I get that, but it means a heck of a lot in our world. It means a future and a bit of security and not having to look over yer shoulder every other minute. He stole the journal to try to do good more than he stole it to hurt me."

"You *do* like him," she says, mounting her pony and looking down on me like I'm a child. "You are lost, Kate, and I cannot help you."

She rides past the ironwood and into the valley.

"Lil!" I shout at her back. "Goddamn it, don't leave me here!"

But she keeps on riding, beyond shrubs and between cactuses, till she stays left at the fork and disappears from view.

I stare at the burro and Will and the note in my hands. Then, 'cus I don't know what else to do, I cry.

I give myself till the count of ten and stop. Wipe my cheeks dry. Push to my feet.

I unfasten Will's pistol belt, wrestle it off his limp frame, and secure it to the burro. Then I check his pockets and find 'em empty 'cept for a packet of dip. The kerchief at his neck is damp with blood, the pale paisley pattern stained dark. I ain't sure why, but I save it, 'long with the dip.

The ground is rock hard, and I don't got the tools for digging, so I start a fire. Close Will's eyes. Roll him into the flames.

I read aloud what I can of the psalm beneath Rose's handwriting.

"'Blessed is the man that walketh not in the counsel of the ungodly. . . . He shall be like a tree planted by the rivers of water, that bringeth forth its fruit in season.'"

I toss the paper into the fire and swallow hard. "I liked you, Will," I says. "I'm sorry our last few exchanges were unpleasant. You deserved better than this."

I don't stay to watch him burn. I can't bear it.

I walk into the valley, the scent of singed hair filling my nostrils.

Before the trail splits again, I work my way up the valley's modest hillside. Dusk is closing in, shadows spilling over the ridges.

Needle Canyon forks at the far end of the valley, rocky earth rising up between the two new paths. The canyon to the left—the way Lil went—looks narrow and vexed. Angry spires and spitting blades and roughly rounded tombstones climb from its ridge. They reach for the sky like the jagged edge of a knife, but one of those teeth, farther to the south . . . it's unmistakably animal. The two perky ears, the crest of a neck, the slope of a muzzle. It's a horse's head. Come dawn, the sun'll rise and shine right over that rock steed's neck, lighting up where the mine's at, and I don't even care.

I can't.

Not with Will's swinging body burned into my eyes, with those words Rose scrawled on that Bible page. Maybe for Lil, life really is that black and white. Maybe Jesse's lying and stealing are unforgivable to her. But I ain't letting him boil.

I look to the right fork, where Needle Canyon continues south. In the fading daylight, I catch something flickering 'long the ridge. It glints like a shiny rock, or light playing off the barrel of a weapon. Could be a Rose Rider, keeping watch. Or Apache keeping watch over the Rose Riders. Either way, it'd mean the posse's camp is near. That's when I see another flicker, different this time. More of a glow than a glint, coming from down on the canyon floor maybe a half mile south of where I stand. I dig through the gear loaded onto the burro and pull out a pair of binoculars.

It's them all right; the Rose Riders. Seven dark shadows huddle round a fire. There were seven of 'em when we holed up in that abandoned house 'long the Salt, but Rose shot one of his own men that evening, which means one of their current group is Jesse. And also that it ain't a Rider's rifle glinting up 'long the ridge.

I sit back, thinking.

I can't go in at this hour. I ain't thick enough to walk into a gang's camp at night and be ambushed, though maybe they're thick enough to think I am. Regardless, I don't got the journal to trade, but maybe I can pretend I do.

And that flash 'long the ridge . . .

I scan again and see it after watching a moment or two. Even with the binoculars I can't make out who's up there.

But it gives me an idea.

Rose ain't foolish enough to believe in the ghost shooter, but I *were* traveling with an Apache scout. He don't gotta know that she left. As far as he's concerned she's still helping me. Maybe all her people, too.

I just gotta walk in there tomorrow, chin held high, and pretend like I got the journal. Then, before we make a trade, I'll change the terms. Jesse's life for the safety of Rose and his men. If'n he gives me Jesse, I won't tell my scout to shoot.

It might work.

It's gotta.

'Bout a quarter mile from their camp, I quit for the day. It's as close as I'm willing to go without risking being heard.

I don't make a fire, 'cus it ain't worth being seen.

I eat stale biscuits and drink a little from what's left in my canteen. I'll need more water soon, but that can wait till after I got Jesse back. There's that creek Lil mentioned. Hell, there's prolly even water just back the way I came, snaking through that shrub-strewn valley. But I ain't 'bout to go digging round in the dark, wasting energy and tiring myself out when I need to be sharp and keen come dawn. Plus, my ankle's finally feeling right, and I don't wanna roll it again with a poor step.

By the light of the moon, I clean my weapons. I know the feel of 'em like a blind man, 'specially my Winchester. I could load and fire it with my eyes shut.

I grip the weapon tight, thinking 'bout Pa and the day I turned eight, when he gifted me the rifle and insisted on teaching me to shoot it immediately after. When I asked why, he just said, "I ain't always gonna be around, Kate. You gotta know how to fend for yerself."

"But you put a horse down up close," I argued. "You kill a chicken dinner with the axe. Why's I gotta shoot a bottle from halfway 'cross the farm?"

Pa nudged my nose with his knuckle. "There are good people and there are bad people. Most folk are good. They mean well and will help a friend in need. I really do believe that. But there might come a day when you need help and the only folk round are bad ones." He lowered his eyes to meet mine. "You gotta be yer own help in those situations. You gotta know how to fire this rifle and not miss. You hear me?"

There were something awful cold in his expression that day. I remember it being the first time I ever wondered if he regretted me being born a girl, if he'd rather've had a son.

"Show me," I said, reaching for the rifle.

He passed it over, smiling. "That's my girl."

When I finish cleaning, I make sure the weapons are fully loaded.

What I'm saying is, rifles are big and require room.

I double-check my Colt and make sure all the cartridge slots on my pistol belt are stocked. I'll need a quick draw tomorrow, an easily maneuvered barrel, plus a fair amount of luck to best a man like Waylan Rose.

You gotta be quicker than quick, ace high, the best.

I sleep, but not well. Every noise in the night is a threat. Every moment of dozing, restless.

Far too soon, the sun begins to rise.

CHAPTER TWENTY-TWO

I approach their camp with my blood tingling. My fingers dance near my holster. My heart beats frantic.

Rose sees me coming first. His head snaps up from where he's sitting, a smile curling over his lips.

"Tompkins," he says, my true name sounding like a whip. He stands slow and walks round their small fire till we ain't more than a hundred paces apart.

Behind him, the Rose Riders are on their feet, hands on their pistol grips. The man from the Agua Fria, the one wearing the fringed leather jacket, jerks Jesse upright by a rope. No, a noose. It's pulled tight beneath Jesse's chin.

Jesse barely looks at me, but it ain't outta shame or regret. He's drowning in despair, crippled by guilt. I know as sure as if he'd said it. He watched Will hang, and there ain't a spark of life left in his eyes.

"I can't believe it," Fringed Jacket says. "She came any-way."

"Course she did," Rose says.

"Even without the journal."

"I's got the journal," I says.

"This journal?" Rose draws it from his jacket and my blood thins. He has it. He's had it all this while.

Fringed Jacket starts laughing, a blistering cackle. Be-hind him, the other Riders join in.

"I want Jesse," I says stern, looking Rose dead in those ice-blue eyes.

One side of his mouth lifts into a smirk. "If'n you want him to walk free, to not face the same fate as dear old Pa, then you come stand in his place."

It don't make no sense. He's got what he wants: the journal and the way to the gold. What good will I do him? Fringed Jacket is staring at me with a wicked hunger, his tongue running over his front teeth. It's some sick game now. Maybe Rose's men want a woman. Maybe Rose just likes to finish off complete families when he starts killing. He didn't spare no one in that coach, after all. Not even the young child.

"I ain't a bargaining chip," I says.

"Then the boy'll hang."

"You string him up and you'll bring yerself a world of trouble."

"That so?" Rose's eyes spark with amusement.

"I had an Apache with me earlier — my scout. She ain't here now 'cus she's tucked away safe." I point up at the ridge where I saw the glint of light yesterday. "Tucked away with half her tribe and their arrows. I think they got a few long rifles between 'em, but I can't quite remember."

"Yer bluffing," Rose says.

"Seems we're playing poker all over again."

Rose slides a hand 'long the opening of his coat, tucking it behind the grip of his six-shooter. A slight breeze snakes through the canyon, flirting with the coat's hem. It sways at his knees.

He ain't that far off. I could get him, right now. The breeze won't persuade my bullet much. He's a flower on a cactus, a bottle on a fence.

I lick my lips.

Rose wriggles his fingers.

No one moves.

No one breathes.

The air could get cut with a knife.

I picture it just like Jesse said—the draw and the aim and the shot and the bullet's path. I picture it till my pulse is pounding in my ears, till my heart sounds like a drum beating out a war song.

Then I go for my Colt.

Reach, draw, cock, aim—

But Rose does it all faster. He fires, and my Stetson goes flying off my head. I flinch, thinking I must be dead, shot straight through the skull. But, no, he missed. Only, Waylan Rose don't miss. He did that on purpose, took my hat clear off. For whatever reason—rose carving, torture, sick pleasure—he still wants me alive.

I straighten, ready to fire back, but Rose is already

closing in. I aim and pull my trigger. No bullet flies. Before I can even curse my misfiring pistol, his knuckles sting 'cross my cheek. I crash to all fours, yelping. Rose kicks a handful of dust in my eyes, then backhands me. I lift my pistol blindly, eyes burning, only to feel his boot come crushing down on my wrist and a muzzle press into my forehead.

Everything hurts. My arm and wrist and eyes and cheek. I look up at him, eyes tearing.

"I knew it," Rose snarls. "I knew there were no guns in them mountains."

I catch Jesse outta the corner of my vision. There's an overwhelming sadness to his expression. Though he don't say nothing, I hear every word.

I'm so sorry. I never meant for this to happen. I'm sorry, I'm sorry. He's dead. We're doomed. Can you ever forgive me?

"There ain't no reason for this," I says. "You got the journal. You got everything you want."

Rose smiles. "But not you."

"Who cares 'bout the girl?" Fringed Jacket says.

"Step down, Hank. You don't know what yer talking 'bout."

"Just kill her."

"Hank!"

"But we got the journal," he shouts. "Like she says, we got everything we want. Goddamn it, the gold can be ours! We oughtta kill the lot of 'em, especially Tompkins! Hell, we shoulda killed Tompkins back when this all started!"

I see that glint up in the mountains again, and immediately following it a gunshot screams. Hank goes flying off his feet and hits the dirt, dead.

Another glint, another shot, and Rose's hat is swiped clear off his person. He ducks and skirts for the shelter of a boulder. I do the same, but the blasts keep coming, screaming from the range. I ain't got a clue who's up there, but they're a damn good shot, unnaturally good. Like a spirit. Like a ghost, shooting.

I peer round the boulder. The gang's scrambling for cover and firing blindly toward the ridge, but Jesse's bolt upright. He darts for the Riders' camp and roots through the saddlebags on their burros.

"Jesse!" I shout.

He finds his pistol belt, slings it on. Then he turns on the still-scattering Riders and unleashes his bullets like a demon.

"Jesse!" I shout again. "It ain't Lil in the mountains! It ain't her shooting."

It takes a second, but then the words register. His head whips toward the ghost shooter's perch. There's another glint, and he dives aside. Dust flies up where he was just paused.

A shadow falls over him, a Rose Rider aiming to slaughter. Jesse swivels, raising his Remingtons, but not before the Rider slashes with a knife. A mangled cry leaves Jesse's lips and he crumples still. I curse my jammed Colt, but before I can so much as blink, a bullet from the ghost shooter tears through the Rider's back. He staggers and falls. I scramble for Jesse, but additional shots battle me back to the safety of my boulder.

Leaning 'gainst the rock, I pant, ears ringing. Rose gives an order to fall back. When I peer next, it's just him and one other Rider flying south down Needle Canyon on the burros. They shoot back at the ridge as they flee. The other Riders are dead, their bodies sprawled and lifeless in the canyon. Jesse ain't moving neither.

I crane my neck over the boulder, looking up toward the ghost shooter. When I squint 'gainst the sun, I can see that flash of light, that glinting barrel. It's moving south, following Rose. It thinks it got everyone in the camp.

Still, I wait a moment longer, then stand cautious. When no bullets come, I run to Jesse. The front of his shirt has been torn open by the knife, and there's blood. A lot of blood. He's breathing, but they're more like gasps, and he seems to look through me when I hover over him.

"Jesse?" I says. He grunts in response. "Can you stand? Walk?"

He manages to sit.

"Yer cheek's bleeding," he says.

I touch the tender skin where Rose backhanded me, and my fingers come away wet.

"That don't matter. We gotta move."

But he's fading already, his eyes going crossways and drifting. He ain't in a state to walk. Ain't in a state to do much of nothing. I don't got the needle or thread to see to his chest. He's gonna go unconscious soon, then bleed out.

I look the way the Riders fled. If I go after Rose now, Jesse won't make it.

I need help. I need . . .

If I go left, I will find a spring and then a marsh and then a trail that leads up the ridge to a broad, flat mesa. Our stronghold is there.

I strip down to my undershirt and tie my flannel round Jesse's chest in an attempt to slow his bleeding. Then I grab the reins of one of the Riders' deserted burros. It takes a bunch of cursing and shouting and me calling Jesse a weak coward before he summons enough grit to stand with my help. He's spent by the time I sling him over the donkey's back.

I lead the creature to my camp and grab Waltz's burro. Pulling both animals along, with Jesse still slumped over the Riders', I hike fast as I can for the Apache stronghold.

It's a long shot. And reckless. They'll prolly shoot us on sight.

But the way I see it, I don't got much choice.

CHAPTER TWENTY-THREE

I find the spring running at barely a trickle, and the marsh a bit farther north. I spot the trail only 'cus I know to look for it.

The going is slow, and a stubborn rattlesnake sunning on some rocks makes me have to circle wide round him. The burros don't like it, and Jesse's already unconscious, my flannel wrapped round him damp with blood, but I ain't risking a bite. I can't do neither of us much good poisoned and dying.

When I beat my way back to the trail, we spend another hour or so climbing. My bare arms are hot and aching, not used to getting so much sun. The tops of my shoulders sting. I'm dripping sweat by the time we get to the mesa, and desperate for water. I shoulda refilled my canteen at that spring. What if I ain't even in the right place?

I glance round. The mesa stretches out, bare except for craggy shrubs and brambles. At its heel, the earth rises again — another climb to what might be a second mesa, or summit.

A trail that leads up the ridge to a broad, flat mesa. Our stronghold is there.

But there ain't no stronghold here. Maybe there once was and they moved on. Maybe Lil's already come here and left.

"Lil?" I shout. My voice echoes off the surrounding mountains. "Lil, where are you? I need you!"

I spot movement 'cross the mesa. Two men step into view, silent like deer. They got Lil's dark hair and stern features. Bows slung over their shoulders. Skin darkened by the sun.

One draws an arrow from his quiver.

I go bone still.

He sets the arrow 'gainst his bow, takes hold of the string.

"Please," I says, showing my palms. "I'm looking for Lil. Liluye." I wish I'd listened to her way back when, tried to learn her name proper. I ain't even sure I'm saying it right. "I rode with her earlier and I need her help. My friend — he's hurt."

The Apache pause. Both sets of eyes drift to the burros, Jesse's slouched form. Then back to me.

Slow, steady, I unhook my pistol belt and let it fall to the earth. "Please. He'll die otherwise."

"Liluye?" the one Apache says, releasing the tension

on the bowstring. He pronounces it different from me, the *e* drawn out and long.

"Liluye," I says back, proper this time.

They look at each other, at me, at Jesse again.

"Come," one says finally. They sling their bows over their shoulders. I grab my pistol belt and follow.

"You ask us to help him?" Lil says. She looks different from when I last saw her. An animal-hide overshirt 'stead of her dress smock. Stone earrings hang from her ears, and a rope of beads lies round her neck. "*Him,* who has shown me nothing but hate?"

We stand on the outskirts of their camp. I followed the two Apache men another half hour before arriving, curving up the steep mountain till coming upon its broad peak. It's rougher than the mesa—uneven, rocky ground—but where it levels out a little, brush-built huts sit scattered, their entrances all facing east. Wikiups, I think I's heard 'em called. Another wall of red earth rises behind 'em to provide some shelter. Curious Apache wait there—women and young children—eyeing me as I speak with Lil.

"I know, Lil. I know he ain't been fair. But he'll die without aid, and I can't do nothing. Yer people are good with injuries and healing, ain't they?"

She gives me a look that burns. She knows I'm just going on rumors and what I's read in Yankee papers.

"I saved you in Phoenix," I add. "You owe me a life."

"And you want it to be his?"

"You ain't my scout no more. Yer not gonna be round to save me if I need it later. But he needs it right now. Jesse needs this."

Lil frowns a long moment. "I cannot make this decision, but I will ask those who can."

She steps away to talk with the others. The women chatter in a language I can't follow. The children look between their parents and me, eyes wide. There ain't many men present, which makes me think they may be off on some trip, maybe even with their chief. The only males are a few younger ones—sentries, prolly, like the two who escorted me to camp—and a middle-aged Apache with his hair pulled into a long plait.

Finally, Lil comes back.

"Apache healing is physical *and* religious," she says. "The injured and his friends and family must believe in Ussen and the Power he bestowed on our medicine man or the herbs will be less potent, maybe entirely useless. I know Jesse does not believe in these things. I know he does not value our culture or God. You may be no different. But Bodaway will see to him if this is how you wish me to fulfill my debt."

"I do. Thank you, Lil. Thank you."

"Do not thank me yet. His life is in Ussen's hands."

"I can pay, too," I says. "Whatever the cost, I'll find the means."

"There is no charge for Bodaway's Power, but a gift of gratitude is often given." She motions for Jesse and I grab the burro's reins, leading him after her and 'cross their camp.

The medicine man's hut is draped with animal skins, while the others bear nothing on their woven branches. Soon as we're standing in the entrance, I know why. It's hot inside Bodaway's place, an internal heat trapped by the hides. The air smells wrong too, full of smoke and incense.

Bodaway's weathered face appears. He says something in Apache.

"This is a place for the sick only," Lil says. "You must wait elsewhere."

I watch two younger men carry Jesse inside. His head lolls limp. His shirt clings to his chest, heavy with blood. He already looks dead.

Lil touches my arm. "Come," she says. "There is much to celebrate."

Turns out Lil's arrived home on the eve of a ceremonial rite for one of the younger Apache maidens. She's come of age. There's to be feasting and song and high spirits, only I ain't invited.

As dusk falls, I stand on the outskirts of camp, watching as the Apache gather to witness the maiden step from the ceremonial hut. She looks barely thirteen. A smudge of white marks her forehead, and as she walks forward people toss something powdery into the sky. It flutters down like flour.

"Hoddentin," Lil says, joining my side silent like a cat. "Pollen of cattails. It is used in all sacred ceremonies."

I watch the young girl accept a drink from a shallow bowl. Polished stone beads hang from her neck and glint in the setting sun.

"She has fasted all day," Lil tells me, "but now she eats. We all do." She hands me a dinner of roasted mule deer and acorn-meal cakes, then disappears again to join the celebrations.

I sit on a rugged bit of rock and try not to devour my food so fast, it'll make me sick. The meat is warm and delicious—better than anything I's tasted in days—and the cakes surprisingly sweet. Filling, too. Mescal's poured and distributed among the Apaches. I don't got nothing but water, but it's no bother. I ain't dumb enough to indulge in mescal, even if it'd been offered to me. Suspicious gazes continue to flick my way from the camp, Apaches glaring and glowering and not at all pleased 'bout my presence. I'm still an outsider here, the enemy. I know my place.

After dinner, women shuffle off, cleaning up and readying for the night. The children bounce round the fire, playing a game with a stick that seems to involve balancing it on yer toe and kicking it into the air so that it lands on a marked bit of earth. One of the younger guards who greeted me on the mesa sits near the fire and begins speaking. The children abandon their game to come listen.

I watch all this from my perch on the rocks, but I watch Bodaway's wickiup more. My eyes keep drifting there 'gainst my will. Smoke's still snaking from the smoke hole, but no one's gone in or come out. If I strain real hard, I swear I can hear Bodaway chanting.

The injured and his friends and family must believe in Ussen and the Power he bestowed on our medicine man or the herbs will be less potent, maybe entirely useless.

It ain't working. Jesse hates Apache, and I don't believe much in their religion or folklore neither. I push to my feet, fast. The few men in camp go rigid, their shoulders squaring to mine. Lil looks up and frowns.

I scramble down from my rock perch, and when I reach the edge of camp she's waiting to greet me.

"I need to move," I says. "I can't sit still no longer."

Lil nods solemn. "I will find you when there is news."

I leave without looking back, though I can feel the eyes of many following me. Watching my step over uneven stone, I keep moving away from camp, till I come to a ridge overlooking the Superstitions. The view is end-less. Beneath twilight, it appears how I imagine an ocean would under storm, ragged and dark and teeming. Not that I's ever set my gaze on salt water before.

I stand there staring.

I ain't never put much faith in God. If there were some-one up there watching over us, he wouldn't let things like this happen: Ma dying so young, Pa and Will hanging, that poor family burned alive in the coach. No almighty being would make a person like Waylan Rose and let him roam the earth free.

I can't bear the thought of being alone again. I know I's kept the Coltons at a distance, built a wall 'gainst anyone trying to get close, but I ain't sure why. I hate being alone. I hate that Pa's gone. I hate that I'm out here in the middle of a wild Territory without a hand to hold.

So I start talking. Not out loud, but in my mind.

I pray to God and heaven and every power that be, Ussen included. I ask for Pa to rest easy, and Will to do the same, and Jesse to be all right. I ask for forgiveness for all those souls I killed, on purpose and by mistake. Tom outside Walnut Grove, those poor men at the poker game, even the bastards in Rose's gang. It ain't like the killing's been making me feel better. I want the blood off my hands and my conscience washed clean. I wanna know I ain't as dark and twisted as Rose himself, and, *Christ, please Christ, God, Ussen, whoever is listening . . . Please let Jesse be fine.*

From somewhere out 'cross the canyons, a coyote howls. I know it's just a wild dog. I know it ain't got the power to change nothing.

But I smile small, 'cus I feel like I's been heard.

CHAPTER TWENTY-FOUR

When Lil finds me a few hours later, I ain't moved from the ridge. It's dark now, stars spilled 'cross the sky like shards of silver. Back in the camp, I can hear the chant of song and drum, the soft whistle of a flute.

"He's waking," Lil says.

I scramble to my feet. "And he'll make it?"

"He is lucky. The cut was long, but not deep. Much blood was lost, but Bodaway treated the wound with nopal and lay a clean cloth down after stitching. Herbs are chasing the heat from his brow."

I's been holding my breath this whole time, and I exhale long. She holds out a lump of cloth I recognize as my shirt, which I grab eagerly, suddenly aware of how cold I am. I slip it on, cringing as the material grazes my sunburnt arms and bandaged shoulder. Jesse's blood's left a faint stain on the front, but the flannel's dry now. And soft. Someone must've cleaned it. Maybe Lil.

"I can walk him to you," she offers. "If he feels well enough."

"Thanks, Lil," I says. "Liluye."

Her chin jerks sharp, bringing her gaze to meet mine.

"I didn't say it right?"

She dismisses the question with a head shake. "You said it. *Finally.*"

"I shoulda been saying it all along. I'm sorry."

"You should be."

"Well, I am." I look at her fully. She is stoic and sure beneath the moonlight, posture held haughty. Her dark eyes gleam stern. An eternity later, she smiles.

"All right, then," she says, and leaves to get Jesse.

I'm flooded with relief and guilt and nerves. My fingers bounce 'gainst my thighs. When Liluye returns, I realize I'm pacing and stop cold. She walks Jesse to me, then disappears again without another word.

Standing before me, Jesse Colton don't look like himself. He's pale and his shoulders slouch. Dark circles sag beneath his eyes. His entire being looks beaten and worn. Even his usually squinty eyes don't have the energy to pinch half shut. His blood-encrusted shirt hangs open, partially unbuttoned, and in the pale moonlight I can make out the bandage wrapped round his chest.

"Hi," I says.

He don't even look at me, just keeps his gaze on the dirt between our boots. I could reach out and touch him, but he feels so far off.

"Jesse?"

He drops to his knees.

"Are you hurt? Do you need something?"

He glances up at me, and I know it ain't a physical pain. This is a cut that runs deeper, a scar that won't never fade. I can see the loss on his features, feel it in my chest like it were my own sibling stolen.

I crouch beside him. He's staring at his hands, which rest 'gainst his thighs, palms turned to the heavens.

"Jesse, I'm so sorry."

"It's my fault." His voice is dry and parched, like he's screamed it hoarse. "I got him killed. I—"

"I dragged you into it. You were tangled in this mess since I showed up at yer ranch."

"You tried to make us leave."

"But I struck that deal in Phoenix. I let you help me at the saloon, asked for yer guns 'gainst Rose, had you ride with me into these mountains."

"I'm a grown man, Kate. I made my own decisions and can claim responsibility for 'em. I didn't have to do any of it, but I wanted the gold. I chose to ride this path, to take the journal, to keep going. Even when Will were saying he had a bad feeling and didn't like it, I pushed on. And look where it got us. Look where it got *him!*"

"Jesse . . ."

"Goddamn it!" He grabs a rock and heaves it off the ridge. "Goddamn it." He keeps saying it, over and over, only each one sounds weaker than the next, till they're nothing but whispers. Till he's coming undone before me. Tears stream down his cheeks and it rips something open in my chest, 'cus Jesse Colton don't cry. He squints and jokes and criticizes and always has a plan. He ain't supposed to unravel.

"Jesse."

But he keeps making that awful sound, that pitiful moan, more animal than human. He won't look at me. Not when I say his name. Not when I touch his hand. Not even when I put my palm to his cheek.

"I shoulda died too."

"You don't mean that."

"I wish I never woke up."

"Jesse, no."

"I don't deserve to be alive. I fail everyone. I should be dead, I should be dead, I should be—"

I lean forward and crush my lips to his, drowning out the words. He flinches, pulls away.

"I'm sorry. I shouldn't've done that."

He's staring at me like he's seen a ghost.

"I don't want you dead, Jesse. You understand me? I don't wanna hear you talk like that, not ever again. You don't deserve to be dead any more than Will. Or yer ma or my pa or so many other folks that get taken before their time."

He don't say nothing.

What a dumb thing to do. What a stupid, desperate, dumb decision. But at least he ain't making that noise no more.

"Why aren't you furious with me?" he asks after a long moment. "I stole the journal and you came for me anyway. You saved me."

"Bodaway saved you."

"But I stole the journal."

"I know why you did it."

"Huh," he says. Jesse turns toward the horizon, dark beneath the sleeping sky.

"Jesse?"

"No more talking. Just sit with me?"

He reaches out, tentatively taking my hand.

And I let him.

The ceremonial rite is over when we get back to camp. The children are gone, likely to bed, 'long with most of the women. Bodaway sits with one of the male guards, smoking tobacco. The other sentries must be off at the mesa, protecting the perimeter.

The Apache watch us as we lay out our bedrolls beneath the stars. I ain't sure when they retire for the night, but soon enough I'm the only person awake. Jesse fell asleep almost instantly. He looks so worn beside me, so beaten. The bandage on his chest rises and falls with each breath. His hat's tipped low over his eyes, but I can see his lips still—slightly parted, full.

I touch mine, something tightening in my stomach.

He pulled away. He flinched.

It shouldn't sting as much as it do. I only did it to shut him up, to keep him from shattering. He weren't in a state of mind for kissing. It's unfair of me to have wanted anything from Jesse in that moment.

But I did. Still do.

Maybe I just want a distraction.

Maybe it's selfish greed.

Maybe I'm losing my mind out in this wild land and think Jesse can help me escape all the darkness.

I frown, running my thumb over the engraving in my Colt, and tell myself to see sense. I got a score to settle with Rose—for Pa, Will, and all those other souls he's struck down—and no boy's gonna be the reason my head's done hopped a runaway train. Not in a million years.

CHAPTER TWENTY-FIVE

"Up. Get up," I says, nudging Jesse with my boot.

He rubs his eyes, grumbling, and squints at the sky. It's still dark and heavy overhead, with a tiny sliver of soft red 'long the horizon. "The sun ain't even awake yet." He looks a little better today—more color in his cheeks.

"Good thing, too. We gotta hike outta this camp and into them canyons before the sun breaks over the horse-head rock."

"The landmark?"

I forgot he read the journal, already knows everything I do. "I saw it when I were scouting the Riders' camp, the evening before I came for you. It's partway down the other canyon, if you take the left fork. We get there in time, we'll know where the mine is. Soon as the sun shines over the rock form's neck, it'll light up a portion of hillside 'cross the canyon, marking the location."

Jesse pauses, bedroll half cinched to Waltz's burro.

"Well, we still got a deal, don't we?" I says. "I'm more ready than ever to see Rose take his last breath. Figured you'd be the same."

"But he's still got the journal."

"It don't matter. Not if those notes 'bout the horse-head rock are true."

I plop my Stetson on my head and fuss with my kerchief a minute, trying to ignore my aching skin. My forearms were red when I woke today, and tender to the touch.

"Kate, 'bout last night . . ."

"Don't worry 'bout it."

"I was a mess. Still am."

"I said don't worry 'bout it."

He frowns. I strap on my pistol belt. When I glance up, he's still looking at me. "So that's it? We're back to chasing Rose?"

"You don't wanna avenge Will?"

"That ain't what I'm saying."

"Well, what are you saying, Jesse? I can't hear words that ain't spoken."

He checks the bandage on his chest and sees to the buttons on his shirt. Finally, he says, "Reckon we should get to it then, huh?"

I pull my rifle from the scabbard strapped to the burro. "Just one thing before we go."

"Give this to Bodaway," I says, passing my Winchester to Liluye. "Payment for his healing."

"What's this?" Jesse asks.

"Liluye explained everything to me yesterday. The payment is a gift, a courtesy."

"I can pay for my own healing fine," Jesse insists. "Don't go giving up yer rifle. I know how much it means to you." He jogs over to the burro and pulls his long-barrel off. Balancing it 'cross his palms, he extends it to Liluye. "For . . ."

"Bodaway," I says.

"For Bodaway," Jesse echoes.

Liluye looks at him long and hard. Finally, she accepts the weapon. He gives her a fair bit of ammo, too.

"Lil . . ." he says.

"Liluye," I correct.

"Liluye." He don't pronounce it quite right, but he's trying. "I ain't been kind to you. I ain't never said a nice word in yer favor, nor looked you in the eye, and yet . . . I'm grateful. You did more for me than I deserved. You and yer people."

"I did the only fitting thing," she says.

Jesse looks shocked. "How's that?"

"When Kate came to me yesterday, you unconscious and halfway to the Happy Place, I looked at my options. If you died, I would not care. As you say, you have never been kind to me. But letting you die, not answering Kate's pleas . . . that path was lonely. I had lost my Spirit Guide, and so I examined again.

"Another path showed me bringing you to Bodaway. My mother—she is my guide—said that your time was not up. She suggested I call on Bodaway's Power. If Ussen

259

was not content to have you live, you would not. But He was. Last night I heard coyotes call in the canyons and owls sing to the skies, and I knew you would heal strong."

A part of me wants to point out that coyotes cry most nights round these parts, but I bite my tongue. I heard them same creatures last night and they felt like a gift, a soul that were listening. Whatever higher power Liluye believes in, there were something in that to get Jesse through a shadowy place. I reckon that magic's the same reason my folk worship the Lord from those cramped Prescott pews every Sunday. The same reason Pa had a crucifix hanging above his bed. I always thought it were a crutch, religion; the Word telling you what to think. Like poetry, it were another flowery thing to suck time away from the stuff needing doing. But now, after everything . . . I ain't so sure.

Maybe religion's there so we feel less alone, so that we have something to believe in when the world goes dark. Liluye speaks of her mother, her Spirit Guide, like she's a guardian angel always there to lead her. I screamed at God after Pa died, cried like a baby for Pa to come back to me, to say something—*anything*—so I didn't feel so lost. But I never truly believed I might be able to hear him. Or Him. And maybe that's my problem. Maybe I gotta believe in something other than my own two hands. I know life ain't always easy or fair or righteous, but going it alone sure hasn't helped me none. And last night, sending my prayers to the wide Arizona sky . . . that were the first time I felt like someone'd heard me since Pa passed.

"I'm sorry, Liluye. For how I treated you," Jesse says.

She nods.

"I mean it."

"She ain't deaf, Jesse." He shoots me a look, but Liluye's already moved on from the matter.

"If you need water," she says, "use the spring. What runs in the marsh is brackish and stale. And be smart. Not all of the tribe was pleased by your arrival. They worry you will violate Mother Earth in your quest for gold. If so many men were not away, I imagine they would track you."

"How many times I gotta explain I ain't after gold?" I says. "It ain't even Jesse's greatest concern no more neither."

He ain't told me this, but he don't speak otherwise, so I reckon it's true.

"It is complicated," Liluye says. "We hear 'White Eyes' speak of gold and can only think bad things. It is all we know from experience. Be careful."

"You got it, boss." I give her a small salute.

"What is that? I have seen it among White Eyes but never understood."

"A sign of recognition. A way to say, 'I hear you, I respect you, I acknowledge yer words.'"

Her mouth twitches into a pinched sorta smile.

"If I don't see you again, thanks for everything, Liluye. I hope you's found what you were looking for."

"You too, Kate Thompson."

We shake like we ain't two souls on opposing sides of a battlefield.

"Liluye," Jesse says, tipping his hat.

She nods, quiet.

And just like that, the Apache girl exits my life as unexpectedly as she joined it.

Jesse and me hike hard. He's doing well despite the injury. That or he's just hiding the struggle.

By the time we get back to the valley, the sky's lightened plenty. On flat desert plains it'd be above the horizon, but I reckon we got another hour or so till it's high enough to shine over the canyon ridge.

Where the trail divides, we take the left fork, moving closer to the horse-head. I lead, Jesse on my tail and the burros trailing us. The back of my neck is tingly, my fingers itching to pull my pistol. I got a notion a Rose Rider is waiting round every bend, fixing to send us to hell. Or the ghost shooter, camped somewhere in the rocky terrain, getting us in his sights, aiming to finish what he started yesterday. But when I scan 'long the ridge, there's no sign of a flashing barrel. The canyon is eerily quiet today. With each step, Weavers Needle grows, reaching into the sky taller than seems possible.

'Bout a half hour later, I point to a steep but small mesa located between the canyon path we took and the one we didn't. "If'n we climb this, we'll be able to see the horse-head to the southeast," I says. "And we should be high enough to view everything to the dead south."

"The light will hit somewhere in those hills?"

"It should. I'm almost positive this were the vantage point the journal said to use—the ridge between these two canyons."

Jesse checks the sky. "We better hike fast."

Nearly to the summit, we have to leave the burros. Jesse ties 'em to a scraggly tree growing from between rocks and takes his binoculars and his notebook with him.

He gives me a boost up the ledge that were impossible for the donkey. I pull myself up and am greeted with an unobstructed view of the Superstitions. The horse-head rock stands proud on the eastern ridge, and Weavers Needle pierces the sky a bit farther south. From here I can see she's tall, but not in the way I imagined. She's a spire rising outta an already massive mountainside. While hiking—when I couldn't see that mountain—I just pictured her an endless obelisk, a sword that climbed and climbed and climbed.

"Kate. A little help?"

I extend a hand to Jesse and help haul him atop our small mesa. The sky is a golden red, the sun moments away from breaking over the horse-head. We couldn't've cut it closer.

The mine supposedly sits in the shadow of Weavers Needle. This early in the morning, the Needle's shadow stretches away from us, toward the west, and the sun rising over the ridge is lighting up land directly before us, to the south. Jesse and I agree that the clue must be referencing the late afternoon sun, when the Needle's shadow will grow back this way, overlapping the same land to the south. So for now we choose to focus solely on the horsehead clue.

Jesse pulls out his binoculars and examines the rock form.

"Couple more minutes, I reckon. Wanna look?" He passes me the binoculars.

The sun's crawling slower than a slug, blocked by the back of the horse's head. Each minute feels like twenty, each new glint of light a tease. And then, finally, it breaks over the neck of the horse, sending light between the two pointy ears and down into the land before us.

The sun marks a larger area than I'd've hoped for. Could be 'cus we're standing in a different perch than the mapmaker, or maybe 'cus we's trying to use the horsehead clue in June when the journal claimed it useful in late summer.

I scan the lit-up earth through the binoculars. The sun's shining on the southern end of a smaller mountain. Or maybe it's just a big hill. What looks like a rough foot trail carves 'long the edge of it, but that ain't in the sunlight.

Beside me, Jesse's pencil scratches in his notebook. I peer over his shoulder and see a sketch of the terrain, an oblong circle marking the area the sun kissed. On the opposite page is a rough drawing of a girl, captured in profile. Her hat is tipped low, dark hair hanging to her chin. Her eyes are squinting, as if looking into glaring light. She seems angry and cold. But also determined. The pattern of her flannel matches mine.

I turn away, feeling like I's seen something private, and study our destination. Already the sun's rising higher, marking a larger and wider area as it climbs above the horse-head and into the sky.

"Maybe we can cut down the other side of this mesa and head straight for the hillside," I says. "Prolly the fastest route."

"Also the most rugged and the easiest to get turned round in." Jesse pulls out his compass and gauges our current location and where we reckon the mine might be at. "Almost due southwest." He clips the compass shut and slips it into his pocket, then does the same with his notebook. "I'll keep us on course. I just hope there ain't a chasm or some giant obstacle we can't make out waiting to turn us round."

"And the burros?" I says. "We gonna ditch all the gear?"

"If we have to. But let's try climbing down a few feet, then going round. We can prolly get past this mesa without going over the true summit."

We take one last look at our destination to the southwest, then scramble down to retrieve the burros. As Jesse unties the ropes, a gunshot cracks in the distance, rattling the still morning. Both our faces snap toward the sound, which is still ringing somewhere on the other side of the ridge we need to cross.

"Rose?" he says.

"Or that ghost shooter."

"There ain't no ghost shooter."

"Then who was up in the canyons during the shootout yesterday? Waltz said something unnatural's been prowling out here. And Will thought—"

"I know what Will thought," he snaps. Then he swallows, don't look me quite in the eye. "Let's just keep moving," he says.

There's a slouch to his shoulders as he slaps the burros' rumps and starts leading the way. It's the same look of defeat I saw in him last night, a sense of vast hopelessness. I wonder how many people Jesse Colton can bear losing before he won't be Jesse Colton no more.

CHAPTER TWENTY-SIX

The day's travel aint nothing but torture.

For every bit of progress we make, the end goal don't seem to be getting any closer. The sun is scorching my back, plus a bit of my scalp from where Rose's bullet stole away some of my Stetson. My burnt arms still ache within my sleeves. I'm grumpy and irritable, and the course is rough: jagged boulders we gotta navigate, cactuses and shrubs throwing up thorns like barbed-wire fencing. Jesse's doing his best to navigate it with ease, but I catch the truth: a hand pressed to the cut on his chest, a sharp breath drawn now and again.

A buzzard follows us for most of the morning, then gives up midday to scour for other food. We find a scrap of shade beside a tall rock ledge and stop for a quick rest. I drink from my canteen. Jesse chaws on some jerky and passes a bit to me. We don't say much, which suits me fine 'cus there ain't nothing to be said. Not till we're on that rough trail and closing in on Rose.

The afternoon is more of the same: rugged land and careful steps. We use some of Waltz's gear to descend a steep section of rock we can't go on foot. Jesse rigs the rope and everything, brow scrunched and focused. By the time we's done with the descent, the burros've found a route that wouldn't have required all that fancy ropework to begin with. We joke 'bout it, but the laughter between us is weak. We're tired and thirsty. Jesse's had too much time to think on Will and what Rose did to him. He's getting quieter by the minute, his features going dark.

When we stumble outta the worst of our downward climb and into a cactus-filled valley, the sky's being painted with a mighty fine sunset.

"We should prolly call the day quits," I says. "We ain't gonna make progress after dark."

Jesse just nods.

I do most of the work setting up the camp. I find a nice spot where our bedrolls can lie on more dirt than stone. I unload the gear. I let the burros graze, but never too far. It ain't worth being spotted, so I forgo a fire for the night. Dinner will be nothing but more jerky.

Jesse eats with his face a blank stone. He don't bother cleaning his Remingtons or sketching in his notebook. His eyes stay rooted on his boots, but he ain't really looking at 'em. Pa got taken from me and I turned into a fuming giant, a trap ready to spring. Will gets taken from Jesse and he's got no drive at all. No fire, no flare.

"Jesse?" I says.

"Hmm?"

"I'm worried 'bout you. You ain't yerself. You's been moving like yer brain is elsewhere from yer body."

He pulls his eyes up to look at me. "Kate, I gotta be nothing till I face Rose, or this anger's gonna destroy me. I gotta feel nothing till it's time to feel it all."

"Yer pacing yerself?"

"Not everybody's like you—enough fuel to blaze for weeks on end."

I push a bit of dirt round with my boot toe. "Maybe you *should* feel some of it. This ain't you, Jesse, and it's scaring me a little."

Will's story 'bout their mother comes to me, how Jesse quit talking and took to practicing with his pistol after her death like it were the only task that mattered. I feel like he's drifting again right now and if I don't pull him back, he's gonna become a ghost.

"Since when do you know me so well?" he says.

"It's been a slow thing. You sorta crept up on me when I weren't looking."

"Sneaky like Lil?"

There's a tiny slant to his lips, the shadow of a smile. Maybe I's just got to keep him talking.

"Nah, more like a rattler. I could hear you the whole damn time and yet I was still shocked when I got bit."

"I don't bite," he says.

"That so? 'Cus my head ain't been feeling right lately."

His smile widens. "Kate Thompson, are you saying you fancy me?"

"I ain't claiming nothing you can use 'gainst me."

In the moonlight, his grin looks brilliant and sharp. Like a small piece of the Jesse I know come burning back to life.

"Dance with me," he says, pushing to his feet and extending a hand.

"What, are you crazy?"

"Come on, Kate. I need a distraction. I need my mind elsewhere." He extends his hand farther. There's still a small upturn to his lips, and I wanna keep it there. I reach for him and he hauls me up. Or tries to. Soon as he's bearing some of my weight, he drops my hand and cringes, pressing a palm to the wound on his chest.

"You all right?" I says, scrambling up.

"I'm fine." He reaches for me again.

"But yer stitches . . . We should sit, make sure you don't—"

"I wanna dance."

His arm's still held out, waiting, and I don't got the energy to argue no more. I take his hand.

"There's no music," I says as we sway beneath the sky.

"Sure there is. Listen."

Alls I can hear is my own breathing. But then there's dirt beneath our heels, wind rustling the shrubs, the song of an owl in the distance. With my face so close to Jesse's chest, I find the drumbeat—his heart pounding between his ribs. Heat radiates off him like a fire. His skin grazing the inside of my wrist is making me warm. His palm pressed surely 'gainst the small of my back is the only thing holding me together. I swear my knees are failing. I swear I'll crumple and fall if'n he lets go.

"Where'd a wild gal like you ever learn to dance so proper?" he asks.

"Wild? I ain't wild."

His brows peak.

"Pa had me stand on his boots when I were young," I says. "He'd twirl me round the house like that till I were big enough to dance on my own. And by then there were gatherings in Prescott, celebrations and the like."

"I bet all the boys wanted to dance with you."

I don't say naught, 'cus there were a few, Morris included. But none of 'em ever made me feel so unsteady as Jesse. None of 'em made me feel much of nothing, to be honest.

"What 'bout you?" I says. "I didn't figure there'd be time for dancing while running cattle."

He spins me away from him, jerky and uneven on account of his injury, then guides me back. His hand presses me closer than I were before. "Not on the range, but we stop in civilization from time to time, and ain't no one passing up a dancehall on those nights."

I picture Jesse twirling some young belle round and flashing her squinty smiles. It makes my stomach coil.

"And girls danced with the likes of you?" I tease.

"If I managed to bathe first and put on a clean shirt, I couldn't fight 'em off."

"Such a gentleman."

"All cowboys are."

"Then I guess I ain't been riding with a cowboy these past days."

"Damn, yer impossible," he says. But his tone is light and he's smiling down at me. I notice for the first time how tall he is. I ain't short for a girl, and he's still a whole head taller.

"Kate?" he says soft.

We're close. Too close. We's stopped dancing.

His gaze trails over my face, pausing where I know my cheek is either split or bruised or both. I ain't sure why, but I reach for him, pressing a hand into his shirt. His heart thumps 'gainst my palm.

"Kate, I'd really like to kiss you."

My heart kicks in my chest.

"Proper, of course," he adds. "And only if you want it."

I look at his collar, speechless, frozen. I *do* want it. I only just realized it last night, but I think I's wanted it since that night in the shanty when we talked 'bout reading. Maybe even since White Tank.

"Stupid," Jesse mutters, turning away. "The other night was . . . you only did that to . . ." He faces me again. "I'm sorry, Kate. I'm stupid and I'm sorry and—"

I grab him at the neck and pull him nearer. His mouth is warm and soft when it meets mine, his jaw rough 'gainst my skin. He leans into the kiss, arms gathering me up, and I swear a part of my head drifts right outta my body. I don't got a clue what I'm doing, but he seems to, so I let him lead. I let him lead like we're still dancing, and I follow blind, praying I ain't awful while trying to keep my knees strong, 'cus I wouldn't be shocked if they buckled and broke right here. Jesse Colton tastes like spice and tobacco and sweet mountain air, like salt and sweat from our travels. He feels like home and smells like mountains and I can't get enough. My one hand grips him tighter at the neck. The other curls into the front of his shirt.

He breaks free. Takes a quick step away and stands there staring.

"Were it awful?" I says.

"Kate, it were so not awful, I gotta keep my distance else you won't think I'm much of a gentleman. The last thing I want is to be on yer bad side."

"You scared of me, Jesse Colton?"

"So what if I am? I's seen what you can do to a man. I don't want that to be me."

"Pest."

He's still smiling, so carefree, it makes my chest hurt. So unburdened, alls I can do is smile back.

We settle onto our bedrolls. Jesse stretches out, ankles crossed. I sit cross-legged, feeling antsy.

"I'm glad you got shot 'long the Agua Fria," he says a moment later.

"What?"

"I mean, I ain't glad for the bullet or the pain. But I'd still be thinking you were Nate, some hotheaded, too-scrawny boy from Prescott, if it weren't for that day."

"Really? 'Cus you were awful to me after the Agua Fria, Jesse. *Awful*. Judging and goading, and what you said 'bout me in that dress!"

"Well, what if I suddenly revealed I were someone else entirely? I felt betrayed, Kate. I felt used. And then it only got more confusing in the coming days when I started looking at you proper. When I started noticing how truly tough you are, and determined, and loyal. And then what you did for me with Liluye, even after everything. I'm sorry 'bout the journal."

"I know. We both wronged each other at least once, but that's the past now. And ain't you the one always saying there's no point dwelling there?"

He smiles small. A moment later he clears his throat, glances at me sideways. "For what it's worth, you looked damn fine in that dress. Not quite like the Kate I know, but that don't mean you didn't do it proud."

I smile despite myself. I prefer to blend into the background, to be overlooked so I can scurry as I see fit. But knowing Jesse's eyes were on me like that, knowing he liked what he were seeing . . . It makes that twisty sensation flare up in my stomach.

We're in this together, the both of us vindictive and driven and vengeance bound. I can't imagine sitting here alone, having to face Rose with just my Colt. I know now how foolish it were to think I could take him myself—one lone girl 'gainst a vicious outlaw. Rose is a two-man job at least, a hellhound needing an army to contain him.

"No matter what happens tomorrow," I tell Jesse, "I'm with you till the end on this. If we go in blazing and never come out, that's fine by me. I got nothing to go home to anyway."

"You got me," he says. His face is pained and serious, brows drawn down as he squints at me in the darkness. He reaches out and brushes the pad of his thumb 'gainst my cheek. Then he draws me into another kiss.

When Jesse's mouth opens to mine, I lose all sense of what's decent. I forget that I'm sweaty and I smell and we both need a bath. My hands move on their own — exploring the shape of his jaw, his collarbone, his shoulders. I push his hat off so I can thread my fingers through his hair. Somehow I end up in his lap, and the tiny groan he breathes into my mouth is like a blow to the heart. He gathers me up and twists, bringing me back to his bedroll. His lips move to my neck and his hands to my waist. He pulls my flannel till it's untucked, starts undoing the buttons.

I want him to go faster. I want him to never stop. I want my shirt off and my skin bared to him and us closer, and —*God almighty, what is wrong with me?* We're in the middle of the Arizona wilderness. A coyote could be creeping into our camp. A Rose Rider could be taking aim from the mountains. Every potential danger has gone and flown my mind 'cus Jesse Colton's hands are on my body and I can't think straight with him towering over me like this. Can't think at all.

"Jesse?"

He pauses, lifts his head to look me in the eyes.

"I think we should stop."

"All right." He sits up slow and watches as I start fastening my shirt. Even though he ain't asked, I feel like I owe him a reason.

"I gotta have my head straight, Jesse. And you make it so my head's . . . not."

He just nods.

"Yer mad."

"No," he says, sincere. "We should prolly sleep anyway. Tomorrow's gonna be a trial."

A trial we might not make it through. Suddenly I realize this mighta been my only chance. This is a thing I ain't done, and for the first time in my life I think I might want it, only I pushed it away 'stead of grabbing it by the horns.

Jesse plucks his hat from where it fell and smacks dust off the brim. He catches me watching and his brow scrunches. "What?" he says.

"Did I ruin this? Whatever *this* is?"

That makes him smile.

"No. Don't ever think that. You didn't ruin nothing." He draws one of his pistols and starts cleaning it. "Sleep well, Kate. I'll take first watch."

CHAPTER TWENTY-SEVEN

By midday, Jesse and I's found the rough foot trail we spotted from our mesa the previous morning. Cutting north, we follow it toward the hillside that supposedly holds the mine.

It don't take long to realize that our perch yesterday made the trail look far less rugged and potholed than it is, and that it cuts into more of a ravine than a hill.

I remember a note in Pa's journal claiming that afternoon light shines into the mouth of the mine, so I tell Jesse to focus on the eastern edge of the ravine. But as we walk the footpath, trying not to roll our ankles, my hope shrivels and prunes. The ridge is overgrown with shrubs and cactuses. Rock pillars rise up like fence posts, and where they ain't towering, they congregate in loose piles. We could prolly walk within ten feet of the mine and not even see it. Unless we take to crawling every inch of this land, I don't see how we'll get lucky.

I grab Jesse's binoculars, looking ahead for any sign of Rose's burros. There ain't nothing but rugged wilderness for as far as I can see.

"Didn't the journal say something 'bout marked cactuses?" Jesse says.

"Someone hacked limbs off a few saguaros so they only pointed you in the right direction." I glance round, but nothing in a stone's throw looks remotely tampered with. "That were years ago, though, long before we were born. The saguaros coulda sprouted new limbs by now."

"And the tree—weren't there a clue with a tree?"

"A palo verde not far from the mine. It's got no bark, according to Pa's notes, and a distinctly odd shape pointing toward the entrance."

We scan the land before us. The palo verdes crop up by the thousands, speckling the rocky landscape like vibrant flowers.

"I'm an idiot," I says. "It all sounded so easy on paper, like I'd just walk out here and find one lone palo verde tree waiting to guide me true."

"Are we even in the right canyon?" Jesse says.

"I don't know, Jesse. I really don't—"

"Shhh! You hear that?"

"Hear what?"

Something clanks in the distance.

"That."

We stand bone still, waiting. A few seconds later, the

noise strikes again. It sounds like a pickaxe on rock, or a hammer. Like a person mining.

"Come on," Jesse says, and starts leading the way off the footpath and up into the ravine. The burros manage to stay with us despite the extremely rough terrain.

We keep climbing, moving steadily north through the pass as we go. But the higher we get, the harder it is to pinpoint the sound of the pickaxe. It bounces off the surrounding rocks, echoing and throwing us off.

"Hang on. What's that?" I point 'cross the canyon to what looks like a small cave. There's something distinctly manmade in its mouth.

Jesse checks with his binoculars.

"Looks like a stone house."

He lets me have a turn.

The house—if it can even be called that—ain't much larger than a horse's pen. I don't remember a note 'bout this in the journal, but I also stuck to the maps and drawings, to the pages that held Pa's handwriting.

"Kate," Jesse says, nudging my shoulder. I lower the binoculars and follow his pointed finger to a shadowy alcove on our side of the canyon, maybe a few-dozen yards ahead. Another cave, perhaps.

But that ain't what's caught Jesse's eye.

No, there's movement there. Something swaying.

I peer through the binoculars and find a burro snapping his tail at flies.

"It's them," I whisper. "Or one of 'em, at least."

Jesse puts a finger to his lips, then nudges his head

for me to follow. Cautious and quiet as possible, I trail Jesse, watching my step round brambles and shrubs, and always keeping a spare hand 'gainst some bit of rock so I don't lose my footing.

We close in on the burro. He's standing in the mouth of what is indeed another cave, only the entrance has been boarded up with rocks and tree trunks. Even standing in front of the cave, it don't look like much.

As Jesse's pistols twitch to and fro, checking for threats, I skirt by him and duck round the blocked-up entrance.

It takes a minute for my eyes to adjust to the dark, and when they do, the first thing I see is the gold.

It glints where it's piled in the rear of the cave. Placer nuggets as large as my palm. Others smaller, but still nothing to shrug at. This ain't the mine, but a cache. And wherever the mine is, it must have one hell of a vein, rich in free gold that can be chipped and cracked out by mere hammer. The burro-driven arrastres in Prescott ground and cracked earth for hours on end only to produce tiny particles the size of pebbles and dust—like what I got left in Pa's leather pouch—but nothing like this. I ain't never seen such large pieces.

I tear my eyes from the gold and take in the rest of the cave. A bit of Rose's gear is dropped 'gainst the side wall: cooking equipment, a lump of clothes, *Pa's journal*.

I dart forward and grab it up, my chest singing as the cool leather meets my skin. I tuck it into the back of my pants and freeze solid.

The lump of clothes ain't a lump of clothes at all.

It's a man, curled up and sleeping with his back facing me.

I cock my pistol, cringing at the noise it makes. Then I press the muzzle into the Rider's back. "Don't move," I whisper.

And he don't. He don't even flinch.

Frowning, I put my hand to his shoulder and pull. The body rolls toward me, lurching like dead weight. His face is a butchered mess; nose broken for sure, lips cracked and bloody, skin stained red from a gash 'long his brow. A nasty raw wound on the Rider's chest suggests a gunshot, but there ain't a rose carved in his forehead, not yet at least, so he must still be—

His eyes flash open, and his hands come up, gripping me at the neck and cutting off my air. I'm so shocked, I drop my gun.

"Tompkins," he gasps.

I reach blindly for my Colt but can't find it. My fingers go to his, clawing and prying 'em back. He's weak and drained, and it ain't a hard fight. By the time Jesse hears me coughing and races into the cache, I's already scrambled free.

"Tompkins," the Rider says again, this time staring down Jesse. "He's gonna kill her."

"Like he tried with you?" Jesse says.

The Rider just laughs, a low, chuckling gurgle. I think he's drowning in his own blood. I think he's already half dead.

"He's got a plan, Rose . . . always. He's got the gold . . . and he'll turn on Tompkins next. Just like he turned on me. Like he turned on all of us." He pants, breathes deep. "He'll kill everyone. He'll send y'all to God with a rose on yer forehead, and he'll whistle while doing it." His eyes lock with Jesse. "Exactly like he did when he strung up yer brother."

Jesse kicks him hard in the side. The Rider howls, and in the time it takes me to blink Jesse's drawn his Remingtons and pressed one to the bastard's temple.

"Don't!" I says, leaping forward and pushing Jesse's arm away. "The mine's nearby. If'n we can hear the pickaxe, you better bet Rose'll hear yer gun. Besides, this guy's already gone. He ain't gonna make it much longer."

A vein bulges in Jesse's neck as he swallows hard. In the end, he holsters his weapons. When he stands, his fingers dangle lazily near his six-shooters, but it's a ruse, a game. I's seen it in rattlers—a steady, indifferent sway before the attack.

"Come on, Kate," he says. "It's time to kill us an outlaw."

CHAPTER TWENTY-EIGHT

The pickaxe sounds like a bell tolling.

When we look careful, we can spot their path—boot prints where the ground's more dust than rock, snapped bits of sagebrush where they walked quickly through a patch. I wonder how long Rose let his last remaining man help him haul out gold before he decided it weren't worth the extra labor, before he left him for dead back in that cache.

Ahead, and a bit to our left, I spot the palo verde tree Pa'd mentioned in the journal. You wouldn't look twice at it if you didn't know it were a marker. Half its bark is indeed missing and it's grown at a crooked angle, buckling over a rock so its limbs seem to motion up the rocky bluff we're already climbing.

I point it out to Jesse, but if he's acknowledged me, it

don't show. He's a man on fire, a fuse burned down to its last bit of wick.

We scramble-climb up the rocky ledge, working our way toward the pickaxe chant in silence. Sweat drips down my back and between my breasts. I can hear my pulse beating in my ears, but I push on. Even when the pickaxe stops chiming, we don't slow.

After heaving ourselves over a wide, flat boulder, we find a somewhat level ledge. Looking back the way we came, I can see the foot trail winding through the ravine below and, in the distance, Weavers Needle looming proud.

But before us . . .

Before us and just beyond a wild bunch of mountain brush and a cluster of angry, jagged rock that piles 'bout waist high is the mine. We walk toward it together and peer in.

It's a deep, funnel-shaped pit, its edges lined with planks of wood to serve as footholds and handholds. Jesse picks up a rock and tosses it down, but it must've hit the makeshift ladder 'long the way, 'cus it clanks several times before going silent, making it hard to tell how deep the mine goes.

We wait, silent, expecting a voice to come up from the depths. It never does. The pickaxe ain't striking no more, but I know we're in the right place. So where . . .

"Where is he?" I says to Jesse.

There's the crunch of gravel back near the ledge, the sound of a hammer cocking. "Behind you," says Waylan Rose.

We both cock our guns and spin round, ready to shoot together, but our barrels pull up at the same time.

He ain't alone.

Waylan Rose has his left arm curled round a woman, pinning her to his chest. His other arm extends over her shoulder so the barrel of his six-shooter points our way.

His hostage ain't much to look at. Streaks of gray mark the woman's dark, matted hair, which hangs to where her faded trousers are belted with a piece of fraying rope. Her shirt is sweat stained and tattered, her skin darkened by the sun. Toughened, too. It looks too loose round her neck, too wrinkled at the corners of her eyes. Like a vulture's. I can't tell if she's forty or closer to double that, though there's something youthful 'bout her fearful expression.

"Toss those six-shooters," Rose says, "or mama dearest gets it."

"Sierra!" the woman gasps. "Sierra, do what he says. Please!" Her dark eyes are locked on me, desperate and wide.

"I ain't messing," Rose growls, and brings his pistol to the woman's temple. She seems to dissolve in his grasp, knees buckling. It's only his grip that keeps her upright as her hands claw at the forearm trapping her.

"Sierra, I'm sorry I left. I'm so sorry. But you don't want me dead for that, do you? We can start over. We can fix everything."

"Who in the hell is Sierra?" I snap.

Her expression pales. "You, darling. Yer Sierra."

"I'm Kate."

"No," she says, shaking her head. "We named you after the mountains where we found gold. We named you after the place that changed our lives."

And just like that, the moments surge before me, flashing in a spark of truth. The bed, always still. The door, always pulled. That memory of a kitchen that weren't ours *was,* only in Tucson. Those bright colors were her heritage, Mexican roots Pa stamped out after we moved north.

I were young. I wouldn't remember it in time—all those childhood memories. 'Specially how he buried her when I weren't home.

'Cus there was nothing to see.

She was never in that bed, or that grave.

She was never, ever sick.

She left us. She left, and Pa moved me north, and he tried to protect me from the hurt. Maybe he thought she'd eventually come back to us, choose family. Maybe he kept the act going as long as possible, till a faked death were the only way to keep my memory of her pure and clean and something worth loving.

I stare at the woman before me, trying to see past the dirt caked in her skin, the wrinkles brought out by sun. I erase 'em with my mind, turn her graying hair dark, picture her in the same dress she's wearing in our family portrait. Suddenly alls I can see is features I recognize: those proud cheekbones, her bronzed skin, eyes that pierce right through to my soul, awakening something that's been sleeping a long, long time.

"Ma?" I says.

"Yes, darling." A tear breaks over her cheek.

"But . . . you left us. Why would you leave us?"

"It's complicated."

"No it ain't! You don't leave. You got family, you stick by 'em. Plain and simple."

"If you just let me explain . . ."

"There ain't gonna be any explaining if you two don't toss those damn six-shooters!" Rose screams.

Jesse only aims his surer, but I drop my arm.

"Kate . . ." he says.

"She's my mother, Jesse. Lower yer damn pistol."

"Kate, it ain't right. Where'd she come from? How'd she get out here? We ain't seen nobody for days."

Which I can't deny, but I also can't have her death on my conscience, and I certainly won't have Waylan Rose murder the last bit of family I got left.

He kicks her in the back of the legs and she falls to her knees, sobbing. Rose presses his gun to her skull.

"Jesse, toss yer damn pistols!" I scream.

His gaze stays forward, and I know he's considering the shot. Rose ain't fully shielded no more, but the bastard's weapon is already aimed, his hammer cocked, his trigger finger faster than the both of us.

"Please," I says to Jesse. *"Please."*

He bites his bottom lip and lets out a small growl but lowers his arm. I toss my Colt in the dirt between us and Rose, then nod at Jesse. It takes a painfully long moment, but he surrenders his twins.

"Finally," Rose says, shoving my mother forward. "Maria, if you wouldn't mind?"

She crawls toward the weapons, retrieves them, and stands. Only, she don't turn round and shoot Rose in the face.

She walks back to him calm as ever and shakes his hand.

"Thank you kindly," he says, accepting my Colt from her.

She twirls Jesse's twins round her forefingers, smiling. "Pleasure's mine."

"But he . . . Yer working with . . . ? How can you *help* him?" I practically shout.

"I hired him," she says plain. "Waylan and his boys have been after the gold in my mountains for ages, but my rifle usually fends 'em off and keeps 'em at a distance. It were only this past winter, when my cache ran dry, that I thought he could be useful 'stead of a nuisance." She keeps spinning Jesse's pistols. She looks like a completely different person now. Not desperate or weak, but wild.

"There are three caches and one mine, see? I used to have maps marking the location of 'em all, but someone stole the journal from me. I searched for six straight seasons and managed to locate only one of the caches — the one farthest from here, and it sustained me a good long while 'cus it were already stocked with gold. But early this winter I showed myself to Waylan 'stead of running him off. Told him a man by the name of Ross Henry Tompkins had a journal mapping the way to the mine and that I suspected he'd gone north out of Tucson. I told Waylan if'n he could get me the journal, he could take all he could carry once we located the gold."

"And he didn't shoot you right then and there?" Jesse scoffs.

"I showed myself from the mountains," she sneers. "With them in my sights and plenty of distance between us. Plus a good bit of dynamite buried right where they were standing. They stayed nice and still and listened to my offer.

"But Waylan left and the months passed. I figured he'd failed, or abandoned the matter. I went back to my search, combing this land inch by inch, not leaving a single stone unturned. Imagine my shock when I discovered Waylan back in the canyons and heard one of his men ranting 'bout gold — how they got the journal, and the ore could be theirs if only they killed that damn Tompkins. So I did what any respectable woman would do. I shot the bastard in the head, and as many of the others as I could get in my sights."

"It was *you* firing from the ridge," I says. That day I thought it were me Hank wanted to kill, but it were her he wanted dead: the ghost shooter in the mountains, the woman who'd get most of the gold if they stuck to their deal. "You nearly killed me!"

"If I'd known you were my own flesh and blood, I'd've aimed different. But, sweet, yer dressing an awful lot like a boy these days."

And right then it dawns on me why Rose changed the details of our trade, why he wanted me in exchange for

Jesse. I were to be a bartering tool. Once he learned I was Henry's kid, he knew I were also Maria's. He planned to use me 'gainst her as he just used her 'gainst me: hold a gun to my temple till she dropped her weapon, giving him the opportunity to shoot her dead and clear out the mine. Why bother sharing the gold when he could have it all to himself?

It explains why he killed off his last man in that cache. Why he only shot my hat that day at the trade for Jesse 'stead of dropping me cold. Why he appeared to hesitate in the Tiger, when I confirmed who I were. He's been planning this since that very moment.

Maria scratches her scalp with the gun's barrel and turns to Rose. "Lucky I missed you that day, Waylan, don't you say? Only got yer hat. And then you brought that journal to me like a well-trained dog." She whistles low. "How was it you said you found it again?"

"We were in Casa Grande when we got word a man done spent a suspicious amount of solid gold ore on a doctor for his kin. We traced the tale to Prescott, then his homestead on the Granite Creek."

The doc who came when I had scarlet fever . . . That joke he made 'bout gold pay that weren't really a joke at all.

Maria smiles. "It were Ross's—Henry's—only slip in all those years, and it were dire."

"I can't believe you," I says through my teeth. "You hired Waylan Rose, a notorious outlaw and bloodthirsty criminal, to get back a *journal?* He killed my father. He hanged him from our mesquite tree!"

"It were a regrettable but necessary action."

"Necessary? He was yer husband once!"

"And he *stole* you from me," she snarls. "He took you in the middle of the night and left. It were *me* who spent months on end in these mountains, gathering ore from the cache and lugging it home. *Me* who kept us rich and living in comfort. And how did he thank me? He took you, a heap of gold, and the maps, then disappeared. And how dare he rename you! I give you a beautiful name like Sierra, and he changes it to something as boring as Kate."

"If you knew me at all, you'd see it fits me better. But that ain't no shock, hearing you were outta sorts with reality. Pa said it weren't safe in Tucson no more, that folks were threatening yous. He said leaving were the only option."

"Yer father was a coward and a yellow-bellied weakling," she snaps.

"If you were even half the person my father were, you'd've had the courage to show up in Prescott and hang him yerself."

She strikes me 'cross the cheek with Jesse's pistol, and my vision streaks white.

"You watch yer tongue. Think hard 'bout who's the villain here. I ain't gonna coddle you like Ross mighta, but at least I ain't lied to you. How honest has yer father been, truly? From what Waylan tells me, there's a grave marker beneath that mesquite tree bearing my name. If'n yer pa's fabricated half yer life, ain't it possible he's the vile one? Everything I did in those early years, I did for our family. And all he did was leave."

"I think a lust for gold drove you mad," I says through a snarl. "If you can't live in peace—if yer fearing yer own neighbors in the night—what's the point of being rich? Gold don't keep you safe."

"But it sure can buy happiness."

What sort of happiness? As far as I can tell, she ain't left these mountains in years. She's prolly been living in that sad stone house we saw, likely trades with Apache for whatever supplies she can't get herself, keeping her quest for gold quiet. I wouldn't even be surprised if the dynamite she mentioned came from a deal with Waltz.

Watching her go on like this, crazed and unsound . . . It causes something to splinter in my chest. Pa lied to me, yes. He spun yarns and told half truths and kept secrets most of his life. But he did all of it to keep me safe, to shelter me, to spare me from knowing the monster standing before me now.

I were supposed to think she were dead. I weren't to know 'bout the gold and the way it destroyed our family. If'n his past came to catch him, I were to go to Abe's and stay there and move on with my life. But I'm too reckless and wild and angry. I had to keep digging, had to avenge his blood. And it makes me wonder if all the bad in me— all those men I's shot and killed—is part of this stranger, this woman twirling Jesse's guns. Is there more of her in my veins than Pa? Am I more bad than good, more revenge than forgiveness?

I couldn't move on. Like her, hunting down the journal, I couldn't just bury Pa beneath that tree and move on.

"For the love of God," Rose says to Maria. "You gonna berate her all day, or can we silence 'em?"

"You expect me to kill my own daughter?"

"Why not? You had no trouble letting me kill yer husband."

"I had it all planned out, my future set," Maria says. "And yet . . . now that my flesh and blood is standing before me, everything's looking different. My, my, this do present a problem." She shakes her head in mock concern. "All this gold finally back in my hands and two extra brains knowing where to find it."

"Christ, just shoot 'em or I'll do it for you!" Waylan Rose snarls.

"I don't think yer understanding me," Maria says, voice thinning. *"One."* She motions at Jesse, then turns to Rose and looks him dead in the eye. *"Two."*

"We had a deal," he says. "If'n I bring you the journal, I leave with as much gold as I can carry."

"I know," she says, sighing, "but I just changed my mind."

She aims and he aims, and Jesse and me drop to the ground, covering our heads as the bullets fly.

CHAPTER TWENTY-NINE

When I look up, Maria is dragging herself toward a stout rock for shelter, one leg hanging limp. Already her trouser thigh is red. But somehow, 'gainst all odds, she were the quicker shot, 'cus Rose is in worse shape. He's dropped to his knees, fingers touching the front of his coat. When he pulls them away, they're wet with blood. He topples backward so he's splayed to the sky, legs bent beneath him.

I dart forward.

A gunshot cracks from where Maria's hiding, and I swear I feel a bullet whiz by my ear. So much for not wanting to shoot her own daughter.

I see Jesse dive for her out of the corner of my vision. He tackles her to the ground, and I can hear their scuffle as he attempts to restrain her, but I don't pause to watch. The only thing in my sights is Waylan Rose.

As I bear down on him, he's breathing shallow, trying to hold his blood in even though it's already seeping from his chest and between his fingers.

He raises an arm, but I stomp my boot on his wrist, pinning the pistol—*my* pistol—to the earth. I pry it from his bloody fingers. His free hand raises the other Colt, and I react. No thinking, all flow.

Cock, aim, fire.

He drops the pistol, recoiling in pain. My bullet went right where I intended: the meaty part of his arm.

I lean forward as he cringes. My shadow falls over him. My Colt's humming as I bring the barrel in line with Rose's forehead.

I got him, Pa. It's gonna end right now. I'm gonna make everything right.

"I'm worth more alive than dead," Rose says through a grimace.

"Yer already dying, and I don't want a single dollar from you. You ain't worth nothing. Even the buzzards feasting on you will be a better fate than you deserve."

He starts laughing, a shrill, haughty wheeze.

"You gonna do it, honey? Or you gonna stand there jawing me to death?"

As I reach for the trigger, he coughs up a heap of blood. His teeth are stained red. His blue eyes don't look vicious no more. They're scared and wide and so damn desperate. Is this what Pa's eyes looked like when he gazed up at his killers?

"Do it," Rose says. A gurgle of blood reaches his lips. "Please."

He's far beyond saving, and for a moment I consider walking away. 'Cus it would make him suffer more. 'Cus he deserves to feel every ounce of this pain. I want it to last a million years. I want him to burn for eternity. I should carve a damn rose in his forehead first so he knows just how rotten he is.

But then I'll be just like him.

I'll be like Maria.

I'll be more bad than good, more revenge than forgiveness. And I wanna be like Pa, a person who believes most people mean well deep down and will help a soul in need. I wanna start living again without this boiling, vile blackness inside me, this scar that feels like it's never any closer to healing. I wanna move on.

So I do the merciful thing, even though he don't deserve it.

I cock my Colt and press the muzzle to Rose's forehead.

"God help you," I says, and pull my trigger.

A well of blood surges on his forehead, trickles down his face. His eyes stay rooted on the sky overhead, as blue as ever but wide and lifeless. I snatch the second Colt from where Rose dropped it, gripping the twin pair tight.

I got him, Pa. It's over.

A scuffle back near the mine pulls me from the moment. Maria's still got both Jesse's guns. She throws an elbow, catching him off guard. As he takes a step away, trying to catch his balance, she raises one of the pistols. There's a smile on her lips.

And even though I know I ain't quick enough, even though I know I'm beat and Jesse's already doomed, I lift my Colts. I imagine it another way, a different ending. I aim, cock, and fire faster than I's ever done in my life. My right Colt, then the left, then the right again.

And in that moment, time seems to slow.

I see every last strand of Maria's graying hair drifting on the breeze. I see her finger stretching for the trigger. I see the barrel of my pistols flare. My first bullet misses. The second nicks her arm. The third strikes her just below the shoulder.

Time snaps to speed.

She drops one of the Remingtons, stumbles backward. She touches her bloody shoulder and her gaze jerks to meet mine. Before I so much as blink, she raises the second weapon.

There's a blast and I buckle, grabbing at my chest. Feeling, searching. But I breathe deep and it don't hurt. My fingers come away from my shirt dry.

I look up. The pistol slips from Maria's grasp, clattering to a standstill at her feet. A patch of red blooms over her heart.

Jesse stands not a few paces away, his arm extended and the Remington still smoking in his grasp. He musta grabbed it when my shot caused Maria to drop one of the guns.

Maria teeters, staggers away. Her hip hits the rocks bordering the mine, hard, and like a flower blasted off a cactus, she loses purchase. Her momentum sends her back, over the rocks, falling headfirst into the funneled pit.

Soon as she disappears from sight, Jesse races for me, but I shove past him in a trance. Move to the mine. Peer in.

I can no longer see Maria Tompkins. She's somewhere at the base of the pit, broken and buried with the gold she loves so much. Afternoon sun filters into the shaft, lighting up the walls. Veins of gold glint and sparkle, snaking thick as they dive from view. It's mesmerizing, almost peaceful.

I slide my Colt into my holster, wedge its twin between my belt and waistband. Then I breathe deep, turn.

Jesse's standing where I left him. He's got a bloody nose and a faint pink line on his shirt. His cut must've opened during the struggle.

"I'm sorry," he says, expression pale. "I only meant to disarm, but I had to fire so fast and . . . I didn't have a choice, Kate. She was gonna shoot you."

I glance at the mine. I feel . . . I ain't sure what I feel. "She weren't my mother," I says finally. "Not the one I remember."

Jesse checks the bandages on his chest, wipes his bloody nose on his sleeve. Then he toes the body at his feet.

"You got Rose," he says.

"I guess I did."

I stare off toward Weavers Needle, words failing me. It's over. It happened so fast and I don't know what to do with myself. I feel surprisingly empty.

"What now?" I says.

"Now"—Jesse squints into the sun—"now we can go home."

We return to the cache to get Waltz's burro.

"Should we take some of it?" Jesse says, eyeing the gold.

"It ain't ours to take. Remember what Liluye said?"

"But think of how much it could buy."

"It's tainted, Jesse, cursed. I don't want it."

He considers that a moment.

"I forgot," I says, reaching into my pockets. "I held on to these for you." I hand over the half-empty packet of dip and Will's kerchief. Then I fuss with the gear on our burro till I'm able to yank Will's pistol belt free. I pass that over too.

Of all the items, Jesse holds the packet of dip like it's the greatest treasure.

"When you found him . . . was he . . . ?"

"Yeah," I says. "I took care of it, said a few words."

"Thanks, Kate."

There's tears building, his eyes big and glossy, but he don't let them fall.

"You know, I think yer right," he says, hardening his features. "'Bout the gold. I don't want it neither."

I nod, and we leave it at that.

We decide to take Rose's extra burros. Waltz can prolly sell 'em in Phoenix and get a bit of extra coin outta the matter. It's the least we can do for the old miner. We'd've been lost without his burro and the loaned prospecting gear. Plus, neither of us feels good 'bout leaving the poor creatures to starve.

When we're back at the base of the ravine and on the potholed trail, I look up at the eastern face of the rocks. I can't see no sign of the mine or the cache. It's like they were never even there, like we stumbled upon another world.

"I think if we take this trail north, we'll join up with Needle Canyon," Jesse says. "Least, it looked that way through the binoculars from the mesa."

I pull Pa's journal from the back of my pants. One of the map drawings says Jesse's theory's true. "And then backtrack to Waltz's?" I ask.

"I reckon so."

A foreign whizz sounds, and something strikes the path no more than five paces before us. An arrow.

We freeze in our tracks. Even the burros seem to stop twitching their tails.

I spin round, scanning the ridges that surround us. One by one, they step into view—perhaps a half dozen in total, all men. They's got bows held in hand, and hide shirts belted at their waists. I recognize a pair of 'em as the young men who greeted me on the mesa two days back and took me to see Liluye.

"Apache," Jesse murmurs.

I know I should be scared. I know everything I's ever heard suggests I should be running right now. But I just raise my palm and acknowledge that I see 'em.

One of the men I know steps forward and raises his hand in response.

I wait, breath held, expecting arrows to rain down on us like they did on the Peraltas. But the man simply turns round and leaves. The others follow, till they's disappeared as quietly as they arrived.

"What in the . . . ?"

"I think they were just checking," I says to Jesse. "We didn't take any gold. We waved 'stead of running."

Jesse shudders. "Let's just keep moving. And fast."

"Fine by me," I says.

So we do.

CHAPTER THIRTY

By the time we stumble outta Boulder Canyon two days later, Jesse and me are sweaty, sunburnt, and damn near starving. When Waltz's shanty comes into view, my legs feel like giving out. The Salt's glistening behind the house, sparkling and looking like heaven.

Waltz comes hobble-running to greet us, and when he sees our group's only two large, he pulls up short.

"Where's . . ."

I shake my head fast. Waltz drops the question, but the grimace remains on his face, not quite shielded by his beard. He's got the decency to not tell us he tried to give fair warning.

We stagger into his tiny house for some shade, where we gulp down fresh water and wipe sweat from our brows. When I'm feeling a bit reenergized, I leave the men talking and head outside to unload the animals.

I take care of Waltz's burro first, separating Jesse's, Waltz's, and my gear into different piles. Then I move on to the creature Jesse rode to the Apache stronghold while injured. Poor thing's still got blood caked into his coat. I let them two go graze and turn to the two remaining burros—the ones we took from the cache.

Their saddlebags look heavy.

Unnaturally heavy.

I flip one open and brilliance flares up at me.

For a minute I think I'm seeing it wrong. I blink, expecting the image to change, but no. The saddlebag's filled with gold. Some pieces the size of a fingernail, others large enough to fill my palm. I race round the burro and flip open the other saddlebag. More gold ore. So much, a few pieces rain out, spilling over my boots.

I don't know how we didn't see it when leaving. Were we too concerned 'bout getting home? Too blinded by stopping Rose at long last and escaping the mountains alive? Unless Jesse . . .

I check the second burro. Not as much gold packed on this one, but still enough to fill the saddlebags 'bout halfway.

I sink my hands in and grab a fistful.

"You damn rascal," I says, plowing through Waltz's door and holding my hands out to Jesse. "When'd you do it, 'load 'em up like that?"

"I didn't," he says, staring dumbstruck at the ore in my hands. His eyes are so wide, I know it's true. "Rose musta been loading his burros before we got there."

I feel terrible 'bout it. Like I lied to Liluye, betrayed her trust and crossed her people after all they did for us. But she did say it were fine to pick gold off the ground. And in a way, that's what we did. It weren't like we dug the gold from the earth, hauled it outta the mine. We weren't even after it. We just happened to walk outta them canyons with an unknown fortune in our pockets.

I shiver, thinking 'bout those Apache scouts that watched us leave. They didn't know, couldn't have. We'd be bleeding out on the canyon floors like the Peraltas otherwise.

Dazed and still half numb with shock, I duck outside and head for the water. I dunk my hands in, wiping days-old dust from my arms and splashing my face. A familiar whinny sounds. It's followed by a shove that nearly sends me stumbling into the water.

I turn and find Silver nudging at my shoulders.

"Hey, girl," I says, putting my hands to her coat and stroking. "I missed you."

She stomps a foot and tosses her mane.

"Yeah, just like that," I tell her.

Mutt comes bounding my way next, but when I drop to a knee to greet him he seems to recognize me and pulls up short, growling. "I see yer opinion of me ain't changed much." He turns and flees the way he came, as if to show he agrees.

"Hey, Kate?"

I lurch to my feet at the nearness of Jesse's voice. He's standing but a few paces off, hat held in front of him.

"I didn't take that gold. I swear it was just chance."

"I know," I says. "I believed you the first time you said so."

He looks over his shoulder at the house. Waltz is standing there, watching, but not in an encroaching way. More like a curious cat.

"When do you want to leave? It's a three-day ride back to civilization. Two, maybe, if we really push."

Jesse frowns. "I gotta ride for Tucson. Clara might still be there, plus I gotta make amends with Benny. Sarah'll be furious if I come home having lost Will *and* one of our sources of income. Think you could ride ahead and tell her where I'm at? I want her to know I'm setting things right, that there ain't a need to worry 'bout nothing else."

I don't point out that there's prolly enough gold between us for him never to have to run cattle again. But maybe he wants to stay busy, try to live as normal a life as possible. Spending gold is what caught up with Pa, after all.

But even still, that ain't what bothers me most. It's the favor, his request that *I* go see Sarah.

"You don't think it'll be better to tell her all this yerself? I can stay a few days in Phoenix till you catch up."

"I ain't sure how long things'll take with Benny. And I don't want you waiting. Go see Sarah. Have a proper bath and sleep beneath a roof. You deserve it."

"Yeah. All right," I says. "I'll leave right away."

"Thank you, Kate. Thank you." He grabs my face and gives me the quickest peck of a kiss that be. For once, my knees don't quake. "Take that gold from the saddlebags too," he adds. "It's yers after all."

He turns back for the house without another word.

I stand there a minute, dazed, not quite certain what happened. This weren't how I envisioned it—me riding out alone. I saw us together: me and Jesse, our horses and Mutt. Why's he think it a good idea for *me* to break such horrid news to Sarah? And why can't I just wait for him in Phoenix? I'd do it, gladly.

Maybe he don't want me round. Maybe I were a crutch to lean on when he first lost his brother. We were nothing before Will got taken—just bickering and chiding, a constant quarrel. What did I really think were happening? I was after justice and Jesse needed a distraction. He even admitted as much. We used each other for a little to get what we needed. Now things go back to usual.

God, I am so thick. I am so blind.

Silver nickers and I jolt to action. I saddle her in a hurry, slip the bridle over her head. I load up my gear and then stare at Rose's burros a moment. In the end, I take one of the saddlebags, leaving the rest for Jesse and Waltz to fight over.

The guilt hits me a second time. I wanted to walk away from all this: the journal and the gold and the greed. But I also got a burned house waiting back in Prescott, and no means to raise a new one. I reckon enough to get me by, set me up for the coming years, ain't nothing harmful.

As I go to pack the journal, something catches my eye

that I ain't noticed before: a smudgy name, scrawled into the bottom corner of the very first page.

Miguel Peralta.

It's *his* journal, the Mexican Liluye told us 'bout. The note Pa left in Wickenburg mentioned how he'd found the journal near the remains of humans and burros. It must've been lying there all those years, just waiting to be discovered since Lil's tribe ran the Peraltas out.

"So you found it, eh?"

I snap the journal shut at the sound of Waltz's voice. "Huh?"

The miner nods at the saddlebags as I wrap the journal back up in its cord. "Gold," he says. "You found it."

"Up on the eastern ridge of a potholed ravine running north and south. There was a footpath you could see from the mine, but you couldn't see the mine from the footpath."

"The old military trail branching off Needle Canyon?" Waltz says.

"Could be."

He shakes his head. "I's been down that way near a dozen times."

"It'd be easy to miss. I reckon you could walk within a few feet of them caches or the mine and never even spot 'em."

I run a hand over the front of the journal. Suddenly, I don't want to pack it. I wanna throw it back among the canyons, bury it with the blood and skeletons it knows so well.

"Hey, Waltz. You gonna head back in there next season?" I jerk my head toward the Superstitions.

"Did you take care of them ghosts done shooting everybody?"

"Yeah, I took care of 'em."

"Then I reckon I might."

"In that case, you should prolly have this." I hand over the journal. "It's got all the maps you'll need."

His gray brows rise. "You don't want it?"

"I ain't going back there, not ever. I'm going forward. I'm moving on."

He shrugs and accepts the journal. "Thanks, kid."

"Just be careful," I says. "It's angry land, sacred land. Gold ain't to be tampered with."

But he's already got his nose buried in the pages, flipping faster than reading allows.

I shake my head and mount Silver, then kick her into a gallop. Mutt runs with me awhile, and when I come to a bow where the shoreline curves behind a low wall of rock, I can't help myself; I pause to look back at the shanty.

Jesse is standing in the doorway, raising his hat in farewell.

I take mine off and do the same.

Then I turn round and fly.

CHAPTER THIRTY-ONE

I ride hard to Phoenix and pause only to visit the sheriff. A short, stocky Mexican deputy by the name of Garfias smirks something doubtful when I inform him Waylan Rose and his boys are dead.

"The Rose Riders?" He laughs. "All of 'em?"

"That's right."

"Well, you ain't getting a bounty without the bodies."

"There's one in an outhouse in Prescott, though I bet someone's moved that corpse by now. Then a couple 'long the Agua Fria, and another 'long the Salt. The rest, plus Waylan Rose hisself, are scattered in the Superstition Mountains."

"That's prime Apache territory," Garfias says, his cigarette near tumbling from his lips. "Ain't no one gonna scour that land for their bodies."

"No bother," I says, standing. "I just wanted to inform the law they're dead and cold."

"You still ain't getting a bounty."

"I figured as much. Good day, mister." I tip my Stetson at him and leave without a backwards glance. I can still feel his eyes staring at me, puzzled, as I step onto the street.

The ride to the Colton ranch feels shorter than the ride south, but twice as lonely.

The weather cooperates the whole way—hot as hell, but no dust storms—and soon I'm back 'long the Hassayampa, following those dry creek beds into Wickenburg.

At the ranch, Sarah deteriorates at the news of Will. I could wallop Jesse for making me do this. *He* should be here, holding her hand and rubbing her back and promising her it'll be all right. *Him,* not me. The coward, running off to Tucson under the ruse of tending to business.

I don't let my anger show, though, 'cus that ain't what Sarah needs. Her husband, Roy, stumbled home a few days after I first rode through, and according to Sarah he collapsed on the bed in a drunken stupor and hasn't hardly moved since. I ain't seen him up 'cept stumbling to pour another drink, so I do whatever needs doing round the ranch: milking cows and beating rugs and pulling weeds in the garden as Jake skips 'bout singing.

A telegram comes from Tucson on my fourth day.

Jesse's found poor Clara, who's been stuck at a dingy hotel where she swears rats sleep in her hair every night. He'll front her a stagecoach fare to Wickenburg, but then he's working a job with Benny, seeing as he turned a blind eye on the last herd of cattle requiring moving and needs to make amends with the boss man.

He don't mention me once in his entire correspondence.

The next day I pack my things and leave.

The first night home, I stay in the barn with Silver, a blanket that used to be Libby's rolled up to serve as my pillow.

I don't sleep much, and in a way it feels like I never left —that Pa just died and I'm still curled up with my horse, mourning.

I thought I'd feel better when it were all said and done. I thought I'd feel like the world had reset, like things made sense. But I'm still just as alone, just as mad Pa were taken from me, just as furious it can't be changed.

The next morning I knock over the marker for Ma's grave and throw it in the creek. Then I clean the barn, sweeping out dust and cobwebs that've congregated in my absence. The following morning I put Silver to the cart and ride into Prescott in search of lumber. Dallying at the post, I draft a letter to Sarah, asking on Jesse, but my pride gets the better of me and I tear it to shreds before I can send it off. I go buy lumber as intended, and Silver pulls it home. What she can't move in one trip I arrange to have delivered.

The next day, I ride the two-mile stretch to see my closest neighbor, Joe Benton. Him and his son are tilling a section of their land, and they pause when they see me draw near.

"Kate," Joe says, grinning. "What brings you this way?"

"I come asking a favor. The house burned and I's looking for some help rebuilding."

"Oh, Lord, I'm sorry. We'll come join you and Henry first thing tomorrow. Fair?"

"Pa's dead," I says. "Got hanged by a gang."

"Lord almighty, when?"

"Over three weeks ago, when you were visiting family in Hardyville."

Joe's head wobbles like a twitchy weathervane. "Aw, Kate. Why didn't you say nothing when we got back?"

"I don't know." I can sense my throat getting scratchy, feel tears welling up. "I just . . . I's been stupid. I know now it ain't a fault to ask for help."

"Course not," Joe says. "And we'll help with the house. Of course we will."

We raise the frame over the next few days, then fill in the walls and put shutters to the windows in weeks that follow. I have it rebuilt exactly as it were before, with Pa's room and everything. Only difference is, this time we lay boards for the floor. No more hard-packed dirt.

They don't ask where I got the money for the lumber, and I'm grateful.

As the days pass I do some woodcrafting on my own. I could buy everything I need with the Superstition gold but figure it's too risky. I don't want people talking, asking questions, and word getting round. I don't wanna be found out like Pa. So I build a kitchen table and put up a few shelves, make a new bed frame. None of it's masterful work, but it'll do. Other things don't need replacing. The stone hearth is proud as ever, the kettle unmarred.

Joe brings over a spare mattress they ain't been using since his eldest daughter married and moved out, plus a chest filled with sheets, a quilt, and a few spare articles of clothing. Still, Joe don't stop there. He helps me see to Pa's homestead claim. A will left the hundred-forty acres to me, but I'm an unmarried woman, unfit to own my own plot of land in the eyes of the law. Joe were listed as a second beneficiary, and even when the land becomes his after he signs the fitting papers, he promises to never sell it.

"So long as a Benton is yer neighbor, that acreage yer Pa secured belongs to you. And if and when you marry, I'll sell it back to you for a single penny."

I says thank you so many times, I sound like a warbler.

When the daughter of a businessman in Prescott marries a month later, I ride into town with the Bentons for the celebration. There's to be dancing and merriment, and it sounds like a nice distraction. I wear one of the dresses from the chest Joe dropped off. A corset 'gainst my ribs and a skirt round my legs feels so foreign, I can't bear putting my hair back. I let it hang plain at my chin.

I drink sweet tea. I tap my foot to the music. Morris asks me to dance.

He's wearing a fitted vest and bowtie—much sharper than his typical Goldwaters attire—and he smells like tobacco smoke. Like mountains and spice. It reminds me of Jesse.

"You cut yer hair," Morris says when the song ends.

"Yeah."

"I like it. It looks nice."

I smile. His cheeks flush. For some reason, this is the moment I know I'm gonna be all right; that the hurt might never fade, and my heart might always long for a stubborn cowboy with squinty eyes, but I'll make do. Sure as the sun will rise.

I work the land best I can in the days that come, managing to save most of the season's crop. I plant some flowers near Pa's grave, and some more near the front stoop. The weather starts changing, daylight slipping from the sky sooner, a break of relief from the heat blowing in by late afternoon. On what woulda been Pa's birthday, I bake a pie and eat till my stomach hurts.

I keep the bulk of the Superstition gold buried beneath the mesquite tree, and a small portion in Pa's leather pouch, which rests safely beneath my mattress in his metal lunch box. The homestead claim sits in there too, 'long with the rest of my documents and the picture of him, me, and Ma. I almost tore her out when I first got home. Now I'm glad I didn't. It might be the only whole thing left in my life.

It takes a while, but I'm eventually able to sleep easy through the night, though never without my Colts nearby.

Summer fades into fall, and on an unseasonably cool October morning, I look out the window to see a lone rider winding up the trail. He stops 'long the creek to let his horse drink, then turns onto my claim.

I snatch up my rifle and step onto the front stoop.

The figure draws nearer, but not in a hurry. He's riding relaxed in the saddle, hips rocking back and forth as he leans easy in the stirrups. The shade of his horse's dark coat comes into focus for me first. Then a swash of burgundy red at the rider's neck.

I set my rifle aside and race forward.

He draws rein no more than a few yards from me and swings offa Rebel.

"Kate," he says, tipping his hat. His squinty eyes take in all there is to see. First me, from boot tip to brow; then the barn, the crops, the house and its yet-to-be-weathered wood. "I thought it burned," he says, gaze fixed over my shoulder.

"I rebuilt it—had all this gold from a reckless chase through the Superstitions."

"I shoulda been here to help."

"Yeah. You shoulda." I can't keep the edge of anger off my tongue.

"I got caught running cattle to Los Angeles. Benny was furious and said I owed him. It were rough land and a long trip and we didn't get much time in towns. I'd've written, but I didn't know if you'd returned to Prescott. Had to ask after you in town just to find my way here." He rubs his stubbled jaw, and I don't point out that he coulda tried sending a letter either way. "I guess I'm saying it ain't an excuse for the silence, but it's the reason," he adds.

He digs round in his saddlebags and pulls out something wrapped in brown parcel paper and tied with twine. "I got you this," he says, extending it my way.

I raise my eyebrows.

"Just take it, Kate. Please? I came all this way to say I'm sorry 'bout the last couple months and—"

"Oh, is that what you came for? 'Cus it's the first time you's said it."

Jesse Colton just keeps his arm out, the package held before me while his eyes plead.

I pluck it from his hand and tear off the paper.

I see the shape of a spine first, then the cover. *Little Women.* I run my hand over the gold-leaf lettering.

"They had an awful nice bookshop in Los Angeles," he says. "And I had all this gold from a reckless chase through the Superstitions."

He smirks, and I can barely fight it no more—the smile threatening to break free on my face. I force my lips thin, look up at him serious.

"What if I'd moved on, Jesse? I'm getting good at that, you know. I ain't just been sitting round waiting."

"I never thought you would. I prayed every day since we parted that I'd find you again and you might still want me. Hell, I said you had me to go home to and then I weren't even there when the time came. It was so hard, though," he adds, frowning. "Every time I thought on you, it brought up Will. Took me a long time to separate the two, to not feel sadness or anger at yer memory."

I stroke the cover of the leather-bound novel, run a forefinger down the spine.

"Did you read it?" I says.

"Got 'bout ten pages in and fell asleep."

"Jesse Colton!"

"Maybe you can read it to me. Aloud. Maybe that'd be better."

"We could try."

He lets go of Rebel's reins and steps nearer. "Tonight?"

"You asking to stay?"

"If you'll let me."

"Jesse, I never wanted you to leave."

"I didn't. I just went away a little while." He puts a knuckle to my chin and nudges up till I'm looking right at him. His eyes are hazel. I ain't noticed that before. "Can I?" he says, so close that the heat of his words graze my lips. "Stay?"

"Yeah," I says. "I reckon you can."

He kisses me slow and deep. My whole being starts going hazy, and for once I don't care. I draw him in and kiss him back, letting every worry fly straight outta my limbs.

He swings me into a silent dance, but I don't carp 'bout the lack of music this time. There's wind and ruffling mesquite leaves and the sway of dry grass out 'cross my claim. There's a bird warbling on the fence and Jesse's heart thumping strong and my pulse burning right on back. A blazing sun rises up over the Territory, and I feel a spark of promise I ain't sensed since before Pa died. It hums at my core.

It's the most beautiful song I's ever heard.

It rings and it echoes and it glistens like gold.

AUTHOR'S NOTE

I've loved the West for as long as I can remember. From childhood literature (*Little House on the Prairie*!) to the Western film genre (Clint!), stories featuring wide open plains and spitfire characters and the trials of homesteading in the late-nineteenth century have always captivated me. I've wanted to write my own "Western" novel for years, but without the right story kernel, there was no tale to tell.

That all changed one evening in 2013 when my husband recounted one of his favorite places in Arizona: the Superstition Mountains. He has family in the area and grew up hearing stories about the Lost Dutchman, a rich gold mine supposedly hidden within the rugged mountains east of Phoenix. As he discussed the legend and the various details surrounding it, my muse exploded. I suddenly had that Western novel idea I'd been chasing for ages: a girl out for revenge, but entangled in a bloody quest for lost gold.

Kate Thompson is entirely fictional, as are the Colton brothers, Liluye, and the Rose Riders, though I'm sure there were individuals like them in 1877 Arizona. However, many of the people Kate interacts with during her travels once called Arizona home. Morris, for instance, was indeed a clerk at Goldwaters, and Garfias was Phoenix's deputy sheriff during the time *Vengeance Road* is set. Then there's Don Miguel Peralta, who only graces the novel through Liluye's words but plays an active role in the infamous Lost Dutchman legend; he was a wealthy Mexican known to have operated a family mine in the Superstitions. While trying to remove a large amount of gold prior to the signing of the Treaty of Guadalupe Hidalgo, his party was allegedly ambushed by Apaches at what is now known as the Massacre Grounds.

And last but hardly least, there's Jacob Waltz—perhaps the most central figure in Lost Dutchman lore.

Waltz's exact role in the legend of the mine is muddled, but there is no doubt that he existed. Declaration of Intent and citizenship papers prove that Waltz came to the United States from Germany and eventually gained citizenship in 1861. Why a German's legend would eventually become known as a Dutchman's is still a bit of a mystery. Some say it's because Americans constantly confused the Dutch and the Germans, and so the two terms became synonymous. Regardless, it is surmised that Waltz went west with gold seekers during the California gold rush of '49, and later prospected his way back east, finally settling in Phoenix, where he took up a homestead claim of 160 acres in the Salt River Valley (about a mile west of what is now Sky Harbor International Airport). Like any good myth, various versions of the Lost Dutchman mine exist, but it's virtually impossible to happen upon one in which Jacob Waltz is not the finder of the elusive gold.

Some versions of the tale claim Waltz had a partner, Jacob Weiser. The two Germans either discovered the mine together by chance or were supplied with a map to the gold by Don Miguel Peralta's surviving son, who wished to repay the Germans for saving his life during a card game turned bloody. Some say that after locating the gold, Weiser was killed by Apaches. Others say Waltz killed him out of greed. Another alternative is that Waltz and Weiser were actually the same person, and that time and retellings have fractured the legend, creating two Jacobs when there was only ever one.

Until the late 1880s, Waltz supposedly spent his winters pulling gold from his Superstitions mine, and his summers on his homestead in Phoenix. A flood of the Salt River in the spring of 1891 destroyed his home and left him sick with pneumonia. His neighbor Julia Thomas nursed him during his final days. Perhaps one of the most agreed upon threads of the legend is that Waltz confessed the location of his hidden mine to Julia while on his deathbed, going so far as to provide her with a map. Armed even with all this information, Julia failed to locate the gold after Waltz's passing.

The Lost Dutchman — if it truly does exist — has never been found. The story continues to be shared and retold, and numerous people have entered the Superstitions in search of the mine and continue to do so to this day. Many of them have been found dead years later, often in conditions that can only be concluded as the result of murder. The blood that seems irrevocably tied to the mine has led to whispers that the gold is haunted or cursed, or perhaps that the very mountains are.

Taking creative liberties is one of the best perks of being a writer, and I have, admittedly, been selective about which threads of the Lost Dutchman legend to weave into my novel. To me, it seemed quite possible that there was only one Jacob, so I eliminated Weiser. The theory that Waltz's gold mine was actually Peralta's, recovered years later, also seemed reasonable, so I incorporated that plot line. Rumors that the mountains are haunted manifested in Kate's mother, the ghost shooter. And though Waltz likely had just the one home (in Phoenix) and entered the mountains only while prospecting, making camp as he traveled, I chose to give him a secondary home along the Salt. There's no indication that such a residence existed, and even if it did, Waltz likely would have returned to Phoenix by June, when Kate and her companions encounter him in *Vengeance Road*. But as you can see, I tweaked things for my story.

As for how Waltz found the gold to begin with? This is where I've taken the most liberties, combining Kate's story with the Lost Dutchman legend. Since the origins of the myth are already so highly debated, who's to say Waltz couldn't have found the gold because a young girl handed him the fitting maps? It was this idea that fueled Kate's story, along with the possibility that all the answers could be contained in a mysterious personal journal, found by her parents when they stumbled upon the remains of the Peralta massacre years earlier. The clues Kate uses to find the mine are the product of my research: a combination of multiple theories and speculations that have surrounded the Lost Dutchman legend since Waltz's passing. They are genuine in that they are pulled from published sources on the topic—but then again, how reliable is any myth?

Simply put, this novel was a joy to write. It is the culmination of years of daydreaming, my opportunity to tell my own "Wild West" tale set against a very real backdrop in American history. While I strived to be accurate, honest, and respectful in my portrayal of the people who populate *Vengeance Road* and the locations through which they travel, it is only fair to acknowledge that any errors or historical inaccuracies are mine and mine alone. Unless we're talking about a detail related to the Lost Dutchman, because, come on—who really knows what happened? That's the best part about legends: tons of holes and discrepancies just waiting to be theorized. It's a writer's dream come true.

ACKNOWLEDGMENTS

I find writing acknowledgments to be an incredibly challenging task. How can I possibly express the true extent of my gratitude to everyone who made this book possible? There aren't enough words, and yet, I'll try . . .

My posse over at Houghton Mifflin Harcourt knocked this out of the park. Kate O'Sullivan, editor extraordinaire: I'm so glad you fell in love with Kate's story and gave me the opportunity to share it with the world. Thank you for your gentle queries and steadfast dedication, for Pinterest boards and constant transparency. You kept me involved from book sale to book publication, and I am so very grateful. To one mighty fine design team, Scott Magoon and Cara Llewellyn: Thank you for dressing up this story so that it shouted *"Western!"* but didn't scare off readers hesitant toward the genre. Teagan White: Don't ever stop doing what you do. The illustration on *Vengeance Road*'s cover is one of the most beautiful things I have ever seen. You captured the essence of Kate's story so perfectly and I still can't believe that this gorgeous artwork graces the front of my book. Additional love to Betsy Groban, Mary Wilcox, Linda Magram, Lisa DiSarro, Karen Walsh, Hayley Gonnason, Ruth Homberg, and every last HMH employee who touched this project: thank you for saddling up and working tirelessly to get this book onto shelves, in the hands of readers, and on educators' radars.

My wrangler? Partner in crime? Whatever the fitting Western lingo, I'd be lost without my agent, Sara Crowe. Thank you for supporting me as I jumped from dystopian sci-fi into a genre that couldn't be more different, for encouraging me to write in a rich dialect, and for then finding the perfect home for this unique little book. I am so lucky to be navigating the unpredictable plains of publishing with you at my side.

The lovely, brilliant, wonderful author gals who read *Vengeance Road* prior to publication and had such nice things to say about it: Alexandra Bracken, Jessica Spotswood, Mindy McGinnis, Megan Shepherd, Saundra Mitchell, A. C. Gaughen, Jodi Meadows, and Susan Dennard. Thank you, thank you, thank you! Who knew there was so much love out there for Westerns?

My trusty critique partners and beta readers, Susan Dennard, Jenny Martin, and Mindy McGinnis: Thank you for weighing in early, for smacking the dust off the less-than-stellar scenes and setting my sights straight. (Sooz, you especially kicked me into gear. The second half of this novel was completely overhauled—for the better!—because of your astute insights. I owe you big-time.) Additional love to Sarah Maas, whose friendship continues to keep me sane and laughing throughout this industry's ups and downs.

To the pioneers of the literary world, the trailblazers better known as librarians, educators, and booksellers: thank you for all that you do. Truly.

I relied on a mountain of texts while producing this book, and am indebted to the writers whose research and documentation allowed me to bring Kate's story to life. Among my most heavily referenced resources were Thomas E. Sheridan's *Arizona: A History,* David Dary's *Cowboy Culture,* Robert Blair's *Tales of the Superstitions,* and the incredibly illuminating *Indeh: An Apache Odyssey* by Eve Ball. I very much wish to thank her and the numerous Apache men whose interviews grace *Indeh*'s pages for allowing me such an intimate look at Apache culture.

As always, much thanks to my family. Dad, I'm so glad for the hours spent sitting on the couch beside you, watching Westerns. Thanks also for driving the van cross-country and showing me the great Southwest as a kid. Just like Kate says about her pa, you're one of the smartest men I know, one of the *best* men I know. Mom, you always find the time to read my manuscripts and cheer me on. Thanks for catching a few historical inaccuracies in this one and providing me with reputable sources to help me address my errors. (The perks of having a librarian for a mother!) Kelsy, I sometimes wonder if I'd be here, writing for a living, if you didn't ask "What happens next?" as I worked on a certain manuscript many years ago. I owe you for that, sis.

Rob, this book exists only because of you. Thanks for introducing me to the Lost Dutchman legend, participating in brainstorming sessions, "suffering" through re-watches of some of our favorite Westerns, and hopping a plane to Arizona with me for research purposes. You are my best friend, my home. I love you so very much.

Casey. Sweet, little Casey . . . You were the size of a grain of rice inside me when I started writing this novel. By the time this book enters the world, you'll be almost a year old. Who knew I could love someone so fiercely? I can't wait for the day you can read these stories Mommy writes. But only when you're old enough. For now, let's stick to board books. Also, stop growing so fast.

And last but certainly not least, don't think I forgot about *you*. Thanks so very much for picking up this novel and following Kate across the gritty plains. I am so fortunate to call writing my job, and it's only possible because of readers like yourself.

ERIN BOWMAN used to tell stories visually as a web designer. Now a full-time writer, she relies solely on words. She lives in New Hampshire with her family, and when not writing she can often be found hiking, commenting on good typography, and obsessing over all things Harry Potter. She is also the author of the Taken trilogy (*Taken*, *Frozen*, and *Forged*).

You can visit her online at www.embowman.com or on Twitter: @erin_bowman.

Don't miss the action-packed companion to *Vengeance Road*:

RETRIBUTION RAILS

When Reece Murphy is forcibly dragged into an infamous gang because of a mysterious gold coin in his possession, he vows to find the man who gave him the piece and turn him over to the gang in exchange for freedom. Never does he expect a lead to come from an aspiring female journalist. But when Reece's path crosses with Charlotte Vaughn's after a botched train robbery and she mentions a promising rumor about a gunslinger from Prescott, it becomes apparent that she will be his ticket to freedom—or a noose. As the two manipulate each other for their own ends, past secrets are unearthed, reviving a decade-old quest for revenge that may be impossible to settle.

In this thrilling companion to *Vengeance Road*, dangerous alliances are formed, old friends meet new enemies, and the West is wilder than ever.

Retribution Rails is coming to bookshelves in fall 2017!